PRAISE FOR CAN'T

"I read C. H. Hooks's last novel, *Alligator Zoo Park Magic*, while in St. Augustine, Florida, where those alligators romp and occasionally chomp. In his forthcoming *Can't Shake the Dust*, set among the strip malls of South Georgia, Hooks writes about people who get sideways at honky-tonks and lose their shirts to payday loan sharks and drive straightaways at dirt tracks, showing the same grit and empathy as his sire, the late great Harry Crews—which is another way of saying that Hooks gets the people of the gray and red clay right."

—John T. Edge, *Garden & Gun*

"The great racetrack in Darlington is called 'Too Tough to Tame.' The same might be said of C.H. Hooks. I kind of expect it on his tombstone, though I hope it's in another 100 years. *Can't Shake the Dust*, told from multiple points of view, never disappoints. It's so easy to say 'This is one wild ride,' I know, but this is one wild ride. It belongs on the tragi-comic shelf with Harry Crews, Barry Hannah, et al."

—George Singleton, author of *You Want More*

"With *Can't Shake the Dust*, C.H. Hooks gives us a raucous, red-eyed ballad of high-test tears and ground-pounding laughs that'll cling to your soul like the red dirt of the title, making you remember the heart is a kind of engine, too."

—Taylor Brown, author of *Wingwalkers* and *Rednecks*

"Strap in and let C.H. Hooks take you on a gonzo ride through the racing circuits and strip malls of South Georgia. *Can't Shake the Dust* is a singular addition to the South's raucous storytelling tradition. As much about aging as coming of age, *Can't Shake the*

Dust takes you beyond-the-track and into the blue-collar lives of those who can't quit this beautiful, DIY sport. At once hilarious, strange, and tender—this brilliant novel you won't soon forget. Long live the Lemons racing dynasty!"

—Caleb Johnson, author of *Treeborne*

CAN'T SHAKE THE DUST

C.H. Hooks

Regal House Publishing

Published by
Regal House Publishing, LLC
Raleigh, NC 27605
All rights reserved

ISBN -13 (paperback): 9781646034994
ISBN -13 (epub): 9781646035007
Library of Congress Control Number: 2023950614

All efforts were made to determine the copyright holders and obtain their permissions in any circumstance where copyrighted material was used. The publisher apologizes if any errors were made during this process, or if any omissions occurred. If noted, please contact the publisher and all efforts will be made to incorporate permissions in future editions.

Cover images and design by © C. B. Royal

Regal House Publishing, LLC
https://regalhousepublishing.com

The following is a work of fiction created by the author. All names, individuals, characters, places, items, brands, events, etc. are either the product of the author's imagination or are used fictitiously. Any resemblance to actual events, places, institutions, persons, current or past, is entirely coincidental.

Printed in the United States of America

For Elizabeth, Margaux, and Brer

The tattoo's removed
but your heart's still black and blue
and the only thing worse
than hitting rock bottom
is rock bottom
hitting you

- Scott Ballew, "High Times"

1

LITTLE

They say my daddy could've been the best racer there ever was, but that didn't change the fact that I couldn't breathe.

Dirt.

My nose was caked, and I could taste it in my teeth when I sucked through my lips, searching for a little bit of air to keep me running even when my car's engine had found the shit-canned end of its own life—again. Might as well have left our house out on the track.

My roll cage rattled like a can. Every time another one of those assholes lapped me, I could feel the whole world rattle, like somehow Jesus was out there playing soccer with me and the car as the ball. My car was named Lemon Party II because Daddy wrecked the first one. More like, Daddy got wrecked *in*. Didn't really do it his ownself. Somebody put him into the wall, but he still wouldn't tell me who it was. I had enough to deal with driving against those folks' kids.

Another car passed, and it felt like I might get sucked out through the window if I wasn't strapped down so tight. Folks called me Little, just 'cause I was the youngest out of me and Daddy and Big Bill, my grandpaw. And I guess I *was* little once. But I'd stretched and leaned out, about as tall as Daddy now, but somehow the name stuck. My daddy got called "Wild" and that still makes sense.

When the whole flock of cars passed they blew more dirt into Lemon Party II. My sleeves got a shower, a loose dust of gray clay and red dirt. The birds would try to bury me. Dang noisy birds flying around, circling and pecking just like those assholes did at school. When the draft tried to pull me out, I thought I might fly into orbit, find some far star even while my own childhood tried to twinkle the fuck out. Believe me, I could blink past the cloud of dust and find some dark sky out past the lights. Someplace I'd rather have been. Then I'd see the whole slew of them coming back around, lap twenty-something by then, and I'd do just like Daddy told me, what he wished he'd have done, and I'd tuck my legs into the seat real tight, push them over to the console. I'd do that, hope I didn't get T-boned, and dream about a place more permanent, a place that wouldn't roll away, and listen to all fourteen years of my life breeze by until they passed again.

Instead, there was more dirt. My foot had slipped off the clutch mid-shift. The car stalled. It wouldn't restart. The only time it turned over, I'd given it too much gas and it sounded like somebody was playing ping-pong under the hood.

Now I was in another race I couldn't finish.

I could read the signs through the dust. Don't know how many times I read the Lucas Oil ad over on the wall next to me. I somehow always ended up parked in the same spot. Usually around lap two out of twenty-five. I knew I couldn't, that it wasn't possible, but I swear I could hear those other kids laughing over the spattering of mud when they passed.

The officials didn't stop the race to move my car. The dirt and mud covered the pair of large lemons and one smaller lemon hanging from the same stem. My mama, Nanny, painted the lemons on the door about a million years ago. She told Daddy the white paint would look like a flash when it flew around the track. Mama didn't come to the races to see that wasn't for real.

The other cars crossed the finish line and I watched Daddy limp over to the tall fence. He propped himself against the chain links and I barely pulled my scrawny ass out before the tow truck driver was hitching up to the bumper.

"Good race, boy," Daddy said. He was trying to smile. Trying to believe his own words till they got gobbled up by somebody's busted muffler. I could barely hear. Dirt was stuck deep in my ears and I knew I'd find mounds like anthills on my pillow the next morning. I'd spit grayish-red when I brushed my teeth. The collars of my school-uniform shirts would have these streaks that would smudge over time, till the whole thing was a different color than the original white. They expected clean and pure at the St. Francis Catholic School. They dragged me along on scholarship when I was for sure the only Methodist.

Flies swarmed the lights high at the top of poles and the pale glow was just bright enough to make me have to squint over at Daddy. Made it a little bit easier to hold back tears.

"Made it longer than last time." Daddy scratched his right leg like he did when he was trying.

I looked back over at my car. The tow truck revved and dragged my car through the dirt, the bumper drawing pictures in the dirt. We'd made the roll cage out of patch welds and reclaimed steel. Now the car didn't have a wheel touching the ground. I'd been drawing pictures in the outfield at T-ball only a couple years before. The tow truck took the turn out of the track too tight. It kept pulling even when the Lemon Party II was stuck around the corner and the rear bumper popped off.

"We'll get it all fixed up," Daddy said.

"I could be the best that ever lived." Don't know why I mumbled those words or chose that second to do it. They say you are what you eat, and I'd been fed that goddamn line so many times from Daddy. He watched the car disappear around the corner too. I missed its tail in a blink. The bumper was still rocking, real slow, in the dirt.

"What I always said." Daddy scratched his leg again.

I walked across the track, pant legs of my racing suit puddling over the tops and backs of my Pumas, and aimed loosely at the gate between the track and stands. The suit was Daddy's from when he was my age. He limped along beside me.

The stairs at the track were cement and the stands were built solid as a tank. Daddy always said we'd hide under there when the 'pocalypse came. I was used to taking stairs slow. Never knew a time when Daddy could move quickly. The tap of his prosthetic left leg, the one Daddy called his "gone leg," kept time and we tapped-tapped up the stairs. Once we topped them, we started down the ramp to a string of windows. All the winners were lining up to cash in. We stopped at a big blue trashcan and Daddy pulled a wad of tickets from his pocket. He looked at them a final time or two, half-expecting the result to change, then dropped them in the can. We kept walking toward the chain-link gate and pushed through the turnstile. Everybody else was getting in their cars and such. I held Daddy's arm without him asking. I didn't even have to look. Was happy to do it.

"Bet for me?" I asked, then looked at his face and watched the squinting of his eyes. Daddy looked straight ahead, wincing a little with each swing of his leg. He had deep-cut wrinkles around his mouth. They could have come from the sun or stress, and were half-hid by shaggy hair hanging down and out from his hat—a Goodyear patch centered on his forehead. He'd picked that up from some podium a long time ago.

Was pretty sure I wanted one too.

"Always do."

"Why?" I asked, but I also thought I knew that answer. Daddy watched his feet while we walked. He sniffed real hard and I waited for a bump of confidence. I'd been racing for two years. Same time as when Mama started working the night shift and I'd been indentured into cutting grass for Daddy's lawn company. I was promised a life of racing. It was one I didn't ask for but knew I needed to love.

"It's gonna happen."

Daddy'd been a dirt track racer and a winner. His career was for sure shorter than Senior's. He told me he'd met Mama when he was winning, and she had dreams of a two-year interior design distance course and was one of the top waitresses at Wing Breakers. Daddy said he'd won races when she was there, and didn't do so hot when she wasn't. He lost the leg when she was at the refreshment stand waiting on a bag of fresh chicharrónes.

I was in her belly by then.

We walked out over the gravel lot. The fall breeze pushed white dust off the ground and the clouds and wisps looked like ghosts. Those dusty ghosts reminded me of being a little kid, just like the smells and sounds of the track. I felt the wisps and the dirt find the holes in my Pumas and looked up just in time to watch this dark-haired lady's jean shorts bounce across the parking lot. Her skin crept out from under the denim like the crescents of white were moving toward full. She reached her car first, parked a few spaces closer than us. It was fancy and shiny, like a pace car, like something I thought a winner would follow back when I thought I could still win. I recognized George's mama in the reflection of the fancy tinted windows. She saw me looking, turned her head over her shoulder and winked, then pulled the denim back down. I smiled, all stupid, and hoped I didn't have dirt covering my teeth.

Daddy somehow missed the view as he searched for his keys and tried to pull them from jeans that were tight enough now to burn his knuckles when he pulled his hand out of the pocket. I kept looking, my head on a swivel till we got to the truck and I nearly bumped into it. Daddy was still searching and I kept my hand on the door handle, tried to get grounded. I felt something else familiar, heard something I recognized too.

"Woohoo!"

My head got knocked from behind, made it tip forward, and I looked down in time to see a Diet Coke can rattle on the ground. I saw the can wobble and thought of my mama, how she used to hold me in one arm, a Diet Coke in the other when she rocked me to put me to bed. I felt the cool liquid from what was left in the can run down the back of my neck. It heated by the time it touched my back, pure from me being pissed. Gravel slung from the oversized tires of the truck behind me. The fancy Dodge Diesel sucked the air real tight and hung out in first gear and when I turned to see who'd thrown the can, the chips of gravel hit me in the face, stung my cheeks, and let me breathe in those ghosts I'd been staring at a second before. I was pissed at myself for turning and smeared the dust when

I wiped the water from my eyes. Thing that pissed me off the most was that I knew who threw it. I already felt like I probably had a callous and a permanent dent in my skull from Coke cans that had caught an edge on the thin skin of the back of my head over the previous two years. It didn't change what I said.

"Fuck off, George!"

The gravel hit Daddy's truck and landed in the bed. George's daddy, "Go Get 'em George," caught second gear and the truck took off into the bright blue night. Only the echoing sound of a giant farting muffler and the floating layer of chalky dust stuck around.

"Watch your mouth." Daddy looked in the truck bed. "We can use some of that in the driveway, anyhow."

I wiped the ghost dust off my face and spat. My lips were bleeding, maybe from biting the bottom one earlier waiting for the race to end, maybe from drying out and cracking. That was the first I'd tasted of it, and in the parking lot light, the drops made a dark spot on the ground.

Daddy was in the cab of the truck and leaned across the seat to unlock my door. I brushed off my pants and climbed in the creaking Ford. The worn-out, red-cloth insides smelled like cigarettes and the faint sweetness of vodka. Daddy slid an old Coke can out of the center console and drank. He pursed his lips and no matter how parched I was, I knew I couldn't ask for a sip.

"I'm pretty hungry," I said. I opened the glove compartment, found a tissue and blew. When I checked the results I was impressed at how scant dirt had come out. I must have swallowed it earlier.

"Yeah, me too." Daddy took a final sip from the can and tossed it out the window. It rattled and bent on the gravel. He'd aimed for the trash can as he pulled away. "Let's find us some dinner."

The night was quiet and it was late. Don't know how late. The clock on the dash had frozen on 9:12 years ago. There was no traffic, only a thick marsh fog that sat fat on the road and misted the windshield. We passed Hungry World, the marquee of the old theater where the Baptists set up shop to give out free dinners for the starved. But it was dim. I think we'd both hoped for a freebee tonight, some sort of win. We drove on.

A familiar glow swelled in the distance. Even the fog couldn't keep its colors from permeating the night sky. My stomach growled because I'd missed breakfast. There was no lunch. The groceries ran out on Thursday. The last meal I could remember had come from the school cafeteria, could have been Thursday too.

Daddy pulled us into the Taco Bell parking lot and slinked into a parking space. A few spots down, two teens, maybe a couple years older than me, sat in lawn chairs in the back of an oversized truck bed. Another sat on the roof of the cab. I turned and looked the other way, pretended they weren't there.

"You getting a chalupa?" I asked Daddy.

"Nah. That's the big money. Go for the dollar menu. Just get me a couple tacos. You got any money?"

I shook my head. "You don't?" I turned back to look at him. Through the window, I saw the boys out there were looking at us. They were having a laugh. I felt some dread in my belly and tried to think it was hunger rolling around in there.

"I bet it on you." Daddy took his hat off and put it on the dash. He held his palms over his eyes and pushed till I imagine he saw some stars. "What'd you do with that fifteen bucks I gave you?" Daddy pulled his hair back, then put his hat back on.

"That was Monday. I got school lunch."

"*What* are you buying?"

"Just a slice of pizza. It's two bucks." I gave him the truth. He held out his hands to his sides, weighing the justice of me having to defend eating.

Daddy moved his lips, counted silently but moved his fingers, and came to a conclusion.

"You should have some left over, then."

"There's taxes. There's taxes every time." I felt my eyes burning again, but the burn in my belly was way worse.

"I swear. Man. Check the seats."

I pulled the handle and kicked the door. The cab light didn't come on. I dropped down to the asphalt below and felt under the seats, more than a little scared of what I might find. French fries. I found a lot of old french fries.

"You gonna eat these?" I held a handful of fries up for Daddy to see. "Or you going to look too?" I was trying to be funny, maybe. I'm not real sure, just felt like our luck was running out, that I wanted somebody between me and those boys over on the other truck. They were standing up trying to see what we were up to.

Daddy opened his door and dropped down from the truck. "We have *got* to get you a win."

Looka there, it's Wild Bill Lemons! came the familiar refrain from the truck a few spaces away. Daddy heard the yell but didn't look.

"First, I need a car that can finish. Goes dead every time," I said, trying to look unfazed.

"Not your mechanic's fault. You flooded that engine tonight. Nerves on the line."

"We got to eat," I said.

"And don't *I* know it." Daddy got pissed, looked across the seats at me. I kept prodding under them.

"You think Senior would help us out?" I looked up, not expecting to catch the glare Daddy showed me. I might as well have yanked on a dog's tail.

"Listen here. That man's no help no-how. Where you getting that idea?"

"Just thought with the car and all—" I didn't get a chance to finish.

Wild Bill Lemons! Look at this pair a lemons! the group in the other truck yelled and whooped.

I looked up long enough to see through Daddy's door. "They're doing the dance, now. Same as school." I pointed up from the floor, trying to avoid any obvious gesture. Daddy looked up from the seat cushion where his arm was still lodged deep. The boys in the other truck bed thrusted repeatedly toward Daddy and me. They held their crotches and Daddy looked at their faces. They had their eyes and lips all scrunched into grimaces. I saw on Daddy's face the familiar look of pain and lifelong suffering, the same one I saw on my own face in the window of the truck when Daddy picked me up from school, or when I looked into the mirror. One of the boys had taken his pants down for the act. Daddy pulled his arm from the seat, stood, and leaned back against the side of the truck.

"Those are about the smallest lemons I've ever seen in my whole life," Daddy called. He pulled his own pants down, grabbed his manhood and began dry humping toward those boys—his rear thumping against and denting the side of the truck as he bumped. I didn't expect it, wasn't ready for all that, but Daddy must've had enough. Maybe it was the hunger, but it was a moment there in the Taco Bell parking lot. I thought I laughed a second, but then I didn't. The boys in the truck looked at each other and stopped thrusting. The one pulled his pants back up.

"Hey, what's your last name?" Daddy pointed to the now properly pant-wearing kid. The boy pointed to himself, but didn't answer. "You look familiar," Daddy said. "Hey, you might be mine. What's your mama's name?" This part of the act was familiar. The boys folded their lawn chairs and got in the cab of the truck.

The pickup reversed from its space, then peeled out. As it passed, the driver threw a can at Daddy. It missed but scratched the side of the truck.

Come on, old man!

Daddy chased after them on foot, forgetting for a moment

the absence of a leg. His gone leg buckled under the strain and he caught the bed of our truck with his left hand, his body swung to a stop with his chin on the bumper. I walked around the back of the truck and the boys swerved onto the main road screeching and cackling, erasing blacktop. I pulled Daddy under the arm and helped him to his foot. He strapped his prosthetic back in place.

"We'll be all right. Got a lawn to do tomorrow."

I held up a dirt-caked coin for him to see.

"Got a quarter."

"That's a start," Daddy said.

2

WILD

Nobody cared about me trying. Folks said if there's two cars on a road, there's racing. I was racing an eight-week clock on a season that hadn't even started yet—before the flag even dropped.

My own boy, Little, hadn't won a race yet. Not even close. He'd chase the other cars around the track with the engine rattling a thrown rod, humping along like a heart ready to beat out. We chased bad money with good till there was nothing left to give but Nanny's house. Nothing would change that but a new engine. We didn't have the money for that, but my daddy did. Driving to his bar for another round of begging, the clock was ticking off colors toward a sunset, peeling and dropping them like the label off a dip can.

I drove out past the concrete bunker-looking strip malls with rows of "For Lease" signs, but for the big-box spots and the Mexican restaurants. I passed ProCreations, where Nanny worked. That was the big pet store with all the animals in it all stroked up on love. They sold the dogs and cats and such in pairs all hot and bothered and foaming, looking for a good time. I felt about the same. She used to bring home about a dog a month, but they'd always run off when food got scarce. Then she started just bringing home that blush wine instead.

It was over there on the left when I drove out to see Senior. So were the folks with their signs. The ones Daddy'd already milked for all their worth.

These goons were always out there on the sidewalk of the last strip center on the way out of town. The tall one, long and thin, walked hunched under a plywood sign roped around his neck. Old goon had scribbled on the wood: *Your sin will find you out.*

I slowed down a little and squinted. Probably needed to slow down anyhow. Another ticket and they'd be trying to take my license again. But I also slowed down, because next to the words he had him a photo of a man taped on his sign. It was a picture of guess who—my daddy, Senior, from a newspaper or maybe his high school yearbook. All on the picture it said:

Theif, Theaf, and Theef

I wondered what he done, but I kept on driving.

Everybody owed Daddy something, but they didn't have to like it. He liked to think I owed him too. A man couldn't owe somebody who'd never done a lick of good for them.

Seeing that man straddled by his sign, his own doing, gave me a real empty feeling in my belly. I was hungry and had been for a while, ever since Nanny stopped coming around so much and the lawn-doing dried up. Every time I tried to go in Pro-Creations and see *my fiancé*, they got on the loudspeaker talking about "Nanny Pet-Pet," and everybody hid.

I was probably squirming from the talk I was about to have with Senior too.

Didn't even own enough wood to make me a sign for all my gripes.

The late sun sat on the edge of falling off, right in my eyes, blurred my windshield like there was something I wasn't supposed to see on the other side. The windshield was like a mosquito graveyard, and there were a couple of cracks in the glass from my slapping at them. I yanked on the sun visor and the goddamn thing fell off in my hand. I threw the visor onto the bench seat and held my hand up to clear the view. My wrist was on the wheel and a hand between my eyes and the sun. The smoke from my cigarette had me squinting a little more, but I smoked it to the butt before I pushed the nub out the cracked window.

The wide-open parking lots tightened up into rows of tall pines that hugged the sides of the roads and the sun dropped behind their tops. Here and there, lines of tire marks were rutted through the thin strips of grass and traced patterns back to the trees. Their bark was scarred with burn marks and bald spots. Ribbons and rough wooden crosses leaned on the trunks. I could've slid my wrist just a little to the right and joined them. I wondered if somebody would've stuck a stuffed animal over there for me.

I pulled up behind a big cage balanced on the back of a flatbed trailer. It hung over both sides and stuck out into the lane of traffic coming from the other way, if there ever was traffic. I swear, no less than six dogs lay on the slat wood floor of that trailer looking bored as shit. The bottom of the cage pressed up through the soft of their bellies and made them jiggle. They huffed in the heat, panted and rumbled along the two-lane road, seemingly happy as could be. When they bounced over a big pothole, the dogs lifted their chins for a second, letting the world know they were still alive.

The truck turned a little and angled off onto a dirt road. The dogs turned their heads only to be greeted by the dust kicked up by the truck's tires directly in front of them. They cruised down the path, heads bobbing and bellies swaying, into the cloud of some forgotten shithole nook of South Georgia.

I passed the county line marker. Senior's bar and the land around it was taped off and measured by stakes with little pink flags, making sure the letter of the law was followed and that he could be left the hell alone. Pink neon ran through the building like veins and the whole place throbbed like some late-night horror show experiment had come to life. The light glowed off the gold paint that covered the building and I wanted to see it melted down. The sign across the top of Senior's concrete-block-and-plywood compound was hand painted and said, *Monkey Palace*—King Kong of Honky Tonks.

Behind a low fence, the parking lot had the whole fleet of Senior's lawn service trucks and trailers lined up, fresh and polished. There were also a few beaters, lifted old model trucks with chipped and faded paint, a Trans Am, and a couple Mustangs angled into straight spots. They sat empty with their windows down. They cooked off the smell of a lifetime's worth of booze. I threw my cigarette out the window and tried to hit one. I pulled along the side of the building through the crushed-up white seashell and lime. My wheels chewed on the chips of the fossils and bones of some old-assed animals and I crunched to a stop next to Senior's truck. It had a *Big Bill's Barnyards and Backyards* sign on the side. Pissed me off plenty. I learned in one of those trucks. I put in my time and my hours and got paid the minimum to help his ass out for ten years. All that and Senior had no problem trying to put me out of business.

His signs were made by the pros at the print shop. The sign on the side of my truck said, *Wild Bill's Whackin' and more* and was drawn by me and Little. We pressed that fat clear tape over it, and it held real good, only peeled from one corner. The rest of the truck was held together about the same.

I opened the door, swung to the side and eased my ownself out from the truck. I looked down and checked my jeans. Senior always had something to say about appearance. My jeans were ripped at the cuff from being walked on, and I was forever yanking the cuff off my gone leg. Had to lean up against one of Daddy's lawn trucks to get it free from my worn-out pants, and my keys scraped against the door as I did.

Saw a cook from the Monkey Palace sitting on a crate and watching me balancing as he lit a smoke. His black apron was covered in powder and his hair stuck to his face. I pulled out my knife from my back pocket and cut the cuff off my pants while he watched.

"You Bill's boy, ain'tcha?"

"Sometimes," I said.

"Uh-huh." He squeaked on the crate a little, settled into his seat. "Saw you race a few time. Just about the craziest thing I ever seen." He laughed, coughed, spit. "Think you were pretty close to my boy's year in school too."

I couldn't place the man. Folks were forever telling me these dumb ass stories. I had yearbooks once. Girls wrote me notes talking about wanting to take a ride in a real fast car in a real bad way. I couldn't remember their names, much less the name of some other dude's daddy.

"He race?" I said.

"Nah, he's dead." Like that told me anything.

"Well, shit."

"Exactly what I said too." He laughed again, coughed, spit.

I got to smiling, if only at the success of having finished the conversation. He was still looking at me, so I tried to think of something else. Walked around from the side of the truck, saw all that powder on the man's apron. I pointed to it, then moved my hand up and down like so.

"He's got y'all serving food in there, now?" I asked.

The cook rolled his lips in and blew smoke from his nose. "Nope." He paused. "That's the co-caine."

"Ah." I took a couple steps and he kept staring. Our talking was for sure done, but we just hung around there in the silence like that man's smoke. I shook my pant leg, turned it back and forth trying to get the cuff to creep down. The cook licked a finger and ran it down the front of the apron, then rubbed it on his gums. He looked back at me, then held the apron out and shook it like an offer. Didn't want him thinking I was rude, so I walked on over and wiped my own finger on the apron and then took to my gums.

It tasted pretty shitty.

"That's flour, son. Get the fuck on inside to your daddy."

I sucked on my top gum and spit. "Sorry 'bout your boy."

"Uh-huh. Me too," he said.

The sun was running out of steam but cooked on the shells regardless. Heat in the swamp was cranked out by the shit-ton. It was the only real thing we made outside of beer, violence, and game birds.

I walked around front, where a woman in jean shorts sprayed off bar mats without looking up. Her shorts crawled up into the crack between her cheeks. The mats splattered water back onto her, but she kept at it and I kept staring as I passed.

Looked familiar is all.

"Hey, Wild," she called. I was nearly at the door.

Didn't recognize her face so much when I turned, but I was pretty sure I'd visited the territory her jean shorts bunched in. I tried to recall. I gave her a little wave before turning back. She let me take another step toward the door, then she sprayed the back of my goddamn pants. I didn't bother turning again. I pulled the smoked glass door open and walked into the dark. I decided I'd be a real gentleman and held the door with one finger for that woman in the jean shorts, but she didn't thank me. Just walked right by and then on behind the horseshoe-shaped bar.

I snagged a bottle of beer from the counter, didn't see its owner anywhere around. Tree branches hung from the ceiling and Christmas lights wrapped the dry wood making it seem like the ceiling itself had caught fire. It made the top of my head warm and I pulled my hair back behind my ears. The insides of the Monkey Palace were dark and electric. Cases of Coors and Miller were stacked to the ceiling and it made me feel a little excited even though I knew my visit could only turn out shitty. The bottles inside rattled and jingled with each beat from the speakers. My fillings rattled in my teeth. Off beyond the stage along the far wall, I saw Senior. He looked greasy, like one of those fries got the skin left on, back there sitting in a booth making his little squares and circles in a notebook. His sunglasses covered his chubby face. A dark cowboy hat covered his head. He looked at me, I think, as I walked up.

He mouthed something, then leaned to the side to peer around him, and nodded at the barmaid. She gripped the volume knob between three fingers, two of them tattooed with C and K, and I racked my brain to try to remember when, where, how, her name, anything. She turned the knob to ten and the live primates of the Monkey Palace pounded Plexiglas. The bar shook to the honky-tonk kick drum that felt like a rabbit punch to my ears. I slid into the booth across from him, left my gone leg kicked out to the side.

"Junior." Nothing moved, but his mouth. Just barely.

I nodded back.

"Go on and tell me what you're here wanting. It's end of lawn season. Got to be something."

Under the table, my foot tapped to the throb of my own heartbeat. It matched right up to the music. The monkeys pounded the edges of their confines, invisible and confusing, to the beat of the song.

A couple on the dance floor next to the juke box wallowed through the tune. Their boots clomped as they stumbled around, drunk and horny. The man was sloppy, the girl's pooch hung over her too-tight denim and I wanted to bite it. They held hands and chafed in their jeans. The apes covered their ears and screeched. I remembered why I was there. I remembered Little and what winning would mean.

"Engine's dead."

"And you want—what from me?"

"Money, I guess."

"You got squat to offer in return," he laughed. "Already got the fat. Got the meat. All you got left is bone." He nodded over to the side of the table, let his glasses slink down on his nose. "And you're missing some of those."

"If I got the right engine, we'd take the whole series."

He shook his head. "You thinking somehow prize money might be coming your way?" He leaned back. "You're on your last leg. Look at you, boy. Can barely drive a goddam lawnmower."

"Not me. Little." He was right, but I'd run his ass over with a lawnmower or a car just to chop up his words and the memory I felt every time I had a ghost-pain. He was always more than happy to remind me.

"Little's a runt and you know it. Hasn't touched a podium all season. Shit, or ever! Boy needs an engine running on fairy dust. Barely got a heart to race." Senior laughed. "Your problem is you just don't know when to stop. You ought to gamble where you know how. 'Cause you for sure ain't winning now."

Senior pulled out a small notebook, flipped it open and was

careful to place it in a dry spot on the table. "You got a tax bill
on the house."

"That's Nanny's house."

"It *was* her mama's house."

We'd moved in once Nanny's mama died off. She never
really took to me. The house was paid off, free and clear, but
the tax bill was something else. We took our time on that when
the hospital'd started asking for money. Might've been off by
a year or two. "You're five years behind from what I hear." He
sat there silent, then he made a little circle in his book. "I could
take care of that. How you're going, might as well be living back
under my roof." He made some kind of note. Then he smiled
like I ain't never seen him smile. "Boy. I just about own you."

I stared at the open book, small numbers and figures
scratched on the page, and I tried to read them, make some
sense of what he had going on over there, but I got distracted
by the heat in my cheeks and the movement of the apes in the
orange and pink light made for the room swaying around like
the lick from flames.

"I need two months. Till the end of the season."

Senior held his finger up and gave it a spin. He was done.

I hung my head till I saw the barmaid look over to the table
and I thought for a second that maybe I remembered her name.
I forced a grin at her. She turned down the knob a little as the
music began to ramp up again and the monkeys settled a bit,
swayed to the lowered tunes, and scratched themselves. Senior
shook his head at her, and she turned the song back up. The
bar throbbed and the casket-sized enclosures for each one of
the monkeys flashed in the strobe light of a disco ball. Some
covered their eyes.

He stood, peeled a beer label off the table, scraped the sticky
with his thumbnail, then dropped it all in a ball in front of
me. Light strobed off his teeth as he grinned. His sunglasses
nearly showed the eyeballs behind them. "You done nothing
but lose." Daddy stood and looked down at me, both hands flat

on the table. "Already lost one race. You got a month. Wipe that goddamn flour off your lip."

I wiped my lip on my arm. He walked off toward the bar, then turned back a second.

"You still got a soul? Might try cashing in on that."

He talked to the bartender for a second, then she walked over to the booth. She dropped a black plastic tray with the bill for three beers and a note with a heart that said, "Already got the tip. Wasn't worth the service." I left her enough for one beer on the table and walked out into what was left of the twilight. The lights at the track would already be bright.

3

NANNY

At ProCreations we sold pairs of mating pets. The animals' cages were made of a magnifying plastic, so that the new owners could hope to witness the moment of conception. At any minute in the store, the mess of sounds could be so overwhelming that we gave free earplugs to anyone who asked. There ain't no perfect breed. Let me tell you. Breeding can't be perfect. That's what my mama told me one time when she was putting her tall white socks on, covering up a roadmap of bruises from my daddy. Looked like small islands, maybe spots like the dogs we'd pick up, not even minding the nips and the scratches, the small spots of blood from their eye teeth when they stopped playing and we didn't know it yet. The bitches were the biters, and for good reason. Nobody ever knew when to leave well enough alone. So, there was no perfect breed. 'Cause breeding couldn't be perfect if there was still the possibility of a man. Instead, it was some kinda screwy science, ended up letting loose a world of hurt on a woman and a burden that somehow never got shared, even though the love and admiration somehow got split up with the money.

I fished in my pocket for my Chapstick, gave my lips a rub and breathed in the cherry off my top lip, blew out thinking about having to leave and go to the house.

It was time to close up shop. The girl dogs whimpered in the cages, knowing they had to share the dark with the boy dogs over there hanging out in the corners with their tongues hanging out, thirsty. That's how it was. They waited till it's dark and they waited till you're tired, and they waited till you're half asleep. Just when you stopped trying to be afraid of the dark, they acted like they were the only ones that got any warmth left in world and it was just for you.

Special.

Special's what they called it.

Special's only special for you 'cause you're the one left holding what's left when they went on to find the next special to warm up. Or you were left mending them when they got hit by a car in the dark.

Mama told me about that too. She said, "You get in your own damn car and you run." She told me that while she wheezed from the cigarettes and the mesothelioma and just about anything else she could inhale. So, she talked in spurts and starts and she spit sometimes with her words. Surely close to one of her last.

I said, "What about the house?"

She said, "Who gives a damn about the house? Dogs always come back where they pissed."

I said, "Where am I gonna piss?"

She said, "Somewhere else. Ain't no worse breed than the one that hangs around hurt. Just makes a mess more of a mess."

I walked through the store, back to front, heard the buzz and the hum of the overheads, turned out the big lights, switch by switch. The hum stopped and I heard the girl dogs start up their whining. They whimpered a minute, then I listened in the quiet and waited. I could hear their little noses whistle as they took their panic breath. They tried to be tough for what was coming. They were the sacrifice. Some would never know a time without the boy dogs. They were the cash for buying time.

But I had one cage set off to the side. They gave me a desk there at ProCreations. I had a cage under my desk with my little baby girl in there, an astronaut, an explorer, spinning in the cage and whacking the bars with her tail like a wire whip. My office was up front, mirrored windows so I could look out on all the world of whining and accelerated life. They say there's seven years of living in a dog for every one of a human. I looked at the papers on top of my desk. I kept them messy to keep folks uninterested and strung a curtain across the leg hole of my desk. When I pulled it back I saw science. Breeding ain't perfect, but I had an experiment working. I was breeding out the boy dogs. I had a girl dog named Lady under my desk. She looked up, barely waking. "Good night, Lady," I said. She was going to make a perfect breed. She was going to end the whining.

4

WILD

Mowing was kind of like racing used to be. Mrs. Haverty's lawn was so burned out and chewed up it felt near just like hitting it full pedal down no braking on the clay of the dirt track, I guess, except for the grass blowing out from under the sunbaked and faded Snapper Riding Lawnmower. I'd hit a patch of straight-up dirt and blow a cloud of dust like I'd caught a wheel and burned out. I'd taken the muffler off; I'd taken the regulator off. It was loud and fast and I was doing laps in that yard to the point of leaving tire tracks in the dust while I hammered around the track. I could do work at twice the speed of most. Even wrote that slogan on the trailer. "Twice the Speed to Cut Your Weeds." I saw the long thin whips of grass with the black Vs of seeds ready to spring up new anywhere they fell. They were my competition. I was taking their asses out.

I pulled my good foot off the clutch and the Snapper lurched into a higher gear, pulled along the ground faster. The tires moved into the next row of ruts, fresh-cut a minute before. Grass, the sap of pines, yanked and whipped me through turns.

I was a kid rolling an inner tube down the hill of a dirt road, whacking at it with a stick to keep up momentum. I ran alongside the black loop, spinning it faster, whipping it with that stick. That hoop snake rolled down the road and I looked at its eyes all wide and dizzy, gagging on its own tail as it rolled end over end, for sure catching peeks of sky, dirt, rock, me, sky. I wasn't looking—not one little bit. The man at the crossroads nearly nailed me, swerved to one side, glanced the bark of a tall pine. I remember smelling pine and pitch. The sap cooked right off that tree from the heat of the friction. That man caught his breath and stepped out from the car and I watched the hoop snake as it spun on its side, tip of its tail slowly inching up from its gullet, gagging out its own tail from its mouth.

I earned my nickname early, never fearing much, and always up to something. I ran my car hard. I was focused. Sort of thing that Little hasn't quite figured. When my car hit that wall, I hit it hard. Made sure to. The impact of my car into the wall knocked a rear wheel loose. It rolled down the track after the car stopped for good. It rolled and rolled, till it finally flopped over to one side, where it sat there spinning all by itself. I knew it 'cause I woke up a second, just a second, and watched the wheel on its side, slowly spinning to a stop, and I thought of that snake. That's about when I threw up blood from the brokenness of my own ribs. It was a good distraction. I barely felt the impact when the next car put its nose as deep as it could reach into the steering column of my car—that's the one that took my leg with it.

I cruised on the Snapper, realized I'd been doing laps around Mrs. Haverty's shed for a bit. Everything was rusted. Every time I hit a pinecone the mower rattled and my back locked up in my brace I picked up from the Goodwill. Clinic said I needed one, but they were gonna charge me. I took it pretty easy after the accident, but the ribs never set quite right. I cruised toward the house and realized my cigarette had gone out long ago. Long enough to stop smoking. My lips were dried out and my skin felt cooked from sweating out the booze from the morning. I was pretty sure it could be from me worrying too. But either way, my Goodyear hat was wet and flopping. I'd heard some-body say fall was coming. Every now and then I might catch a breeze, but I was still sweating. I was out of lawns. Maybe that's why I kept looking for grass I'd missed. If I kept driving, maybe we wouldn't run out of work. But the daylight was running out.

Over in the corner of the yard, three ancient trailers screamed POPCORN at the twilight, wrapped in weeds and kudzu. I watched Little while he got after the vines with a weed-whacker. They tangled around the head of the machine and he had to cut the engine a few times to pull handfuls of slimy vine to clear the head. Our shit was forever breaking. When I first got rolling, trying to get the yard business started, I'd offered all these old ladies some free work. I needed lawns and Daddy had them all locked down. Me and Little would go door to door, chatting up ladies and trying to spread the word. I cut the worst of the worst yards. Shut-ins and miscreants, shacks of the dead for hard-up relatives. But folks started thinking that's the way it was, the way it was to be. None of them ever had the cash for the follow-up.

Little was over there near neck-deep in the vine, yanking green ropes and working like he meant it.

I yelled over the noisy Snapper. "Don't stick your whole arm in the leaves. You might come out with a snake."

Boy nodded back, looking right into the setting sun. The last light of day glowed through the neon lights and bulbs of the old midway carnival signs. Thought for a second maybe I could hear some music, maybe sniffed a sausage dog in the cool breeze.

Mrs. Haverty sat on top of the three cement back steps of her house, watching me and Little trim back a summer's worth of growth. She just sat there staring and I kept my eyes looking down. She tried to catch my eye every damn time. I'm sure of it. She caught me at First Methodist last Sunday and hit me up for some service. She was last on the list, but the list was short. Hell, she was the only one left on it, but I put her off as long as I could anyway. Started feeling guilty, so I rallied the boy after school and we jumped in to rattle her bushes. Mrs. Haverty rested a cold glass of ice water on the edge of her dress, her knee just below the fabric. She had scars where her wrinkled skin wouldn't get tan and I shook my thought off how she might've got 'em. Her water glass left a ring on the pale blue dress and I sat there watching the glass sweat, watched the water roll down the sides. I panted a little bit. Shit, I was thirsty.

Mrs. Haverty pulled the dress back a bit and rested the glass on the wrinkled skin of her knee. The beads of water rolled down her leg, and it got me shook when I realized she was staring over there at Little. I took a hard turn on the mower to help break up the gazing. Little was over there yanking the pull-cord on the weed-whacker. Saw him looking at her too. Mrs. Haverty pulled her dress back, slipped it a little more up her leg, crept it away from her knee, then she took a long drink from that glass.

I pulled around the main house and aimed the mower at a black snake. It tried to whip itself up under the steel-sided shed. I might've have caught that tail, but I'd never be able to tell in the mess of gravel and old brick that kicked out from under the Snapper. I rolled up next to Little right about when he finished edging next to the shed.

The boy cut the engine on the weed-whacker and let out a sneeze from the grass and the dust of the mower, looked like a keg got tapped. He blew out his nose and the snot mixed with sweat made a nasty mix that he shook off his hand. I looked back over at Mrs. Haverty to see if she caught all that so I could point and say "eww" about what I'd just seen, but she was busy with her water glass. I pulled up the blade and turned off the mower. Everything always got so spooky quiet when we cut the engines. The birds came back slowly and the cicadas filled in where the engines left off. Sounded peaceful.

"Look good?" I asked Little, and I really wanted to know. He still had snot in the makings of a mustache. The boy looked around the yard. The rows of cut grass were tight and the space looked like a fresh haircut, bald in a few spots like the razor dug too deep.

"It's good," he finally said.

I eased off the mower and made my way to the back steps of Mrs. Haverty's house. She wasn't sitting there anymore. I pulled myself up the three stairs with the help of an old crusty iron handrail. The black paint flaked and the supports wiggled in the busted-up concrete. Her back door was about the same, but it was green. I knocked on the wood frame of the screened door, then looked back over my shoulder at Little and gave a last once-over at the tidied-up yard. Mrs. Haverty stood there behind the screen when I turned back around.

"Been nice to have you boys around here since Jim kicked off." She sniffed deeply. "Company's good."

"Yes, ma'am. Company's good," I said. The screen made her look like a troll or something. Hid any of the good parts. Just a voice coming from some dark. I was happy when she pushed through the door and into some light.

"How's he doing in school?" She nodded toward Little. He turned the mower on and pulled it over to the trailer behind the truck, then drove it inside.

"He's all right." I figured that just about covered the spread. She killed the last sip of water from the glass. The ice cubes rattled in the bottom, and she rubbed the glass on the top of her chest. I felt like I was breathing dust compared to what she had going on. The glass sweat ran down her sun-cooked skin and dribbled more stains on the thin makings of her dress.

"How are you?" she asked me. I had to think about it a second.

"I'm all right." I looked down at the top of my shoe. I thought about Senior's dark glasses. "I mean—we're a little tight on cash." I tried swallowing again, but I was dry as could be. My throat was hurting from the thirst. My skin was tight and my face was raw from wiping my eyes and forehead about a million times. The corner of my eye burned as I peeked through it.

"Just look at you," she said. She wiped that glass along the rim of my forehead, pushed the bill of my hat up. "Just too warm out here. You want to come in?" Woman got me spooked. Had me feeling like a boy.

I took a step back. I mean, I was used to the advances of some ladies, but she was messing. "We're all right. Nothing we ain't used to." I wiped that water off my forehead. "Cooling off again, anyway." My skin was raw and burned from the dirt

on the side of my hand. I tried to bring her back around, out
of all that heat talk. "Ma'am, you think we could get settled up
for the work?"

"Thought we might could work something out. Don't get
much from Jim's pension."

"Yes, ma'am. I see." All these ladies and their "pension" talk.
Couldn't even tell you what a pension was.

"What you mean, *you see*? I think it looks right good around
here for a widow-woman."

"Not what I mean is all. It's good to be good help. It's just
that we don't get paid, we don't eat." I pointed over to Little,
watched as he picked up the weed-whacker. Little walked it over
to the trailer, then placed it inside. He was a pretty gentle kid. I
swear most would've tossed the thing in the trailer. I called to
him. "Get it wedged in there good." Little gave me a thumbs-
up, then closed the ramp of the trailer. My old racing number
was the size of the entire back door. It was scratched and grass-
stained, nearly turning the white door green. I turned back to
Mrs. Haverty and she put the glass on the concrete-slab floor of
the porch. Then she crossed her arms over her chest.

"How'd you get so hard up, William? Thought you were
gonna do something with yourself. I watched you since you
was his age." She pointed at Little, over there snotting again.

"Yes, ma'am. Me too. Just trying to take care of me and my
boy is all."

"And your wife?" Don't know why she had to be bringing
Nanny into it. No better way to kill off my thinking about the
water glass and dress and all.

"And my fiancé."

"Hmph," she said. Wasn't even a word. Just walked back in
and closed the door. Left her water glass on the porch and it
was empty as she was. I walked back to the truck, watched the
birds hop through the yard, pecking at the ground and digging.
There were plenty of fresh-chopped acorns on the ground. I'd
probably run over thousands when I was mowing. The birds,

scavengers, got to enjoy the fruits of my laboring. Little sat there in the truck, windows down, vinyl door panels hot and faded. I pulled open the driver's side door, climbed myself up into the cab and onto the bench seat. I turned on the truck in silence and felt the boy watching me. I shook my head and felt my skin pull, felt my ears wobble and my nose was somehow heavier than what I could recall. I cleared my throat, pulled the shifter, and put the truck in drive. I was still struggling to swallow. The truck crunched over gravel and acorns and the birds scattered. I hit the pedal and fishtailed a bit on the dirt driveway, then stopped hard at the end of it where the driveway intersected Highway 17. Little nearly bumped his nose on the dash, then looked both ways quick like some kind of bird.

"All clear. I mean—think you got it," Little said. "Nothing's coming that fast." I'm sure he was right. The cars that came were probably still quite a ways off, but I was feeling cautious with traffic ever since I nearly got gobbled up by one.

"Don't you tell me how to drive." I took a breath and waited too long in the quiet for the cars to pass. I looked both ways myself out onto an empty highway, then pulled out onto the main road. The truck hiccupped a bit as the trailer caught up and pulled on the ball hitch.

"Sorry," Little said. Got me feeling bad. I looked out at the broken stripe of the road. If I didn't look back, it would seem that the truck gobbled them up like Tic Tacs.

"You get paid?" the boy asked.

I looked over to Little, then reached my hand down into the tightness of my jeans pocket. Jeans tried to bite me, but I pulled out two moist twenties and fanned them between my fingers as best as the wet bills would let me. I'd found those twenties stuck in Nanny's pocket that morning. I couldn't help but smile when I saw him grinning. "Should've seen how much she got tucked down in her bra." I held the bills over to Little's face, tried to brush his nose with them, and Little jerked back toward his window.

"Ew." He was trying to climb up in the corner of the truck.

"Haha! Boy, we got paid. That's the smell of success. Let's go get your car out of impound."

"That's the smell of that old woman's boob-sweat." He was smiling. "Need to go wash your hands."

The ride was quiet down the old highway and through the pines. The light flickered like one of those old movies but the picture never changed. The passing pines were identical and the fading glow down near the thick butts of their trunks looked like it might try to sink into the roots. We finally pulled through the opening of busted civilization and the landscape flattened back into the familiar strip malls. Trucks parked at the edge of the concrete lots, closest to the road with signs selling "shrimp, fresh off the boat." Old men sat on the tailgates under umbrellas, trying to sell off their stock before the season ended. But I wasn't hungry for food.

"Need to stop off real quick," I said. I pulled into one of the parking lots, and the shrimping folks watched the truck, hopeful. I pulled to a side spot, a few spots shy of the store and turned off the truck, stuck the keys in my pocket. "Back in a flash." Boy just stared out the window. I rattled the Diet Coke can in the console, but it was empty, so I ticked another dollar off in my mind. Opened the door and walked head down toward the ABC store. They were waiting on me inside. Guess they saw the truck out the window maybe. But I was quick, came back out with a can of diet and a small paper bag hanging out my back pocket. "We're good," I said, and nodded to Little, still looking out the window. No telling what he was staring at. I looked in the rearview and said it again, blew out the rest of my breath, then backed out and drove on to the house.

The single story house with yellow, chipped paint sagged under the swampy air. Nanny's car wasn't in the drive, so it was easy enough to pull the mower out of the trailer, then the weed-whacker. I sat in the truck, still running, and polished off my Co-Cola while I watched the boy get everything out and put it away. Little climbed back in and the empty trailer rattled as we pulled out of the driveway again.

It was basic to get anywhere around there. Point and push a pedal. Could do it with a full head of booze. Had to make do with pints and half-pints till we got us a win. The main roads all led out of town, every highway slightly older and more cracked and beat up than the next. The sun cooked the pavement until it was barely there at all. I turned onto a pot-holed and disappearing street that wrapped around the bend of the track. The white tower haunted the timberline and the grandstands hung back off the road. The whole racetrack was dark except for a light in the press box tower. That was where the office was too. I pulled us onto the dirt road leading to the parking lot and the truck bounced and slid around the ruts. I barely had to touch the wheel. I swear the truck knew them on its own. The springs of the trailer squeaked and the safety chains jingled. I didn't even bother with parking in the lot, pulled up to the gate of the barbed-wire fence.

"Let's see the damage," I said. The fence was full of all sorts of shit and I was having trouble finding the Lemon Party.

"You got enough?" Little asked.

"Haven't even counted it," I said. It was a pretty thin wad.

Little pulled his door handle and kicked the door out. The hinges creaked. I joined him and we walked toward the tower real quiet, knocked on the box office door. The blinds were all shut tight, but they cracked and somebody looked out. Then the door opened to a squat man, Don, the owner of the track. He was always pretty-well gussied up and his skin glowed in the backlight of the room behind him. He held a root beer can and his fingers were ropes of skin-wrapped bone. Never knew another man that squat with fingers that long. Like he was supposed to be bigger but his body forgot to keep up with his potential.

"Evening, Donald."

"What you needing, Wild?" Donald looked back over his

shoulder into the buzzing lights of the office. Somebody laughed and he smiled at them.

"Our car." I stuck my thumb to the right, like Donald needed to be reminded of who Little was. Donald turned back around to look at me, and his smile faded.

"You got fifty bucks?"

I pulled the bills from my pocket. Forgot to pull the receipt from the ABC store out from in the middle of my change. I held the wad out toward Donald's palm, avoided his fingers like they might get me.

"Might be a few shy," I said. He took his hand back, left me hanging there with the money.

"I got a business to run, Wild." Donald didn't bother to look, much less count the cash. "Come on back when you got the money. Till then." He started to pull the door. Pissed me off.

"You know how much I brought in around here during my winning days? You know I'm good for it." I pushed the bills at him, nearly touched his shoulder with them as he turned. "I'll settle up for the rest on our next entry. Meantime, got to get our car right."

He paused, stood there a second.

"Ain't been right in a long time." Donald snatched the bills, receipt included. "Won't be no next entry if you don't. Not even charging you the daily storage fee. That's just for the towing. I got to pay my guys," he whined.

"You made enough off my bets to pay them."

"It's a business, Wild. You got a business? You like to get paid?" He looked back in the room. "Be right back." Donald held up a finger to whoever was in there laughing, then pulled the door shut and the yellow light gave way to evening. "Let's walk." I saw him looking down at my gone leg. I could always tell when somebody was looking. He sighed through his nose. "Known you a long time, Wild. Y'all need a win if you're going to keep up with this."

"Don't we know it." I nudged Little with my elbow. Little's

lip kind of curled up over his teeth, tried to smile, tried to break one out of our mess of a situation. We walked back over to the gate of the barbed-wire cage. Donald pulled a full ring of keys from a janitor loop on his belt and searched for a second for the key to the gate. I leaned myself up against the fence while we waited. Blew a breath of vodka into the night and my eyes watered. Little stood back with his arms crossed. It was cool out. Little wore a T-shirt and tucked his hands into his armpits. My own sweat from the day's work was long dried, but a light breeze chilled me and I shook it off. Donald pulled the gate open and the chain links dragged the ground through a well-worn rut of gravel. A dog came over to greet us.

"Hey, Kitty," Donald said.

I held my hand out to Kitty.

"Hey, baby girl, how you?" That dog snapped, nearly took my damn finger with her. I yanked my hand back. Couldn't afford to lose another piece of my body.

"Easy, girl. Ain't seen Wild in a minute, huh? Kitty's a sweet one, but her memory sucks pretty hard. Nice's just not what she's for." That dickhead smiled and pulled her away by the collar. "Go 'head, boys." He smiled at his own charity.

"Go on, boy." I waved for Little to go first. He walked in, then over to the car. It was pushed in up against the fence. The rear bumper bent the chain links and bowed them out. The front bumper sagged to the ground, looked like a broken mustache. I followed Little in and pointed to the car. Looked back over at Donald.

"What the hell happened to the bumper? It broke down, didn't wreck."

"Can't say. These things ain't my responsibility." Kitty didn't stop pulling on his grip. She rumbled under her thin skin. "You left it here."

I opened the passenger door and waved over at Little. Looked like his eyes leaked a bit. "Come on, boy, help me roll it. You got school in the morning."

5

NANNY

Standing in the back doorway of the house, I felt the cool fall air creep through my bathrobe. It smelled like wet oak trees, and drops of dew fell like flecks on my neck, like god sneezed. The mold stopped creeping around the edges of the patio a long time ago, and now it covered the whole patio in the gray morning light that reflected off the windows, the same ones I used to look in from the yard, watching Mama and Daddy, hearing their voices but not making out any words through their shouts and their volume. It was time for Little to get up. The lights were off inside and there was no chance that Wild would wake up before Little.

I held the piece of paper with the apartment complex's number on it. Let the phone hum its dial tone till I thought it might stop itself, but it never did until I finally hung it up. The pole in the backyard is rusted. It used to have a chain on it to hold the dogs. Daddy sank that pole in the cement. I was there the day he did it, or at least I think I was. I'm pretty sure I can still see him cussing and pushing 'cause the cement would have been drying up faster than he thought it would and he would have had a couple more beers than doing work like that would allow. I'm sure I would've snuck a sip of the beer.

This was always Mama's house. Before her, it was her mama's house. That always bothered Daddy. He chained up the dog in the back yard because the outside was his. He said nobody could own outside. He said a lot of things that weren't true. When he tried to outrun his lies, he took my baby dog with him in his truck and drove away down the street. My dog looked at me, probably hoping for something that would never happen; like ever seeing him again.

Thirteen years. Whole ones. Not some half-assed rounding-up years. What did I want? I wanted a dog that'd come back when I called it. What did I have? Holes under the fence. Big ones. Spots for escaping. I wanted a dog that would come back just to smell food on my hand, some sort of *can't resist* because it smelled like home, like it would be there because it always has been. Has been. Those couple of words hurt when they bumped into each other. "Has" was like you had something in the first place. Like you got it still. I wanted it still. I wanted it tomorrow and I wanted it today. I felt like I earned it, for sure. My hands smelled like somebody else's pets. Mine had all run away.

I'd been in the backyard looking. Looking at fresh patches of dirt from filling holes under the fence, feeling air on my face that doesn't smell like the booze breathed out by Wild laying there on the floor. It was gray out, and I might just blend into the air. I filled the holes in every time. I brought home pets and they split, like they were predicting the future. Like they knew somehow that the smell of food was out there on somebody else's hand but all they'd get around here was starving. The special was always somewhere else. They only stuck around a day or two. We barely got to where we could say their names without tripping over them and calling them somebody else's. But my breed would never need anything or anyone else to exist.

I was a girl when I thought I needed somebody else. The rumblings of the track made Little kick in my stomach. I was in the refreshment line when Wild hit the wall. Wild had never had control. He was reckless and fearless. He flew around the track like some lost ghost. The concrete shook. The air cracked when the car T-boned him. It took away our stability. He lost hold of the control he never had. I've tried to get two feet under us, between us, ever since.

I wanted to shiver at night because the AC kicked on, not

because it was cold outside and my boy was shivering at the turn of weather. His daddy stole the only blanket in the house to mop up a fifth of vodka on the floor of the truck, wringing the soaked towel out in his own mouth.

I wanted the dent in my ring finger to feel metal roll into place, not watch metal roll up in the trailer again, roll out with my boy in it, roll around a track and hold my breath he doesn't wreck into a wall just to be like his daddy.

My feet ached as I walked across the creaking floors. There were scratches across the pale wood from where the furniture was moved across the floor lazily, without lifting it, like it didn't matter if it scratched the surface because no one would ever care again. The furniture was gone, because Wild gave away the house when he gave away his leg to the hospital. I opened Little's door; his chest rose and fell and I saw the baby I thought I remembered through the haze of a thousand vodka and Diets. The present was clearer than the memory. His hair looked like Wild's and Wild's faded like Senior's. Every time Little grew, he inched closer to the gas pedal. He looked like he could dig a hell of a hole. Leaving wouldn't reconcile time with feeling, but if I left first, maybe a dog would follow me.

6

LITTLE

When Mama knocked on the door of my room, I pretended I hadn't already been awake for an hour listening to her go off on Daddy to somebody on the phone. Every wall in the house was hollow as could be. I knew it from hearing every word of every bickering Mama and Daddy did and I knew it from the holes I saw that matched up with Daddy's fist. Most of the neighbors heard them too. They wouldn't look when Daddy and me would walk out to go to school. If it was Mama, they'd just stare and shake their heads.

"Time to go. You're late," she said.

I rolled over and sat up, adjusted my boxers. "Hey, Mama."

"Hey, Little."

She was a ghost, still dressed in her white nighty and dragged from her own bed. She was one foot out the door of my room, and the back of her hair was matted.

"Got you a Toast'em for the road." She shuffled out, arms lean and veins glowing bright blue through the thin skin of her hands—a neon sign showing off exhaustion.

I could smell the off-brand Pop-Tart from the kitchen. It had burned, and I heard Mama curse when she pulled the pan from the old-assed, creaking oven. She dropped it hard on the stovetop.

Yesterday's shirt was still clean enough. I turned it inside out and pulled on last week's jeans, then found two socks similar enough to call the same. I stuck my feet in my driving shoes, an old pair of Pumas that still felt fancy enough in my mind to call new, even though they were so busted through with holes that I could feel the pedals through the soles. Daddy said those were the best kind, that it took a long time to get shoes to feeling like that. I'd worn them for over a year. They stretched, but still pinched when I walked. I kissed my hand and slapped the poster of Dale, Jr. on the wall. Down the short hallway, Daddy was passed out on the floor, a towel over his legs, but otherwise still wearing the same clothes from last night. He still had his shoe on. I brushed my teeth in the bathroom and dunked my face in the sink. When I came out, Mama was kicking him in the foot. Daddy covered his head right about the time she started kicking him in his ribs.

"Get up, you sorry—" she said, but I went on and ducked into the living room.

I searched the usual spots, under cushions, behind chairs, but no one had any coins or cash in so long that there hadn't been a chance to drop any. If they had, Daddy probably beat me to it. We raced each other on the change circuit, but there was really never a winner when it came to finding lunch money. I walked back to my room, careful not to look down the hall where things were getting louder and more pissed. I searched the bottom of my closet and my dresser drawers. I found a couple pennies, but pennies wouldn't be enough, and I gave up, grabbed my old empty lunch box from the closet. At least if I had that, I could look like I had something during lunch time. I put it in my backpack on top of papers from a couple weeks back.

When I came out, Daddy was sitting up and Mama walked out the back door. I watched through the window. She pulled her hair back and lit a cigarette. I looked back to Mama's room and Daddy smiled at me, gave me a thumbs-up.

"I'm all right. You all right?" he called.

I nodded. "I'm all right."

"Got your stuff?" Daddy pulled himself up onto the very edge of the bed, careful not to invade unwelcome territory. He strapped his prosthetic on. I had never known him without it, but still struggled to watch, knowing that my own left leg more than likely resembled the one Daddy lost. I felt a small wave of guilt at the thought.

"Think so."

"Let's hit it."

I grabbed my Toast'em from the stovetop and tapped on the glass of the back window at Mama. She looked over her shoulder and the skin of her face looked gray. It was overcast out, but I couldn't blame the weather in my mind. She blew out a cloud of smoke and nodded to me, then waved her fingers like she would at a pet in a cage.

I picked up my hoodie. It settled two finger widths above my wrists but would keep the chill off. The truck was parked deep in ruts in the yard. I pulled open my unlocked door and climbed onto the cold seat, ate a bite of Toast'em, and breathed out a warm fog onto the glass. In that first bite, I realized how hungry I was and had to fight the temptation to eat the thing whole. Instead, I went after the charred parts first, and left the candy innards for the ride to school. I struggled to focus my eyes as Daddy started driving. We had finally rolled the car into the carport behind the house around eleven the night before. We'd agreed to get under the hood when I got home from school.

Daddy tapped the steering wheel as he drove, pulling a hand off here and there to sweep the hair back from his eyes. It was a ten-minute drive to St. Francis Catholic School. Everybody knew I was there on a community scholarship. They were happy to let me write their papers. I was happy to take their cash. I usually passed it along to Mama. I squinted and watched the veins throb through Daddy's temples. I knew him to not be feeling his best during that hour of the morning, and left him to his own thoughts. Daddy surprised me when he spoke up first.

"Engine's dead."

I looked from the window back over to Daddy.

"*Dead?*" I pulled on the strap of my seatbelt. It started feeling too tight.

"Dead." Daddy still looked straight ahead. "Fired a piston

into the hood." He reached over and rolled down his window. The cool air blew in and he breathed. His eyes stretched open wider and he motioned for me to push in the cigarette lighter. It was one of those weird things that still worked in the truck when nothing else did.

"Thought we weren't gonna check it out until tonight."

"Couldn't sleep. Donald got me all pissed off. Shit, I remember when he was still Donnie."

"What're we gonna do?" I asked. "We still owe him money, and we don't got a car to enter in a race."

"You let me do the worrying." The lighter popped and Daddy pulled a single cigarette from his pants pocket. It was bent and he chased the sagging cigarette with the lighter as the truck bounced along. "Besides, I think I found one."

"One what?"

"An engine."

"What kind of—" A man in a sandwich board walked the gutter. We both looked. "Where? And, how?"

"Got a text from Early. Said he got a fresh one in." Daddy looked over at me. "Kind of felt like this was getting close. You know? Last couple of races we didn't finish out."

I looked back to his window. Daddy's admission came as a little bit of a relief, having blamed myself for the previous car troubles.

"How are we gonna afford it?"

"Stop being such a downer. I can figure it out. Always do." Daddy reached over and slapped my leg across the bench seat. "The guy says it's pristine. Says the whole ass-end of the car blew off, really everything behind the engine wall—gone." Daddy fanned his fingers on the wheel and smiled. The thought made me squirm on the seat. "Said the engine's just fine, turned right off when the gas was gone. Just like it should."

We pulled to the front of the school, on the playground side. There were tall oaks, heavy and sagging under Spanish moss. I had Daddy drop me a good ways away from the drop-off line where the expensive cars dropped kids off to the waiting teachers in neon sashes. I'd walk behind the teachers, hoping they wouldn't see me. We weren't on time. At my last parent-teacher conference, we'd been given a goal to be on time once a week.

"Bye, Daddy."

"Bye, Little. Hey," he said. I still had a hand on the door. I don't think Daddy realized I was still so close to the truck. He'd been watching Ms. Watkins, one of the teachers, and her titties in a curve-hugging dress as she crossed the road in front of him. "You all right?"

"I'm all right."

"We're gonna look at this thing this weekend."

"Sounds good."

Daddy sat with the truck in park for a minute and watched the traffic as I walked off, head down, thumbs under the straps of my backpack.

At the front of the school in the drop-off line, I walked behind a teacher as she pulled another car's door handle. George, not young enough to be a child and apparently not old enough for the responsibility of logical kindness, dropped from the car to the covered walkway.

"Bye, Mrs. Kelly," said the teacher.

The kid, George, spotted me as the teacher closed the car door.

"You like recycling, Billy?" he said, hustling for the words to catch me, as I walked through the school door. I finally looked back to see George looking to the teacher, who smiled at him. George pointed at me. "Same shirt as yesterday," he told Mrs. Kelly.

I walked down the hallway to the right, passed other kids' bright construction paper crafts hanging along the walls. The art got better with the passing of each classroom and the passing of each grade in the wing of the building. I walked quickly, knowing that George was not far behind. The papers fanned in my breeze. I could hear them rattle against the wall.

"Where you going, Billy?" called George. "Feeling some heat behind you?" This time I didn't look back. George drove in the races too. We were too young to drive on the street, but just old enough to strap into a machine with enough horsepower to break every speed limit in the country. Besides, everybody'd been doing it forever. "Going the wrong way, Billy. Hustling yourself straight into the fire. Know you can't outrun me."

I walked faster, made a turn to the left at the next hall, and nearly ran directly into Mrs. Florence, my homeroom teacher.

"Wow," she said. I think I spooked her. She looked at her watch, then back into the room at the clock on the wall. "You're—on time."

I got to own that moment for a second, but then got rammed from behind by George.

"Sorry. Blind corner," he said. I tripped into the classroom and looked back at Mrs. Florence who rolled her eyes at George who was dark-haired with arms that filled his short sleeves. We were sent to separate sides of the class a while back. We dropped our backpacks at the back, then split at the rows of desks for our opposite sides of the room. The classroom was covered in orange and brown crafts. Dead leaves dangled on yarn strings and a small pumpkin moved through the days of the calendar. A poster for the Fall Festival was taped to the chalkboard. Other kids moved through the door and the room filled up with talking.

I took my seat, a cold gray desk, ancient, with the scribbling of generations of the town's finest and fanciest, and me.

"Hey, Billy, you going to the Fall Festival?" the girl next to me, asked.

"Don't know. It's here, isn't it?"

"Think so. I guess," she said, her cheeks turning a rose blush like the spritzers Mama drank oceans of. Her name was Sedona, and she was the closest thing I'd known to warmth at school. Her blond hair kinked-up and reminded me of the permanent my grandmother used to get every Wednesday.

"You?"

"Yeah," she said. When she slowed a word down like she did, I imagined I could probably slide down it all the way to her mouth. "I want to. Who's taking you?" Her nose pointed, like she was selecting me while she talked at me.

"Don't know yet, Sedy. Just now thought about it."

"Well, maybe I can see you there." Her smile showed off her two large front teeth. I felt some heat in my collar. Felt like flames that lapped at my neck when I dropped my pencil and caught the sweet smell of Sedona. She'd told me she had recently found her grandmother's perfume. The smell of flowers and honey caused me some confusion but got me all bothered anyway. Her eyes sparkled like the flashing lights that sometimes lit up the windows of my bedroom when Daddy had to find a ride home from the bar, or he and Mama's talking got too loud for the neighbors. I'd gotten good at sleeping through those nights, but when my blinds lit up blue like that I always thought of Sedy.

Halfway through the morning in homeroom, I bumped my pencil with my elbow, and the yellow stick bounced eraser first, then rattled on the floor next to Sedona's left foot. Nobody turned their heads, 'cause they were used to me dropping my pencil. I did it at least once a day. Sedona kicked the pencil toward me and smiled. When I leaned over to grab it, I took a big sniff, pretending to be worn out by the act. Right about the time I got a finger on the pencil, my desk started to lift from one side like I took a corner too sharp, then the entirety of my personal space toppled and fell to the middle of the aisle. I hit my head on the seat of Sedy's desk on the way down and flopped onto the cold tile floor.

Tom was a sonofabitch. His foot had done the work of lifting my desk in my off balance moment. He was bigger, taller, blonder, had a couple hairs on his chest and a deeper voice than most everybody in class. He was dumb as hell, but good buddies with George, and was laughing behind me. He was also faster than George. His daddy had worked for Senior some way or another. Most folks around town had either worked for him or been owned by him.

"Another crash for Billy!" George called from across the

room. Tom's feet kicked triumphantly in the empty space behind me. The week before, I'd done some homework for him. Thought Tom might slack-up on me for a minute, but his kindness was short lived. I was going to give that twenty bucks to Mama, but it had disappeared from the pocket of my jeans when I went to look for it the next morning. "Can't finish a race without choking," George said. Tom put both hands around his own neck and pretended to gag.

I pulled myself up off the floor and my knee hurt like hell. My chin did that thing where it trembled and I knew if I tried to say anything it'd come out warbly. I limped up. I couldn't keep them off my back.

"Are you okay?" Sedona asked. She reached out a hand, but I could barely see through the tears in my eyes. I wiped my eyes on the back of my hand, then picked up my books and pulled my desk upright. Mrs. Florence watched from the front corner of the room. She'd sent a note home the week before about my "antics for attention," and she stayed put where she was.

"William. We've talked about this," she said.

We hadn't talked about it.

I sat back down in my seat and looked out the window. The leaves blew off the trees with a gust of wind that rattled the panes. When I looked back to the front of the room, Sedy had placed my pencil back on my desk, along with a folded note. There was a smiley face and a heart. I picked it up and unfolded it.

I'm sorry. ☺

As soon as the words had settled in my head Tom reached over my shoulder and snatched the note from my hands.

"Billy's got a note!" he called and laughed more. "He's in love!" Row after row of desks caught what he was saying and giggles came out like a wave. Sedy covered her head on her desk and Tom whispered in my ear, "Gonna end up just like your old worthless, limpin' daddy." Then he reached around and tried to push the note into my mouth. I tried to bite his fingers.

It was nearing lunchtime.

By the time I sat down in the cafeteria, I was a mess. I was heaving and honking, and I could see the heads turning table by table, but it got to be where I couldn't see anybody's faces, just these blurred bodies through my tears. The people sitting next to me weren't there because they wanted to be. They usually moaned when they got assigned to my table. Now they sat back in their seats and attempted a long view at what was going on with me. I saw a couple of them making the sign for choking. Chairs squeaked over linoleum until the whole lunchroom was focused on me.

But I wasn't choking.

When I'd opened my lunchbox, I found another note, a picture scrawled on a napkin. It was the head of the devil, jaws open wide, waiting for a man in a wheelchair to roll into his mouth. A boy was pushing him from behind.

Mr. Davies, the gym teacher, was the first to get to me. He slapped me on the back a few times, but this didn't help my heaving and crying. I tried to wave him off.

"Help. Somebody help!" Mr. Davies yelled across the room.

Mrs. Florence, in heels a couple sizes too large, clomped and scooted across the floor toward us, testing out the fresh coat of wax. She wrapped her arms around me from behind and began pumping her fists into my stomach. I couldn't tell her to stop. It was like picking up one of the neighborhood cats and slinging it around by the belly. The picture, my tears, all the snot, her fists. I farted super-loud and then threw up a little. Couldn't believe I even had anything in my stomach. But I remembered the Toast'em with some sadness, and stared at the puke in my lunchbox, finally half-filled with something. I stopped crying. The heat I felt all over was either coming from the fires of hell, or maybe from the blood rushing to my face and fists. "He puked!" said George. He was a table over and that asshole stood and pointed. Mr. Davies walked over and yanked George by the shirt toward the door. But everybody'd already caught on. Laughter rolled through the cafeteria, pulled out the voices and chuckles of both relief and hatred.

The whole thing reminded me of church camp and the time I walked out of the bathroom in my towel just to have it yanked away. When I tried to fight to get it back a boy had thrown a broom, handle-first, at my head. The wooden handle knocked me senseless for a second, and I vomited and fell over naked in a pile on the floor. That had been funny to other kids too. It earned me a nickname. Anytime a broom was nearby at youth group, somebody always found a way to stick it up between my legs.

I was pissed. Had no regard at all for how much worse it could all get.

I stood up and followed George, still getting pulled by his shirt toward the door. When I got close, George turned around to me and mouthed, "Fag."

I punched George's mouth, knuckles catching one tooth each. His teeth cut my hand and that man-child held his mouth, moaning, eyes wide in shock. Mr. Davies dropped George's shirt, left him in a pile right there on the floor, then dragged me to the office instead, while Mrs. Florence was left to work on George.

My classmates prayed to a woman, Mary, and a host of other folks for a million different things. I experimented and said a Hail Mary on my way to the office, 'cause I knew the meanness of the woman I was going to see.

Sister Theresa, the principal, sat straight across from me with her toes crammed in orthopedic sandals and crossed like spaghetti junction. Her office had a single desk lamp that glowed over a *Take a Number* grenade that sat on her desk. That was about all the decorating. I forgot about the note and cried for my own actions. Sister stood, and I wondered how she balanced with her toes like that.

"You're here on a scholarship, Billy." She handed me a towel for the string of snot and vomit running down my chin. "It's revocable at any time. I'm having some trouble extending the grace of Christ, over and over and over again." She walked around my chair, circling like a shark. The habit on her head was kind of like a fin. "Eventually I have to shake the dust off my sandals." She shook a foot toward me. I couldn't take my eyes off it. "That's your dust, Billy." She shook her foot again. The pale beige panty hose couldn't contain the pile-up inside the sandals. My reactions were all mixed up. I felt threatened and laughed a little. I was a mess. She put her foot down and placed her pointer finger below my chin like a pistol. I sucked in a breath. "I'm not sure that you grasp the gravity of your predicament." Sister Theresa lifted my chin with that cold, bony finger. "We'll see if you're here another day." She said the words slowly and left a halo of a threat to hang around my head. "Get out."

She stepped back, and walked to her desk and sat down. I stood but before I opened the door, I looked back.

"I'm sorry," I said. My eyes blurred again and I blinked out a couple tears.

Sister leaned back in her chair, away from the lamp's glow, and crossed her arms over her chest. The chair creaked and the dark panels of the walls cast a shadow over her eyes. "So was Judas."

7

NANNY

"That apple never fell," I said. "It hung tight on the stem and drank its own cider."

I'd gone out to find Senior. He was standing there in the parking lot at the Palace, shouting orders at some old cook, trying to drag one of the monkeys out through the back. Poor thing looked like it got knocked over the head with a beer bottle. Probably did.

Senior looked at me like I was growing another eye. That man wasn't used to a soul having something to say about his work, much less a woman.

"You one to talk, miss." He never used my name. I'm not even sure he knew it. Family was unnecessary. Family didn't take care of itself.

"I'm gonna need a minute."

He looked at that cook, didn't say a word to him, but that man had the look of some horror movie victim. Senior kept looking at him, but talked to me. "You got exactly one." Senior pointed at the Palace and that cook went inside. Left the monkey right there on the gravel, tongue hanging out and knocked out cold. "What you needing?"

"I've got a complaint about that son of yours," I said.

"Got plenty of those my ownself. Hope you got something more groundbreaking than that. Your time is near up."

"I need your foot off our neck."

"Small town. Got nowhere else to stand." He spit. "Plus, I'm owed."

I couldn't see beyond his glasses. Never could. After years of being around him, I still didn't know the color of his eyes...

"I'm a man of principle. I've got wealth to maintain."

"And taste, huh?"

"That's right. So, what's got you puzzled?"

"I want Wild out of my mama's house."

"Honey, that's my house now. Clocks ticking. You got more than that?"

My eyes started watering.

"You came up here all strong, but never done a thing about getting that cripple out of your house your ownself." Their sex was the perfect example of broken. They planted a seed, an awful misconception of necessity for creation, watched it grow, watched it break, left it to rot.

"He's your son."

"Not no more." He paused. "A son is an investment. From the time a son's born, there's a limit on how much gets put in. There's no limit on what that one'll take from you. He's cut off here. Not mine no more."

"Little's there. That's the roof over his head too. Your son is going to ruin him."

"Time's up," he said. Senior walked back inside, left that monkey right there in the lot.

8

LITTLE

After school, I walked to the edge of the playground where Daddy would usually pick me up. My stomach was pissed, it twisted and rumbled after I lost my Toast'em at lunch. I was hungrier than when I'd gotten there. At the front circle of the school, the car line was fancy and flashed. The sun bounced off the shiny metal of polished machines and they whirred around all perfect. Everybody was getting picked up, ready for their after-school snacks and some cartoons on their couches.

I sat down on the curb and watched the ants move in lines along the busted ground. Their red bodies tapped along on all their legs, low to the ground, lower than me. They carried crumbs twice their size home to their beds. They circled my feet and I took off a shoe and crushed a generation of them. I only wished I could steal their crumbs.

Every now and then a breeze blew leaves from the stalks of the pecan trees. The reds and oranges and browns rattled through the gutter and onto the tops of my Pumas. I didn't move them. My eyes were cold and dry, but when I blinked it didn't help. They were worn out from the day. The sun was setting earlier and earlier. It sank in the afternoon sky. As the teachers walked out, they'd glance over at me real quick, sneaking glances and scooting to their cars quick. Then, finally, I heard a familiar rumble. A single headlight rounded the corner too close and hit the curb. I scooted back to the dirt and grass so as to not get hit by Daddy. I got up and shook off my feet, walked over to the truck as it stopped. Daddy was in there behind the window, shaking his head. I pulled open the passenger door and dropped my bag on the floor. Smelled like Daddy in the car and I must've made a face.

"What's wrong with you?" Daddy asked. He hiccupped for punctuation.

"Just hungry is all," I lied. I rolled down my window.

"Got running a little behind. Was out looking for some lawns. Totally got away from me." He kept his next burp, held it in his cheeks, then blew it out his nose. Even with the window down, I caught a gust of vodka as it floated through the cab of the truck. "I could get hungry myself."

"Where's Mama at?" I asked. Sometimes she'd roll up if she knew Daddy was riding the struggle bus.

Daddy shrugged off the question, kept his eyes on the road as best he could. It was a routine. I buckled my slack seatbelt. I would've needed to hang onto it if we ever rear-ended somebody. I held the extra to my chest and watched the road better than Daddy did.

"Not around. Far as I can tell."

"She working?"

"Not sure. Either way, we got to find us some food."

"You have any cash?" I asked, knowing the answer.

Daddy smiled with his mouth, but his eyes didn't change. "Looks like we're headed to Hungry World."

"They running it tonight?" I asked. I got a little excited, my stomach did a flip, even though when we went there I tried to hide my face so folks wouldn't see. But I was too hungry to be cool. "Worth a shot. Could be our lucky night."

Daddy drove us through the streets as dusk settled. The trees in the spring and summer made a tunnel over the road. Now they were gray, rough-bark posts. Orange plastic skeletons were taped around the trunks and they flapped in the breeze. When our headlight tapped each one on the shoulder, they seemed to wave.

"Weird shit," Daddy muttered, but the words weren't meant for me. I grunted and nodded anyhow. I felt like I was near passing out. "Must've put those up this week. I for sure didn't see them last week."

The orange plastic bones led the way to the end of the road, where it finally ran into the overpass of railroad tracks. Graffiti scratched the large stones of the land-bridge—words of love and hate, religious pleas and curses. At the bottom of the bridge, a three-story square building looked like it stood on its own shoulders, supporting the weight of faded bricks and tubes of a scribbled neon—Hungry World—across the top of a rusted theater sign. The letters were painted in white across the rust, like they glowed out from under old. Under the awning of the sign, the Baptists set up a buffet line of plates and food. Flakes of rust shook from overhead like orange snow when the swinging doors opened and shut for the workers. Folks in line shook their heads and blew off the plates when they walked under the shower. They ate the food anyhow.

Most pulled up to the curb and parked along the street. That or they walked or rode old busted bicycles. But Daddy always parked in the empty lot next door. The lot connected the crumbled old Mason's Lodge and Hungry World. It was also where the local kids parked on the weekends when the town shut down. The patchwork of crumbled cement and grass was blocked in on three sides and gobbled by new growth. Spray paint on the wall said, "Thus saith the Lord" and there were corners of the lot that would never see light. The grounds were haunted by old mistakes that seemed new with every saved life and Daddy had parked there many times, at several stages of his own. He'd been coming to Hungry World for some time.

The truck bumped over the curb and the bench seat bounced through the lot. Daddy put it in park and bent over the steering wheel for a moment. I was drawn by hunger and slipped out from the truck. I left my window down and kicked the door closed. Daddy tried to straighten up. The Baptists wouldn't serve if he was drinking, so he pulled a few deep breaths and peeled a piece of gum from under the dashboard. He looked over at me, and I twisted my face up when he put the piece of

old Winterfresh on his tongue and chewed. Daddy pushed back
from the wheel and breathed through his mouth to try to suck
some life from the gum. I hung my head and stood there waiting in the lot. I kicked a chunk of old brick free from cement
and dirt while Daddy eased down from the truck. He held on
to the truck bed and stepped gingerly toward me.

"Why you limping so bad?" I asked.

"Just a little out of it." Daddy shook his head, still searching
for any trace of mint freshness with his tongue. He grabbed my
shoulder, and I felt his fingers dig in; he was for real struggling.
"Got kicked too," he said. Daddy didn't say any more. He held
on to his breath as we rounded the corner of the building.

The sidewalk in front of Hungry World was wide awake. A
praise band wore matching T-shirts and busked for our souls.
The lady shaking the tambourine was sweaty, but wiggled in a
way that made it seem right. Her shirt rode up and she flexed
her stomach as she waved her body. It was George's mama and
she opened her eyes long enough to look straight into mine.
Pretty sure she got a deep look. I moved around to the other
side of Daddy to stay out of view. They sang "Dropkick Me
Jesus" on repeat for the line of us, hungry and near homeless,
and they jittered for the Lord.

Me and Daddy joined the buffet line. The smell of toasting
rolls crept from the kitchen vent and my stomach burned. It
was lasagna day, and the Styrofoam plates were stacked with a
wedge of meat and noodles. I waved off the salad and asked for
an extra roll, wrapped it in a napkin and shoved it deep in my
pocket. At the drink station, one of the teachers from school
handed me a cup of RC Cola and pretended not to recognize
my face. I kept my head down. I'd seen her there before, working the drink station, and us pretending it was nothing new. At
the end of the line, a plastic grocery bag full of cans and dry
goods was looped around each of our wrists. The bags were
topped off with a flier talking about our ever-elusive salvation
and I managed to only spill a splash of my drink. I waited for
Daddy, who spilled his whole drink under the weight of the

bag. They gave him another one. We walked to a curb, far away from the rest of the folks. Daddy didn't want to be lumped in. I ate my lasagna fast, felt like my own actions were out of my control. My throat burned from lunchtime, but it was just a speedbump.

"Got some on my pants," Daddy said. He didn't look at the blotch of dark cloth.

"I know. Saw it happen," I said, my mouth full of roll. I chewed hard. The roll was tough and I realized the challenge that waited in my pocket. I pulled the roll out and put it on my plate.

"You sharing?" Daddy ate his roll while he was still in the line and had somehow ended up with a salad that he scooped from the plate and sprinkled onto the sidewalk.

"Only got the one extra," I said. I eyed the roll and wished I would have left it in my pocket. "What about your salad?" I pointed with my fork.

"Can't eat the stuff. Bad on my stomach. It wrecks me."

"You go ask for another one." I looked over my shoulder. The line was long, wrapping around the corner of the building. We were lucky we'd gotten there early. The place always ran out of food. I felt a pain and a sadness for that roll, but Daddy looked at me, all bummed out. "All right." I sighed and broke off half the roll and handed it to him.

"Like I never done nothing for you." He smiled.

I mopped up the rest of my sauce from the plate. I put my plate down and rested my arms on my knees. My stomach hurt and was confused by the stretching and movement. I'd started to recognize the feeling as satisfaction. Daddy mopped around his plate with the piece of my roll and I looked away.

"You ever been with an Italian?" Daddy asked.

I watched the street in front of me and pretended like I didn't hear him. The streetlights came on and the neon of the Hungry World sign buzzed behind us. The Baptists would start the movie soon. Daddy waited, watching me for a minute as I stared and ignored him, then he dropped the question.

The sounds of ancient previews came out muffled from under the heavy swinging doors and seeped out over the noise of the kitchen in spurts. The volunteers pushed the doors open and the other diners milled around and attempted a line. They shuffled in excitedly to the low glow of the projected light.

"That's us." Daddy pointed a thumb over his shoulder. "You ready?" He elbowed me, and I broke my stare from the buzzing swarm of giant moths and other heavy bugs flapping in the warm yellow hum of the streetlight.

"Sure thing," I said.

I felt unwieldy, light-headed when I got up from the curb. Automatically, almost mechanically, I offered my grip to Daddy. He took my hand and raised himself; all his weight pulled on me and I leaned back. Then we walked. My legs were asleep from the curb, and I limped along with Daddy toward the door.

The insides of the building were red. Old stained velvet walls that would have once been fancy now looked like the open and bleeding innards of some dying animal—safari game from the wilds of the South Georgia swamp. The crackling sounds of the speakers hammered just enough to make the building breathe heavy. The folks that slinked into the room shook the folding chairs before they sat down. They tested the old wood. Most of the broken chairs were marked with a black X on the armrests, but there was always a new one to break. The surprise was greeted with the cackles of the people who had picked better in the surrounding rows.

Me and Daddy found a row toward the back of the room. We weren't super interested in the movie, but there was something comforting about the creak of the chairs as we leaned back, propping our feet on the broken seat backs in front of us. The movies were always boring. They sputtered onto the screen in black and white. The lessons and morals of faith and imminent judgment landed in someone else's heart, warmed someone else's soul. Daddy dozed, his chin tucked to his chest. I watched a few minutes of the movie, sandy men in robes, their mouths not quite lined up with the sounds of their words.

I heard the chair next to me creak and looked over. It was George's mama right there next to me. I nearly pissed myself. She looked over at me and then at Daddy. He was sleeping hard. "Don't you worry," said George's mama. "I won't bite." But her teeth sure were shiny. They kept flashing in the movie light. She had real dark hair and it hung down around the sides of her face, then kept going low till it swished like a horse's tail across her rear. I'd watched it before. Only her pale face glowed through. The corners of her eyes were bent in a way that only the tip of a sharpie could draw. I imagined she hid things in those corners. I held on tight to the arms of my chair, afraid to move, but the sweat from my palms made it difficult. I dug in with my fingers and felt like somebody else was driving.

"Let me see you smile." She put a finger, warm and gentle, under my chin and turned my face toward her own. Made me look at her. "You know what they say—somebody said," she paused. "An eye for an eye, a tooth for a tooth, and all." She was smiling and I looked to the corners of her eyes. "Smile, boy." She still held her finger under my chin. I squeaked out a grin, stretched the muscles in my cheeks to defy the feeling in my stomach. "You've got you some nice teeth." She took her index finger from my chin, then touched my cheek with the rest of her hand. "Little Georgie had it coming. Just like his daddy." She made a little pouty face with her lips, held up her left fist in a tight ball. Her hand was pale and smooth and glowed in the dark. I tried to remember to breathe as I felt the buildup of waxed wood under my fingernails. She took her hand down from my face and let it rest on my knee, her other hand she kept on her own knee. I noticed her chair was missing an armrest. Figured she just needed a place to put it.

"I'm Margaret. Pleased to meet you."

I teetered someplace between aroused and terrified. My pants were confused too, and she smiled when she looked down at me shifting around.

"You racing this weekend?" she asked. I nodded my head, tears in my eyes. "Do you talk?" I nodded.

"Yessum. Hope to."

"Good. I'll be seeing you there." She sat for a minute and watched the screen. Then she brushed her hand up my thigh as she stood and walked away. Her spring-loaded chair clapped, wood on wood when it folded. Daddy snorted in the seat next to me and I couldn't move. I stared at her and her at me as she walked away. Then she was gone. My hands cramped and I relaxed my fingers. The exhaustion of relief, a wave of sweat and cool air, drowned my face and shoulders. I sank down deep into my chair and was asleep in moments.

I woke to a poking from a bony finger. In the backlighting of a wall lamp, fully illuminated, the small figure in front of me poke-poke-poked with the bone of an index finger, a cold digit to my chest. The shape of the figure's face was scraped into sharp angles, carved up with the knife of time.

"Get up," that skeleton said. I got startled, and leaned back hard into Daddy, who also woke. The theater was empty, the movie was over. I shook my head and breathed. My eyes adjusted.

"Shit," I muttered at the sight of the rigid old woman.

"Watch your mouth, young man." The woman, satisfied with me waking up, moved on to the next row, sweeping under my chair as she shuffled along. She continued up the slope of the theater and I nudged Daddy, elbowed him hard. I swear, we both slept better in the theater. Never interrupted by the sounds of fighting or the feeling of being fought. Daddy sat up and looked at me.

"Got school tomorrow," he said, spit all dried up in the corners of his mouth.

"Shit. You're right."

The old woman looked back over at me.

Daddy pushed himself up from the armrest and stood. "And gotta get the engine." I was turned around in my chair watching the old woman walk from the room. The bones of her body pointing at angles from the oversized T-shirt of the church group. I was still trying to convince myself that I hadn't seen the very figure of death. Daddy stood there patting his pocket and there was no jingle. "Keys." He looked over at me. "You got 'em?"

"Nah. Never do." I stood up. "You check under the chair?"

Daddy shook his head, still patting his other pockets. Then he pointed over at me, telling me to look. I leaned down, and groaned as I pulled myself out of my grogginess. Under the chairs was a mound of dirt, wrinkled and aged generations of popcorn missed by the delicate brooming of the skeleton woman. The keys sat on a mound of buildup. The lights flickered.

We walked out into the night. The glow of the streetlamp lit up the last of the volunteers.

"Thanks," I said to the bustle of people. The group loaded trays of leftover food into the back of an Astro van.

Margaret was nowhere around.

9

LITTLE

After a final ring, the outgoing message for Daddy's lawn service played, then the machine clicked. "Good morning," started the voice of Sister Theresa. "After much thought, prayer, and consulting with the family of George Mackey, we have settled on a one day suspension for your son, William Lemons the Third, pending further deliberation on the matter."

It was only eight in the morning.

I was awake, and stood in the kitchen, staring at the machine as she continued.

"This, of course, will begin a review of your son's scholarship, and could very well jeopardize his continued attendance of St. Francis Catholic School, an institution that prides itself on bettering the young men and women of…" she rambled. I got the point but saw no fix. I watched through the oven window as the heating element turned orange and blew wisps of smoke. "I look forward to speaking with you first thing on Monday morning."

Daddy'd scrambled into the kitchen and stood behind me. The sound of another woman's voice in the kitchen was probably unsettling. Seemed like anytime there was a woman in the kitchen other than Mama it wasn't any good. We'd had visits from Child and Family Services and some of his former lovers.

"Sounds about right," Daddy said. "What'd you do to that kid?"

I rubbed the knuckles on my right hand. "Nothing."

"Don't sound like nothing. Got tooth marks on your knuckles." Daddy walked past me and over to the sink. He turned on the faucet and the stink of sulfur water filled the galley in a cloud. Daddy cupped his hands and splashed the water over his face. His hair was matted to his cheeks.

"Those guys are assholes," I said. It was the truth.

"I know," Daddy said through the lines of water streaming from his lips. "I know their daddies. I whooped all their asses too." He toweled off his face on a dishrag. "Still...got to take it out on the track." Drops of water fell from the tip of his nose. "You signed something or other." Daddy was talking about the code of conduct I signed when I accepted my community scholarship. "Signed a thing for the track too. They sure ain't gonna let you race if you're out there dicking around at school. It's part of the deal."

I watched Daddy as he shook out his hair like a dog. Droplets hit the kitchen window and sparkled; they disturbed the scum and buildup of dirt and grease.

"Can't race anyhow. Not without no engine." I grabbed half of a snack bag of chips from the counter. Mama left them there when she came home last night. We were fresh out of Toast'ems.

Daddy pulled himself up on the counter and sat. "You in luck. We got that covered." He motioned for the bag of chips and I handed it over. Daddy ate the last one and tipped the bag back for the crumbs. "God, I'm hungry."

"Me too." I pointed to the bags of canned goods next to Daddy. He looked over at them.

"No opener. Your mama bring home anymore of those chips?" Daddy motioned to the cabinet. He was tapping his leg on the cabinet. I opened the door and looked in. The cabinet was empty aside from napkins and a single bulb on a chain that hung from the ceiling.

"Nothing. For sure."

"Well. You're missing school. *That's* for sure." Daddy slid down from the countertop, balancing on one leg until he got his footing. "Let's get on. Think we got one last yard we can hit up." His stomach growled, a hollow, empty reverberation that sounded like creaking pipes. "Shit." He put a hand on his paunch, a small round belly distended from his otherwise thin build. "Then we can go see my man with the go-fast."

I felt a chill, maybe a shiver of excitement. It made the hair on my arms stand up. I never got excited for the races, only nervous with a floater of dread. But the idea of getting something new, something we never did, was enough to make me break a cold sweat. It was similar to the feeling I'd got the night before, when Margaret's fingers brushed my jeans. My teeth gave an involuntary chatter and my head shook. Same as I felt when I was up to no good, but going to do it anyway.

"First," Daddy held up a finger, looked down to burp, looked back up, "line for the weed-whacker," he said.

We drove down Highway 17. Daddy's phone rang and he picked up. He leaned toward his window and I knew it was best to lean the opposite way. I tried hard not to listen. Daddy spoke in short bursts. "I get it," and, "No shit." The words grew sharper, and I could hear Mama's voice through the treble blasting speaker. Still, Daddy held the phone close to his ear.

The other kids at school had their own phones. They played games and sent messages to friends. The only phone that I knew personally was Daddy's, and he never wanted to have a conversation on it. He cussed at it every time it rang. The calls never ended well. Daddy snapped the phone shut and looked over at me. He wiped his nose with the back of his arm. "Well, fuck it," Daddy said to the windshield. "You all right?" He nudged my leg.

"I'm all right. You?"

"Yep. I'm all right." He stuck the phone in the ashtray. His eyes were lined with a thin creek of water, small enough to jump into the void of the darks of them. Maybe it could figure out what was going on behind them. I would sit there and wonder, but never got to ask questions.

The shopping mall was a khaki sprawl, closed and shuttered.

Daddy turned the truck onto the feeder road and we circled the dinosaur of a building draped with signs, bright red banners, weaving around speed bumps long useless. Daddy parked the truck right in front of the store. The landscaping had expired. One of Daddy's former racing buddies, Stevie, propped himself on a fire hydrant, letting the top push through the seat of his pants. He leaned forward onto the four-foot arrow sign that he was supposed to spin around his body.

We stepped down out of the truck.

"Hey, Stevie," Daddy called.

The man didn't move. He wore dark sunglasses that wrapped around his head and his headphones hid behind stringy dark hair. The hair was attached to his oversized hat, a costume I was pretty sure. He slept. "Used to drive with him," Daddy said. Man was propped up, arms cooked in the sun. Looked like a work glove got colored with a highlighter.

I followed Daddy and we walked on toward the store. A crack in the glass of one of the large metal doors was covered in masking tape. Inside, the aisles were empty except for the occasional spool of barbed wire or empty plastic tank for gasoline. The sales folks, dressed in light jackets, huddled around a small portable TV borrowed from the shelves. The sounds of a sitcom rerun crackled through the fuzz as Daddy waved to the crew. They didn't move.

We moved on toward the section labeled *outdoor*. I looked down at my hands to make sure we existed and that I didn't look like a work glove too. The fluorescent lights flickered a pale pink shade on my hands as we floated between aisles. The building hummed with the AC, still on despite the break in temperature. Even the floor throbbed in the mechanical buzz. Daddy disappeared down an aisle and whistled for me to follow him. We looked up and down the racks for the last leftovers of merchandise—a display of yard gloves with only one glove left, used shears with a frosting of rust. The line for the weed whackers glowed yellow and stood out from the end of the lane like a large spool of thin whip. Daddy reached down and picked up the spool, nodded, but didn't say another word. We walked out of the aisle, toward the front of the store. Daddy looked at me again and smiled. I held my breath and looked up to the lens of a security camera. The red light was off. Daddy stuffed the line under his jean jacket and we walked out the doors into the daylight. I kept my focus on the truck and moved as fast as I could, making a gap between me and Daddy, who looked inside his coat.

"Hey, Wild!"

Daddy heard the voice—I knew he did—but he didn't stop. He limped along faster.

"Wild! It's me, Stevie!" That time, Daddy stopped and turned to look. Stevie was awake. He was still propped on the sign. He'd barely moved, like maybe he was still dreaming. But he barked over at Daddy. He sounded like somebody held his nose when he yipped, "Hey, man, you going to the race this weekend?"

"Yeah. Yeah, Stevie. For sure!" Daddy called back. He gave Stevie a thumbs-up. "Good to see you, man."

Daddy climbed up in the truck. I was ducked down nearly to the floor.

"Should've gave me the keys," I said. "Would've picked you up over there."

"All good. Quit your worrying. Tell you what," he said, taking a breath while he turned on the truck. "Stevie like to scared the shit out of me." Daddy backed the truck out and caught his wheels when he hit the gas. His hair flipped back, then settled on his neck.

The yard we were trying to cut wasn't far away, just a few blocks. Daddy pulled the truck into the drive, just as the owner opened the front door. The trailer bounced behind us, rattling and squeaking. The truck humped along with the weight.

I looked out on fresh-mowed grass, like a flat-top buzz cut. "That grass is cut," I said. Daddy stooped his head toward the steering wheel and looked out on the yard. He breathed through his mouth. The old man from the front door walked up to Daddy's window, and he rolled down the glass.

"Hey there, Wild," he said, smiling. "Youngin'." He nodded at me too.

"Mr. Sanders, that grass is looking cut," Daddy said.

"Yessir. Sure is. Your daddy didn't tell you?" The man looked around real slow, with pride. Had a big smile on his face. "Had him a crew sent over here just yesterday. Said they'd let you know." Mr. Sanders rested a hand on the windowsill of the truck.

"No, sir. He didn't let me know." Daddy rubbed his hands on his jeans. Our last lawn of the season was sitting over there wrapped up in a debris bag with Senior's logo screened on it. "You know, we aren't working together these days. This is me and my boy's business now." Daddy grabbed my shoulder without even looking over. It was taking everything he had to try and squeeze out the words as mild as possible. His jaw was clenched tight and the skin rippled and rolled over the bone. "We're making a go."

"Hmm." Mr. Sanders squinted into the truck. "Y'all are going to have to get to moving faster than my grass grows then." He tapped his ring finger on Daddy's door. Daddy gripped the steering wheel tight. The leather, all raw and flaky, still managed a squeak under his grip. "Supposing that daddy of yours was doing you a favor. Lesson's in that for sure."

"I learned me enough lessons from him." Daddy looked into the man's eyes deep enough to swim to daylight through the back of his skull. Thought his jaw might cut right through the skin of his cheek.

Mr. Sanders blinked, but Daddy for sure didn't.

"Let's get on," I said, practically whispered.

"Listen to your boy." Mr. Sanders spoke the words slowly. "Ought to be respectful to your elders, even if you can't be to your own daddy." He pulled his hand from the door like the metal was flaming hot. Daddy blew off the spot where his hand had been, then put his own elbow there. He put the truck back in gear and turned the truck and trailer like a snake wrapping around Mr. Sanders in his own freshly mowed yard.

"Goddammit," Daddy hissed as the trailer followed us back onto the road. "Don't need no more lessons." Daddy grabbed the weed-whacker line from the bench seat and threw it out the window. I looked in the side-view mirror and watched the trailer wheels bump over the hard plastic spool. The line squiggled over the asphalt behind us. "Let's go get us an engine."

"Got to pay for it, right?" I looked back over to Daddy. "How?"

"We got options. Your mama. The pawn."

"Mama's working. What're you gonna pawn?" I asked, still confused by him throwing away our spool. I looked back to the mirror, watched the wire unfurl like a giant glowing snake. "We just got our tools *back*."

"You know I'll get it figured out." Daddy kept looking forward. He pushed the gas pedal harder, like he was outrunning the lashing-out he'd left behind him. I pressed back in the seat.

We drove back toward town. ProCreations sat on a hill at the top of a parking lot in a strip center. When it rained the runoff would wash down the lot and form a wave as it hit the curb at the street. I loved it when Daddy would drive two tires through the puddle, splashing water and oil over the roof of the truck. Today, there was no rain, there were only food wrappers that blew like tumbleweeds. Daddy pulled into the parking lot and the truck's engine strained as we mounted the hill toward Mama's work.

Daddy parked along the emergency lane, in front of the red curb, and left the engine running. Mama was on a smoke break, and had been standing behind one of the yellow brick columns in front of ProCreations till the lawn truck rolled up to the curb. She stepped out from behind the column. She wasn't looking like she was surprised to see us. There wasn't a lawn at the strip center. Daddy, however, was surprised when I pointed over there behind him and he saw Mama, cigarette in one hand, the other on her hip looking straight through the glass.

"You want to go ask your mama?" he asked.

"No way," I said. "Knew you were gonna come here."

"'Course I was. She's your mama," Daddy said, rubbing his eyes with the palms of his hands. "She can help. She used to like watching racing too." He didn't look at me. Kept his eyes straight over the wheel. He knew that he was out of asks. "All you got to do is walk in." Daddy motioned with his fingers. "Walk yourself up to the counter, and say, 'Mama, you got some cash for me?'"

Daddy rolled down the window. "Hey," he said, his fingers still in the formation of legs.

"Hey yourself." Mama put her other hand on her hip. "What are you wanting?"

Daddy stopped walking his fingers and tried hard to fake a smile. Somehow, the corners of his mouth turned down when the rest of his mouth tried to go up. "Me and Little were just coming by to see you."

"You must take me for some kind of fool." Mama didn't smile back. She pointed over at me. "Get on out, Little. Why don't you go look at you some pets." She didn't need to ask twice. I pulled the door handle and got out and started walking toward the entrance, even though I knew the conversation would be quick. I didn't go inside. I just stood there on the other side of the column peeking and listening.

"What are you wanting, Wild? A cigarette, some booze, money, some pussy? Last of all that. All gone." Mama held up her cigarette, turned it back and forth for Daddy to see, then flicked the ash. "Nothing's bottomless, except the chips over at the Chili's."

"You got to contribute too," Daddy mustered. "I'm with the boy all the time."

"'Cause. You. Don't. Work." She stomped out her cigarette.

"Speaking of which. Time for me to get back." She turned to go inside.

"Nanny," he said, all sorts of busted. "Twenty bucks?"

"That all?" Mama stepped back toward the truck and Daddy leaned back into the cab. "You know you need more than that." She was talking way too quiet. Her eyes were wide, and her nostrils grew and flared. Daddy supported himself on his right hand and leaned back hard. "You're such a piece-a shit, Wild." Mama reached into her pocket with no trouble and pulled out a crumpled bill. Lint blew from between her fingers in a cool breeze. The pieces of fluff looked like dandelion seeds as they floated up and off, just wishes of dust. Mama threw the crumpled bill in the window of the truck. Daddy didn't catch it and it hit the floor. He leaned over, scrambling and searching for the balled-up bill, all frantic. He sat back up and had it snatched in between two fingers.

"Thank…" he started to say. But Mama was already walking back to the doors.

I stepped in front of the sensor for the automatic door and it opened, then walked the long way around the columns, and looked out from around the bricks at Mama. "Neat stuff in there, Mama," I said, but she didn't hear me.

10

NANNY

I took a fifteen and stomped around my office.

Wild's ass came to my work and it set me boiling. He was always needing. That was just like my daddy. Men were always needing something. I had no time to wait around on Wild, scrambling and searching for that twenty. Folks were waiting inside for a demo. I had to walk back in stone-cold faced and tell about how some other species of animal was getting sexed. Wild could keep the twenty.

I wanted to keep something. My mama's house, maybe. I wasn't that broken up about the house. That house had seen the worst of my days for nearly every year I'd been living. Work felt more like home to me. All it would take with Wild would be a splinter in his finger and it was like we should be starting all over again with the surgeries and hospital stays. The first round of all that wiped me out. Wild didn't see it.

Sometimes when Wild took money from me, I'd find a few rolled up bills with a note from Little with some money back. I never expected them or asked for them, but those were coming less and less. When does a boy become his dad? Does he have to? I knew I needed Little with me as fast as I could make it happen, but it felt like every day he stayed with Wild was another step closer to him becoming Wild. I felt some defeat. All I wanted was a moment and a cigarette. Instead, I got a visit. Is there a final straw? What does it lead to when you give it a suck? Nothing was ever enough. I knew from experience like he knew the bottom of a bottle or used to know the feel of a gas pedal. He'd go searching for the last drop at the house. He'd be surprised.

I watched Lady in her cage. I'd dissected and distilled, watched late at night in the whimpers and the whines, tried to understand if creation came from the brokenness of a late-night romp or an acquisition, a transaction or a wish, or an agreement for momentary pleasure, a hope for a future before being left in the dust? Nature was broken as soon as the boy dog saw that there were other girl dogs besides the one with her ass up in front of him. He couldn't get to the next one without humping his way through the one right in front of him.

I checked on Lady's cage up under my desk. She was looking plump and unworried, and I was hopeful. She was free from any boy dog's influence. She had a male, somewhere in her bloodline, in her genetic pool, but she had taken flight, escaped the late-night escapades of a shared cage. She was perfect and unpossessed. I wanted to isolate and capture the god inside, the self-breeding, self-conceiving god. I wanted some cosmic understanding. I said a silent prayer for her immaculate conception and watched her roll to her back. Her fur was unruffled, and I dreamed for her future.

11

LITTLE

We pulled up in front of the house and Daddy pointed the nose of the truck straight at it and parked in the brown-cooked sandspur grass. He craned his neck this way and that, looking at the concrete-block house like he'd never seen it before. We sat there in the quiet for a minute. The house had always been yellow when I saw it in my head, but as we sat there I saw the green and black running down the sides from the drips of a sagging roof. The oak trees blotted out sunlight and hung heavy with moss. They dropped branches here and there and tested the roof's ability to cope. Daddy, with all his craning, finally said something.

"Got to be something here we can move. Something I missed." The look on his face looked real similar to the one I saw on the squirrel that got stuck in our kitchen vent, head poked out through the wall looking at me, desperate, but also curious at the surprise of company. Daddy was climbing out of the truck and I watched him. "You coming? Need a fresh set of eyes on this stuff." He pointed to our house.

I got out and waited there on the front steps, watched Daddy as he looked through the window next to the door. Then I walked over and turned the knob on the front door. We'd left it unlocked.

"Our house," I said to him. Daddy nodded and I walked inside, with him following behind. The camp chair sat all alone in the living room. Daddy checked the blinds—they were a long shot for a dollar at the pawnshop—but they were cracked and broken anyhow.

I had noticed over the course of growing up, but it was

never mentioned, that things disappeared—toys, gifts, family. It was like Daddy was letting me in on some poorly kept secret. I watched Daddy as he took his inventory of nothing. I followed him to the kitchen, opening cabinets. There were a few plastic cups. The microwave had disappeared a while back. Daddy'd told me it needed fixing. It never came back, and I guess I thought it was just too broken to make its way home. The pantry door opened into empty, but Daddy pulled the string of the single bulb to show off his frustration.

"Goddamn nothing," Daddy said as he pulled the string again and yanked it right out from the light. It would stay on until it burned out. Daddy slammed the door to the pantry and I followed him back to the living room.

"Check that bedroom," Daddy said. He pointed in the direction of my room. I walked down the hall and it felt like I tumbled out of some rocket, like I was walking through space. It made my room feel like somebody else's. I was an explorer. I was a burglar. It was my mattress on the floor, but it wasn't. I hadn't slept in those sheets the night before. I hadn't left them like that. My backpack sat next to the three-legged dresser propped up on one corner by a book. I checked the book to see if it could be sold, but it was a bible, a copy given out in a hotel room I'd never seen. It said, *Placed by the Gideons* in the corner. I saw a little plastic sword down there on the floor and wondered where the toy that used to hold it was. I was done playing with toys, too old to care about them, but wondered where all the toys had gone. I stood up to a headrush and walked down the hall to Mama's room.

Daddy was standing there looking at the row of trophies on his dresser. He picked them up one at a time, held them to his ear and knocked on them. He held a trophy in his palm, bobbed his hand up and down, then put the metal-plated plastic to his mouth and bit it. He frowned. The only thing metal on those trophies was the screw and bolt that held the fake wood bases to the shiny plastic men and cars up on top. Daddy turned and looked at his own bed. It sat on the floor, too, right next to the pile of sheets he slept on at night. He limped across the room to the closet and pulled the door off the track. A few coat hangers dangled. Mama's clothes were usually all that hung in the closet. They were gone. Daddy pulled out the drawers of the dresser. He checked Mama's drawers, but they were empty. I stepped back from the doorway and leaned against the wall.

Daddy came out of the room empty handed. He wiped his forehead with the back of his arm.

"Nothing left," I said. I shrugged and felt as empty as the house.

"Thinking she might be gone." He looked around, then snapped-to. "But something's left," Daddy said.

I followed him down the hall, through the hollow living room. His prosthetic echoed off the floor and ceiling with each tap and creak and we walked out the back door. The back yard was mostly mud. One of the last pairs of dogs Mama had brought home had grown large. They were nearly pure bred, and Daddy had thought for sure that they could breed them and sell their puppies. They stayed fenced in the yard until they'd gotten hungry. They fought and dug and bit but wouldn't have a litter. When they got out through a hole in the fence they raided a neighbor's chicken coop. Then they ate a few cats, even a smaller dog. The yard still smelled like them.

In the carport sat potential. Daddy pulled back the large blue tarp and revealed the embodiment of failure. I'd lost every race I ever entered in the driver's seat of that car. "You gonna sell the car?" I asked. I couldn't even tell if I was hopeful or just surprised. Daddy shook off the question, yanked his head back and forth.

"See any tools laying around?" Daddy asked.

"We need our tools. How we going to fix it without tools?" I walked around the racecar, saw things that needed fixing every time my eyes shifted. I knew how much work lurked under the tarp. Daddy kicked the rocker panel and I flinched. From my angle, I couldn't tell if Daddy kicked it with his good leg or the other. Either way, it was hard and genuine, not something I saw all that often. I knew we'd have to pound the dent out, that we needed a hammer to do that. Daddy took a second, his arms resting on the body of the car. His shoulders gave.

"Come on, boy. Let's go." Daddy stood and I followed him out to the truck.

We didn't bother to lock the doors of the house.

We drove out of the yard in quiet. Daddy dug around in his pocket and pulled out a bent cigarette. He snapped the filter off and threw it out the window, then lit what was left. I had seen him pick it up from an ashtray outside the hardware store earlier. Daddy didn't know I'd seen him, or maybe he did and just wasn't worried anymore about keeping up the jig. No use once I'd seen the mess behind the curtain.

We turned onto the highway and I flinched as all the wheels barely missed an armadillo, fresh, fat, and dead in the gutter. I watched the side-view mirror. The carcass rolled on its back, one way and back the other.

We'd stopped through the pawn shop pretty regular, but Daddy'd always said he wanted to say hey to his friend. He didn't come up with a fresh reason this trip. I knew the pawn was a heavy player in the family economy but wasn't schooled in how it worked. Daddy parked the truck in the handicapped spot and the trailer took up another couple parking spaces behind us. Fast Rabbit's Lending and Payday Loans was painted white on an otherwise blue building. They advertised "$50 to $10,000—Fast!" in the front window. Daddy opened his door and looked back at me.

"Hold on here, and wait," Daddy said. But I was already climbing out too.

"Nah, I'm coming in there with you," I said.

Daddy almost protested but didn't say another word. I followed him into the building. Two large sleigh bells hung from a string on the front door. They rang when we walked in.

"Well, well, if it ain't Mr. Broke-ass Gas Blower." The large man, like the big stump of an old tree, walked out from behind the counter as soon as he caught sight of Daddy. "Look, we even put a tag on it says, *Broke-ass Gas Blower.*" He picked up an orange leaf blower from a pile of power tools in front of the counter. He held the tag out for Daddy to see. "What kind of broke-ass bullshit are you bringing in for us to not be able to sell today?"

"Fuck off, Teddy," Daddy said.

"No, you fuck off, Wild," Teddy replied. "And who's this we ain't minding our language in front of?" He pointed over at me. I stared at the blower, recognized it, not realizing it had ever left.

"He's all right. That's my boy, Little."

"Like you don't know it—that daddy of yours is a shyster." Teddy held out his hand and shook mine. It felt like a piece of wood in my hand, bark on and everything. "We got some talking to do, why don't you go on and take you a look around." Teddy motioned to the aisles with a fat finger from a heavy hand and I started walking around.

Daddy walked up to the counter, following Teddy. I walked the aisles of stuff. TVs and saws and guitars lined the walls. After a minute, I heard the bells ring again and watched Teddy walk out the door with my daddy.

A row of microwaves in alternating colors of black and white and silver sat on a folding table in the middle of the room. A white one with a burn mark across the top was ours. Reminded me of a time when we used to cook together. I had begged for mac 'n' cheese and was excited to see the kitchen in the new house get put to use. Daddy made burgers instead, caught a pan on fire and put it down on top of the microwave. The kitchen smelled of grease and smoke. Mama and Daddy fought for days after that.

I walked on, looking at the devices and trinkets. Deeper in, I found the toy section. A giant stuffed bear sat on a shelf along the back wall. I remembered when I'd first named it. I reached for the bear and squeezed its paw. Howard the bear had once played, "We Wish You a Beary Christmas." Now he sat silent, eyes dead and black with his fur dusty.

I heard the bells jingle behind me. Daddy and Teddy walked back in.

"This thing don't even got a line on it." Teddy laughed. "How we going to test it out?"

"Come on, Teddy," Daddy said. "Next win and you know I'll be back around."

"Wild, you ain't won since god knows. What's to make me think it's gonna change now?"

"Need to get a bump for the engine. Car's all right, just needs more horses."

"Wild, I was *at* the race last week. That horse is plum dead. Barely even made it off the track without the thing falling out of the car. And that was when it got towed." Teddy put the weed-whacker on the counter. He still rested his hands on it. He held his breath.

"You're talking about credit, Teddy. Sign out front says no credit checks. You know all about me. Not exactly fair to a customer."

"That ain't credit, that's personal experience. That's common sense, Wild. Besides. Talking about customers, the blower didn't even blow. Thing is toast. I actually sold it—to a customer 'cause *you* didn't pay it off. The dude that bought it—he brought the damn thing back."

"I just need a hundred."

"Thing won't even sell for a hundred. Be lucky if this thing sold for ten. Not exactly fresh from Sears." Teddy looked at me at the back of the room. I turned around and pushed the paw again, not wanting to see the scene up front. But I could see it fine in my head as I listened. "Here's ten bucks, from my own pocket, Wild. Get your boy, and y'all go get you something to eat." He paused. "Don't come back."

"What?" Daddy's voice got all high. There was a pause, like the air stopped moving. I clicked Howard's paw again, not thinking and it stuttered out, "We wish you…" before I clicked it again.

"Don't come back, Wild."

"Come on, boy," Daddy called. I turned. Daddy hung his head and started out the door. The bells slapped the glass. As I passed the counter, Teddy had his head down too.

"Thanks," I said.

"Uh-huh," said Teddy.

I caught up to Daddy on the steps.

"What the hell was that?" I asked.

"What are you meaning?" Daddy said. "Watch your mouth."

"Just left our weed-whacker. Got nothing for it."

Daddy didn't get a chance to respond. I didn't get a chance to ask another. A big, shiny black truck pulled up between us and Daddy's truck. Senior rolled down his window. I could see our reflection in his sunglasses. We weren't shiny.

"Boys," Senior said.

"What you want?" Daddy replied.

"Came to see my grandson. Funny, the places I got to go to do it." Senior nodded over to me. I got a little excited. "You still losing, boy?"

I felt like I'd been busted for something. I looked over at Daddy first, for some sort of thought on how to answer, but he was clenching his jaw. I looked up at Senior. "Yessir."

Daddy tilted his head toward me, eyes wide and pissed. He turned back to Senior.

"Fuck off," Daddy said.

Daddy and Senior's relationship was some awful mystery. The temperature heated at least fifteen degrees anytime they shared the same space.

"I'd say you got you a smart mouth." Senior looked out the front windshield, then ducked his head out of the window and glanced over at Fast Rabbits. "But you're just not even a little bit smart." He looked over at me again. "What you selling, boy? I know he ain't got nothing." Senior pointed at Daddy.

Wild held a finger out at me, which meant, *Don't you say a word.*

"Nothing. And for sure nothing for you to be snooping around here about," Daddy said.

"You want to sell something? You know I'm always buying." Senior opened the door of his truck and stepped down. "Besides, I'm sure you know I bought this place up six months ago, right?"

Daddy pushed me by the shoulder. "Go get in the truck." I started walking, real slow, and watched them.

Senior started to walk over to our trailer.

"Get out from behind there," Daddy said. I got in the truck and left the door open.

"You still got a mower? You sell that yet? Think I gave that to you, didn't I? High school graduation? Still amazed you made it out." Senior followed Daddy. "But I paid up. I stayed true to my word and paid out what was owed."

Daddy climbed in the truck and started it. Senior walked around to my window. I looked up and directly into the mirrored sunglasses. "You still got a mama, boy?"

Wild put the truck in drive and threw me back in the seat as we left Senior standing in the parking lot. Senior's voice chased us. "You just let me know when you're ready to work for a winner."

It was late in the afternoon. I could hear Daddy's stomach talking across the truck. My stomach said something back. We took the ten dollars from the weed-whacker and headed to the Taco Bell. We each got a bean burrito from the dollar menu, and I had hopes for the change. I could make it stretch for a few meals. But Daddy held on to it.

"How we going to get the engine?" I asked. "Thing cost a hell of a lot more than ten bucks." Daddy squeezed the money into his pocket.

"You let me figure it out," he said.

We ate in the truck and watched as the sun glowed low and

orange in the sky. I felt our options melt in the puddle of the glow.

We rode south out of town where the four lanes turned to two. A water moccasin was draped over a stop sign—someone's pride and a warning for what hung around the bushes.

The pines pushed in toward the road, narrowed the drip of light that trickled toward the blacktop. The air grew cooler, then the tongue of land unspooled into a stretch of cause-way through the marshlands. The sun flickered off the dying marsh grass, a strobe effect that made me dizzy. I closed my eyes and let the air blow down the collar of my shirt. It was a simple, cheap pleasure. I opened my eyes again 'cause I wasn't sure I deserved it. We passed the old rice canals, flooded lanes switched back and forth, soil and water. The thin strip of road tucked back into another hollow of pines, which were inter-rupted by the occasional dirt road punctuated with a mailbox. Daddy squinted and stretched his neck to read the numbers.

"Can you see those for me?" he asked, pointing to the posts with the peeling foil number stickers.

I rolled down my window and read the numbers out loud. Daddy slowed onto the shoulder and pushed his emergency lights button on the steering column.

"That's it," he said.

"So, where's this thing coming from?" I asked.

"From my buddy, Early."

"You know—" We hit a pothole in the dirt road. I braced myself with a hand on the ceiling. "You know what I'm saying," I tried to clarify. "*Where's* this thing coming from?"

"You know it was a wreck. What're you gonna do? You gon-na start being choosy?"

"No. Just don't want some wrecked piece. What're we gonna do with some dead-ass engine?"

"Watch your mouth." Daddy looked over at me. "Besides. It's not a dead engine. Should be running just fine. He's got it pulled out from the wreck already."

"Don't really mean dead like, not running—"

"I know what you mean. Don't be worrying about luck or whatnot. You start worrying about that, you get this." Daddy pointed down to his gone leg. "Besides. Can't be no worse luck than what we got." He reached over and ruffled my hair. I wasn't feeling eased. My head was tight with concerns, dozens of them swimming around.

The dirt road dusted up behind us and we pulled into a clearing. Pieces of machines were scattered, a thousand projects planted in weeds and tangled in Spanish moss. A carport stood in the middle of the clearing. The grass was high enough to hide behind and the scrapyard was the haunt of lazy billy goats and rattlesnakes, I imagined. I couldn't tell if it was cicadas or a thousand rattlesnakes, but the pines seemed to vibrate. I felt thrown off. A burned up Astro van with fake, painted flames rested in the shadows.

A man stood in the glow of the overhead fluorescent of the carport. We got out and walked toward the light, past the blackened wreck. The seats were bubbled and crisp.

"Pulled it from that? There's still stuff cooked on the seats," I said. I pointed to the mess; charred fat peeled from vinyl. There was nearly nothing left of the back end, like it had vaporized in its demise. The front seat was pushed into the steering column. Daddy held his breath as we passed it. I didn't look any closer, didn't want to own the ghosts.

"Early," Daddy said.

"Wild, how you doing?" They shook hands. Early was a huge, hunched lump of man, skin dark red like he'd hugged up too close to a fire. His scraggly beard half-covered his broken smile. Early didn't look at Daddy's face, just his leg. Daddy stood with his gone leg hidden behind his good leg.

Early toweled off his hand on a rag and turned to me. "Well, I'll be." He kept wringing his hands. "Dang, boy, you grown. Remember you when you were looking like this." He leaned toward the ground as far as his gut would let him and held a fat hand flat and steady, to show me how high I had been. He was

constricted at the waist and his voice strained as he said, "Holy
smokes." Swear I saw a little smoke come out of his mouth, but
he wasn't smoking a cigarette that I could see.

My eyes struggled to adjust to the buzzing bulb overhead
and I couldn't see Early's face. What I could see was the swarm
of insects like a frenzied crown behind the round silhouette of
Early's head—a halo of squirming bodies. It made me shiver.
Early noticed me shaking.

"You feel that moon pulling on us?" Early pointed out from
under the roof.

"Huh?" I asked.

"Sir?" Daddy corrected me. "It's tough, man. Don't learn
nothing in school now. Not like manners."

Early's head slowly came into focus, and the bugs looked like
they flew in and out of his ears. He was still pointing, and I felt
obliged to look. The giant chalky moon was near full. The circle
rim glowed like it was a hole punched out of the sky, waiting for
the sun to drop out completely. In the last of daylight, it seemed
like a child had scribbled it into being.

"What you looking at, boy?" Daddy walked up behind me
and pulled on my sleeve. Early shuffled over as well.

"Think that's something? Want y'all to have a look at this
here." Early put his hand on my shoulder and pulled me toward
an engine hanging by chains from the ceiling. It hung there with
hoses plugged in to the right places. They dangled into buckets
of fuel and oil below. Early walked over to a battery on the
floor. He crouched over two lines that lay on the ground. He
held them up to us.

"Watch this."

Early pressed the cords to the battery and small sparks
popped from the terminals. As the sparks bounced off the cement and landed at our feet, the engine grumbled. It twisted in
its chains. The hoses jerked and sucked from the buckets below,
pulling juices into the slowly throbbing machine above. If it
had eyes, they would have opened, sleep crusted and blinking.
The engine was awake and alive. It was a heart beating, begging

for some poor body to inhabit. Early hooted over the noise, his own eyes wide as he cackled like the sparks. I didn't see what was so funny. Early dropped the cords and stood. He pressed a small lever and revved the engine, made it louder, more alive. It stretched and grew hungrier. I covered my ears and Daddy elbowed me in the arm. He had a strained smile on his face. I'd seen the same expression when Daddy greeted Mama in the kitchen some mornings, when he still attempted to keep the show going. Think it was fear.

"They tell me he howled," Early shouted. He pointed to the charred chassis outside the light of the carport. "The devil himself blessed that machine and when the tail end caught fire, flaming like the very gates themselves, that beast only blew faster. Said you could see the fireball all the way in Jacksonville." Early was sweating like he'd touched the fire he spoke of. The grease of a thousand engines was so embedded in his skin that the beads of sweat rolled over the black marks but they didn't streak. "Somehow or another he jumped right in the air and lifted off, ramped it right there in front of all the crowd to see. *Howl!*" He tipped his head back and I watched that man's Adam's apple lurch like he was drinking. "Said it happened just like that. I believe 'em, for sure."

The engine backfired and the noise got me, made me jump. Early cut the engine. The buckets feeding it from below were nearly dry. His fingers sizzled when he touched the metal. "Sonofabitch," he said in the new quiet. My ears rang and Daddy paced. Early dipped a rag in oil and rubbed it on his singed fingers. "Bit me," he said, looking at his hand. "Screams, don't it?" Early looked over at Daddy. He still held his fingers and his eyes squinted.

"Don't change how much it's costing," Daddy said. I watched his face and saw that it had lost its flush. He looked sober.

"Come on with me, Wild. Let's do us some talking." Early turned and walked out of the light. Daddy paused like he had a thought, looked at the engine, then to me. He held my gaze for a second before he turned and followed Early.

I walked up to the engine, held out my hand, then remembered the sizzling sound Early's skin made. I felt the warmth on my palm from a few inches back. I swear the engine looked like it was sleeping, chained to the ceiling. It smelled of smoke, burned oil, and gasoline. I turned my ear to the machine and listened. It felt like it had something to say. In the quiet, I could hear the faint words of Daddy and Early, urgent words, Daddy's of desperation, Early's calm and opportunistic. In between the words, I heard the creaking of cooling and contracting metal. I rubbed my arms with my hands, then pushed my ear a little closer to the engine. Liquid and air bubbled and hissed, the innards gurgled and slurped, and I couldn't help but feel empathy for the engine's hunger. My stomach did the same.

"Lemme show you this, boy." Early's words shook me, and I pulled my head back. He guided by the shoulder around to the back of the engine. The block was black, smoked from being licked by flames. Early took the oiled rag and wiped the bottom plate, an otherwise smooth, flat surface. The poem was hand etched in script. I reached my hand to the words, slowly, thinking instinctively that perhaps the machine would snap at me. I read out loud, didn't get nervous like in school. Did it without a stutter or start.

And what should we do with the horses and corpses?
I guess that we'll hang them from trees.
And what of the pyre, the funeral fire?
It'll likely consume you and me.

From the corner of my eye, I could see Early grinning.

"What's it mean?" I asked.

"Means this thing packs a bunch of horses and blows fire," he said with a quick laugh and a look over his shoulder at Daddy, who shuffled and paced.

"What else?" I asked.

"Means we'll settle up when you win."

I looked to Daddy, not sure if I should be smiling or not. "*Really?*" Daddy nodded and raised his eyebrows, flashed the same strained smile. "How're we going to get it home?"

"You're gonna leave that mower," Early said.

I squinted at Daddy in that low light, searched his face like there was a mistake, that we weren't there to gamble the last of our livelihood. He looked back at me.

"All in," he said, and nodded to me.

It felt like the thousand pounds of engine hung on my shoulders. We rolled the mower from the back of the trailer and lifted the engine in with the chains and a few wood supports. My work felt the heaviest, even though I saw Daddy and Early sweating too. Fluids from the hoses and buckets leaked strings across the ground and into the back of the trailer. I borrowed Early's rag and wiped up what I could. Early sat on our riding mower and grinned as Daddy drove us up the dirt road. I looked in the side mirror, back at the glow of the light in the carport. Early was bathed in the light, a fat cherub swarmed by bugs.

We drove in the quiet. The windows were cracked and crisp night air filtered in over the smell of stale cigarettes and gasoline. I nodded off, and then came to when the truck bounced into our own yard.

"Now what?" I asked.

"Time for a heart transplant." Daddy backed the trailer up to the blue-tarped patient in the garage, then we set about the task of prepping the recipient of the beastly machine. I was in a fog, still groggy, and felt my way around, pulling the tarp back as Daddy hit the lights. The carport buzzed as we worked. Daddy talked to himself, muttering under his breath in his focus, as he freed the space of the old engine. We lifted it with the crude ceiling pulley we'd installed the last time we replaced an engine. It hung, limp and battered, seals blown and flatlined. We would scrap the metal to hustle some cash.

We rolled the fresh engine from the trailer out on furniture movers. It was uncaged and hugged low to the ground. It seemed like an animal sniffing and orienting itself to a new space. It drained oil and gas from its hoses, marking its territory. While Daddy cut metal with a torch and made room for the new muscle, I grabbed kitchen towels from the house. They'd been stuffed under the sink during the last major pipe leak. They were dry enough now, and I used them to clean the engine. I scrubbed and tried to make the head gleam. We each hoisted a chain on the pulley. The engine lifted from its rollers and swung, twirled. We held the chains and looked on as the engine stilled. It hung in the light, as if to receive some blessing. I thought of Sister Theresa, wanted her to genuflect, bring Mary's blessing as the hoses dripped with gravity.

We lowered the engine into the chassis.

"Careful—careful, easy," Daddy said.

I could barely hear him in my concentration. My muscles ached, my body was worn and my head was weary with the learning of the day. "Easy does it. Let it settle. Weight's coming at you." But it felt like I was surely holding all the weight already. There was no difference when Daddy let his chain go. He lay down and pulled himself under the car to line up the descent. "All right, boy. Let a little off." I let the chain slide a bit. It ran smoothly through the pulleys. There was no clank of metal, no heavy crunch or scrape. The engine soggily settled into position. The car sat lower. I swear I could feel it throb through the chain, satisfied for the moment with a new host.

I let go of the chain and neared collapse. Even without the burden of weight, I felt pulled to the ground, and sat, draped my arms across my knees.

"Go on to bed if you can't hang," Daddy said out from under the car. I looked over and saw him, focused and red-eyed. I rolled to one side and picked myself up. Each step was the shuffling of a bag of Quikrete. I got inside and fell asleep in the tub.

I stirred to the slam of the front door and morning light coming in through the bathroom window. It was race day, and it hurt. Daddy hummed through the house and I hoped the car would hum too. It was time to roll to the paddock.

12

LITTLE

Daddy was sure he still had fans. He kept up the same track-day champ's routine for the races I was driving. We dropped the car at the corral, the dirt pit where he'd look over everything one final time, twist the gas cap till it clicked, and push the car back and forth to make sure the tires were squishy. He wanted to see it sway, to know that it could corner and hold him tight in the seat without flipping, even though it would be me driving. Then he held my helmet and left the car in the corral. I followed him from the pit, around the side, to the main entrance. He stood there at the gate, took a couple deep breaths and waited for the ladies at the turnstile to say, "Hey, Wild, come on through," and they unchained the side gate. He was still deep breathing, eyes all squinty, when we walked through the gate. I walked in behind him, just far enough back to see those ladies, his fans, look at each other and roll their eyes in a way I'd grown to cringe at. Their eyes rolled like whitewalls, while I prepped myself for another blowout.

We walked up to the raceway; the giant, domed lights overhead were never the first things to see—they were blocked out by the grandstand. It was always the little orange dots along the railing. The line of men and women, each with one foot resting on the bottom rung, elbows leaning on the top, cigarettes held between two fingers or lips. The burning floaters would alternate and grow brighter as one after another sucked on their smoke.

"Don't know why we still got to do this," I said.

"Keeping the tradition, man. How 'bout the smells and such?" Daddy asked.

"Kinda smells like dirt." I had trouble keeping my teeth from chattering. My nerves made me cold. I didn't wear much under my racing suit.

When we got close to the folks at the railing, the dots extinguished in a wave. One light after another fell four or so feet to the ground, a shower of haloed embers before they were rubbed out. For a second, till our eyes adjusted from moving to the shadows of the track lights, we couldn't see much. In this brief spell the quiet of the pre-race time was broken as the voices behind the orange dots grew to a rumble. The crowd came to meet Daddy. He liked to call them fans, but they all wanted his bet. They wanted to be on the collecting side of his money.

"Evening, Wild, what's the spread?" The questions came, smoke still spilling from their mouths. Daddy shook hands and high-fived.

"Never know." He skirted the questions. Daddy kept his head down but gave me a sideways glance. I picked at a sticker on the helmet, a former sponsor of Daddy's. That company asked for him to remove the sticker, even the chipped pieces, to avoid chipping their reputation. Daddy propped himself on a handrail as more of those folks asked for his take. I wandered away toward the concession stand. The lady at the counter offered me a cup of Coke and placed it on the counter. I put my helmet on the ground and sat down on it. I chewed on the waxy edge of the cup and watched as Daddy was offered a beer to loosen up his pockets. His eyes grew wide and he began to crack some jokes.

"I'm betting on my boy!" He offered the crowd to a chorus of laughs and cheers. "As always!"

"You got money left to bet?" one man said to more laughs. He lit up another smoke. I blew into my cup and felt the coolness of it bounce back from the icy drink.

"Hey," came a voice much closer to me, just to my right. "Didn't know if you'd make it tonight." The track lights lit up Margaret as she leaned down to me. She may have been George's mama, but she still had a couple zits like the girls in my class. Her tank top barely covered her belly button, and she hovered so close I could smell peaches and cinnamon and vanilla from her body spray. It made my Coke taste funny. She propped a foot on the lower rung of the rail, next to my head. It looked like somebody had squeezed a tube of toothpaste the way her white legs shot out of her jean shorts all spread out like that. Margaret was close enough I could see the goosebumps on the cold white skin of her legs. I was lost, bumping along those bumps. She wore an old letterman's jacket with a football stitched to the chest. The jacket was unzipped, and it seemed as if, were the football ever to land, it would surely split the uprights. "Hope you win," she said and looked down at me. "Sure would like to see you give 'em hell." I felt heat on my neck, near burning, and my teeth stopped chattering. She pushed her hips closer to the rail. The leather of her ankle boots creaked next to my ear. "Why don't you stand up, let me give you a little luck." I don't remember standing, but I did, maybe I floated. The ice in my cup shook. "Can I get a sip?" Margaret took the cup from me.

"It's only ice left," I squeaked.

"All right by me." She took a cube in her mouth, sucked on it a second, rolled it around her tongue, like some wild beast was flopping around in her mouth, then pushed it back from her lips real slow and into my cup. "Good luck." My stomach and head swam around like I was in that cup.

She handed the cup back. There was a rim of dark-red lipstick that looked black in the low light. And then she turned and walked away, the heels of her boots clomping. I imagined that if she had a tail like a horse it would swish as she stepped.

A minute later, Daddy walked up. A smile stretched across his face. His eyes squinted from the beer. He burped and blew fumes of beer out his nose.

"Cheers, boy." Daddy held out his beer to me. I tapped my cup to the bottle.

"Cheers," I said, still in a light state of shock.

Daddy must've seen the smear on my cup. "You wearing you some lipstick these days?"

"Huh?" I pulled the cup down, cube in mouth, with a question in my mind as to if I'd chosen correctly. I held the cup away and turned it. "Oh. Yeah. I guess." I forced a nervous laugh. "Must've given me an old cup."

Daddy pointed to his own chest. "You know, I'd know the look of that on a cup any day." Daddy twisted at the waist, stretching out his ego. He tapped his finger on the empty bottle in his hands.

"Drivers to the pit. Drivers to the pit." The voice came over the loudspeaker, and I was thankful for the distraction.

"Go time, boy." Daddy winked at me. I picked up the helmet and tossed the cup in a nearby trashcan with a bit of regret. All the confusion of my body had the racing suit rubbing me the wrong way.

"I gotta pee real quick. Meet you down there." I walked around to the back of the concession stand and into the yellow lights of the men's room. Both stalls were stocked full of heavy bodies with dropped jeans, and I chose the corner urinal from the three that sat empty. It was tall for me, but I unzipped the racing suit and the legs of the suit puddled around the backs of my Pumas. I aimed up. A few seconds into my stream, George's father walked up next to me and let his mule out of the pen. He breathed heavy till his own stream splashed the porcelain. I focused on my own work, aiming for the pink urinal cake. The smell of peppermint was overwhelming.

"Knocked my boy's teeth out." That man looked over at me. Thank Jesus I was finished. "What do you say?"

I thought of the ice cube. Mumbled, "Yessir."

He laughed. "I guess I could be more pissed if I wouldn't a helped that daddy of yours lose a leg." He held his right hand out to me, his dick still hanging out of his pants like some sad flag. It dripped on my Pumas. I paused, but before the words could settle, I put out my hand and shook. George's daddy smiled. "Smarter than your daddy, but you're still gonna need all the luck you can get." He took his hand back to task.

"Better go." I walked past the empty urinal to the sink, doubled up on soap when I washed my hands. George's daddy shuffled behind me. I saw him zipping up as he walked out the door. I scrubbed until my hands hurt.

"Start your engines!" came the voice over the loudspeaker. I hustled toward the paddock.

Daddy had the car running by the time I got down to the pit. The noise of the muffler-less cars was overwhelming. My own engine vibrated and shook the shell of the car. I'd heard it when Daddy cranked it up briefly at the house. He'd had this wide grin, eyes big, and laughed like the car told him a dirty joke. The noise was a heavy rumble, like the car itself was hungry.

"You all right?" Daddy asked.

I swung my legs through the open window. The doors were welded shut. I looked over at the other cars, saw Tom two rows back. George was ahead. The lottery had been kind to me, and I had a good position for the night.

"I'm all right. You?" I asked.

"I'm all right," Daddy said. "I'll be more all right you win this thing." He looked away when I glanced over at his face. I pulled on the helmet and Daddy tapped me on the hard plastic. "Hit that gas good. Feed the beast."

"What if it don't work?" The words slipped out before I could catch them.

Daddy looked at the hood, then me. His jaw was tight like one of those hungry dogs right before it dug a hole under our fence and disappeared.

"Has to." He slapped the top of the car. "Be the only roof we got left."

I nodded, then dropped through the window and settled into the cold seat, pulled the harness over my shoulders and strapped myself into the piping of the roll cage. The clutch was tight, but I worked it a few times, shifted through the gears, made a cross, genuflected through the tree of gears and the engine backfired in protest. I put it back in neutral and pushed the gas down to cycle out the backfire. The pedal was spongy with resistance and the engine roared as I teased the throttle. It seemed to ask a question out of hunger, an angry desire to consume. The driver to my right startled and looked over at the noise. A look of fear changed to confusion at his realization that the noise came from me. The boy next to me hit his own gas pedal to listen for a difference, to see if his ears had deceived him. I couldn't contain my smile as I eased the car onto the oval track. We started the lap in two lines, a formation for all the crowd to inspect us like cattle. In the stands, money changed hands. Hotdogs were choked down real quick to free up napkins that bets were scribbled on. The rows of cars throttled up and I wiggled my tires to warm them in the cool night air. The bets were on. I was raised going to the races. I could imagine what they were saying.

Charlie's car has a fresh ding in the rear quarter—no good. Tommy's rocker is lookin' lean—bet. I'll take that! Two on that! Little Billy—ha-hahaha!

Daddy sat in his usual spot on a big knobby tire behind the chain-link fence. It was in the Red Zone, beyond the cones and beyond where it was considered safe for cars and drivers. He sat there, motionless, all topped-up on people and all betted-out of money he didn't have in the first place. I made my formation lap and felt my own nerves prickle, could feel every blond hair on my arms reach for air and touch the underside of the second-hand race suit.

The official pulled the rolled up green flag from the back of his jeans. Everything slowed but my vision. I could see the EMTs working over in row fourteen, unplugging some over-zealous hot dog eater with the flesh rolling in the undershirt—freed waves with each pound to the chest—beating, beating, beating on his heart—and my own heart throbbed in my ears. And I saw the sweat stain on the flag as the official unfurled it, teasing us like dogs after a rabbit just as we took the final turn of the oval. The front fenders and grilles of the cars lined up facing the stands, rolling and slinging mud, revving out of the turn. The engines competed with the voices and screams of the crowd—then the official wagged the holy hell out of the flag and the hearts of the crowd and the hearts of the cars and the fringe of my soul all touched redline.

We rounded turn one.

Five rows back and the Lemon Party II was losing position. I tested the engine twice, pressed the pedal to find its growls, but each time I felt a cold trickle down my spine that froze me to the seat. I only revved it to the five on the tachometer. The wheel jerked when I touched on any higher revs. Like they were somehow linked. Going into turn three on the first lap, Tom slid alongside of me and rubbed the front bumper on my quarter panel as he passed. He held out his third finger for me, the signal of his intent to pass. I pressed that pedal again, and where once I'd felt ice, started to think for sure there were flames. That heat welled up, and I checked over my shoulders to make sure the car wasn't on fire. I sniffed through the mud in my face, spit to breathe, but there was no smoke, nothing thicker than the exhaust of the cars in front of me. The heat rose from the holes in my Pumas, burned up my legs. It rose from my hand on the wheel, and from my hand on the shifter. It moved through my knees and my elbows, up my arms and shoulders and thighs and hips, through my empty stomach, and cycled through my heart. My neck flushed and my face burned. I punched the gas pedal to the floor.

The engine rumbled, laughed, coughed out the dust of char and the choking stink of death, a cloud that humbly descended to the track in a fog. It gnashed the teeth of its pistons and fired, reveled in the gasoline and huffed the flaming fumes as it screamed—low at first, guttural. It permeated the metal of the cars all around, I saw the other drivers' looks of surprise and fear, like some dark angel had knocked on their roofs and yanked them by their bumpers. I bet it could be heard a county away. The other cars seemed to stop. The dirt swirled in clouds, small bits and particles, tiny planets spinning, but suspended in quiet, and waiting to collect and fall under their own weight.

I lost control—but I didn't need it. The steering wheel turned and the wheels slid. I let go and was obedient to its whims and it held each loop of the oval like it was on rails. My hands guided and the wheels bit. They ate up the track until no one was in front of me. It was an empty road, mine to enjoy traveling. I whooped through the exit of the next turn and hollered, a primal howl from somewhere deep.

The car stole my breath and other drivers' glances, stares, and mutters. Drivers that had shoveled heaps of shit on my suffering got lapped, uncontested—like their cars had a governor limiting their speed, but the Lemon Party II had no such leash. I turned the wheel to drift and looked over my shoulder as a spray of mud, thick globs of oil and dirt, the puked-up chunks of my own years' worth of wasted tires, flung into the open windows of the cars behind me. They wiped off their goggles and visors as they watched the spectacle of my flight. Nine laps later, and the official waved the checkered flag. The race was done.

I eased off the gas, and the engine rested, barely winded from the trip. But there was no noise from the stands. I pulled the Lemon Party II up to the grandstand and cut the engine, not real sure what to do next. The rest of the pack of cars stopped short. Some drove straight back to the pit. In the silence, the official rolled up the flag, then pointed to me. I pointed to myself, and the large, balding man nodded, then waved me out. I sat there a second, then unbuckled the helmet from my chin, looked around the car, and unstrapped myself from the harness. I was shaking, felt a little frantic, and started to pull myself through the window just as I heard Daddy's drunk-rambling.

Daddy stepped onto the track, just got missed by a car that crept through the access gate. The driver was dazed. Daddy hustled and limped toward me and the car. I had it parked right in front of the podium. I held my arms out toward him, gestured a *can you believe this* when he took a sharp turn and walked over to the podium instead. I saw him take a big sniff and look all around with his eyes watery. I slid one foot over the door of the car, then the other.

I walked over to where Daddy was already standing on the podium. Years were pulled through his cheeks. A new line appeared on each side of his mouth, below the eyes and running straight toward his jowls. He stretched out his arms, held his hands out toward the grandstand and expected the embrace of the crowd. He let the track lights blind him, didn't even blink as he stared out there into the bright lights.

"Wild, just what the hell you think you're doing?" asked the race official. Daddy turned around blinking. He held his hand out, waiting for a shake, but the official didn't offer his in return. He stepped around Daddy to get to me. Daddy flattened his back against the rail, and let the man pass. The official shook my hand. I was still in disbelief. The crowd murmured, and the official held the night's trophy out to me. The bleachers began to empty, to leak people out into the night. By the time the announcement came, "Ladies and Gentlemen, our winner is 'Little' Billy Lemon!" I looked out and the stands were nearly empty.

I smiled, regardless. The lights kept me looking down at the trophy and a check. I held the check close to my chest.

"We sure do hope you'll catch us next Saturday for race number three of the season. Only four races left!" he announced to the stands, but the stands were empty.

"Good race, boy." Daddy had walked down from the podium and sat on the hood of the car. He patted the spot beside him. "Good machine."

"Look at this here!" I held the trophy out to Daddy.

"Seen a couple of these in my day," he said. He spun the trophy a couple of times, held it up in the lights, then knocked on the plastic racecar topper, just in case.

"Let's go do some celebrating," I said, trying to make my excitement contagious, trying to get it to catch on him somehow. "Let's get some dinner." I held up the check.

"Let's get this thing packed up first." Daddy pointed at the car. He still held the trophy. "Don't be getting too ahead of yourself." Daddy took the check from my hand. "Besides, can't be cashing this tonight."

"How much we win?" I asked. "We got to go cash in!"

A car rumbled by. "Still a fag," Tom said as he passed and drove to the paddock. Daddy flicked off the boy. "You too," Tom called back to Daddy.

"Fuck that kid," Daddy said. "Go on, boy. Get that thing to the pit."

I walked back to the car and slid my legs through the window, then settled back into the seat. It felt cold. I cranked the starter and the engine reluctantly yawned back to life.

"Hop on?" I asked Daddy, motioning to the back of the car, but he waved me on, and I steered around him. I watched out the window as he stuffed the check in his pocket. I didn't want him dropping it.

I pulled the car into the pit, up behind Daddy's truck and the trailer. George and Tom stirred around with their families. They were smiling somehow, even though I'd just beat them. I kind of wanted what they had, just another Saturday night. They talked about Pizza Hut and watching movies. They touched arms without leaving the room afterward. They didn't have bruises. George's teeth were shiny and his jaw looked just like his dad's, his eyes like his mom's. He saw me staring at him and I thought he may say, "Congratulations" or something. He gave me the bird.

Daddy walked up and put the trophy in the cab of the truck, then lowered the ramp from the trailer. I turned off the car and it sighed, then chortled a bit, like a snore. I listened, scared for a knock in the engine, but it never happened. I pulled myself out the window. Daddy and me leaned back against the rear of the car and pushed until we got some traction. I realized how sore I was from the previous night, and how I hadn't even noticed it in my nervousness. I grabbed a side and Daddy grabbed a side, and we lifted the ramp and each locked it. I looked around. The pit was nearly empty.

We walked up the sidewalk to the box office, and there was still a smattering of cars in the lot. Margaret's unmistakable rear poked out as she leaned into the window. I came to a quick stop when I saw her.

"Stay here," Daddy said.

"Why?" Didn't matter, I wasn't moving anyhow.

"'Cause I said to."

Daddy walked to the window and Margaret walked away from it. The window closed and locked. I stood at the corner of the concession stand and Margaret walked up.

"Nice win tonight." She unfolded a wad of bills in the palm of her hand and peeled one off. "Guess I'm the only one that bet on you. Think I might owe you a little more than this." Margaret stuffed the bill in the pocket of my racing suit. She let her hand hang on the rim of the fabric. I held my breath. "Soon, I guess." She brought her finger up to my chin and gave it a pinch. My breath followed her as she walked away. It took me a second to get it back. She was parked close; her BMW took up both handicap spots. I turned to see what Daddy was doing but he was still standing over there at the window. He looked frantic, so I stayed put and did my best to pretend I didn't see him banging on that window.

The light was on inside. Daddy knocked on the glass until Donald pulled the blinds back. He shook his head when he saw Daddy standing there. The door unlocked and he cracked it rather than open the window back up. Like he was going to be letting in some stinking breeze if he did.

"What's up, Wild?"

"Here to collect," Daddy said.

"You lost. You didn't bet a winner." Donald scrunched his

face, confused by Daddy's request. "I'm all paid out." Daddy tried to sneak a look my way. I looked down to pretend I didn't hear. My eyes followed my stomach as it sank.

Daddy held up the check from my winnings. "Bank don't open till Monday."

"We don't cash checks." Donald was no longer confused. "You know that."

"Come on, Donald." My suspicions kept meeting their confirmations. Dinner scooted further away in my mind.

"If you're wanting to collect on that, I might as well go on ahead and take out what you owe me for towing and storage. Want me to?" He held out his hand.

Daddy folded the check back in two and put it in his pocket. Margaret had reversed out of her spots. "See you next week," Donald called after him. I heard that door slam shut. I had my hands in my pockets and adjusted my pants under the race suit. I could feel the bill in my pocket, like it was giving off some of the heat Margaret gave off when she was real close, but I shook off the temptation to look at how big that bill was. She drove that BMW out of the parking lot, slinging gravel on its way.

"Sweet car," Daddy said. "Seven series."

"Oh," I said, and gave a look after the car, pretending to notice it for the first time. "Uh-huh."

"Let's get moving." Daddy walked down the sidewalk, back toward the pit and the truck, and I followed, still struggling with my pants.

As we climbed in the truck, I asked Daddy, "How much you win?"

Daddy turned on the truck and we started to pull out from the pit. Donald walked down behind us to close the gate. I felt a little sad leaving my moment behind, my win, as we drove away.

"Didn't have nothing to bet. Just trying to settle up with Donald."

"For real? But I won." I tried to act surprised, shocked, floored.

"Boy, you got to have money to make money." He tapped

his pocket. "Now we got some for next week." I thought of the small bills that had disappeared from my pockets, the lunch money I'd saved that would mysteriously vanish.

The dark had settled and the lights of all the fast food spots blurred in a neon glow. "You bet against me?"

"Nope. No way." He wasn't convincing. I watched his face and waited for him to glance left and cough like he did when he fibbed. Daddy squeezed the wheel and pushed the pedal. I saw his teeth grinding under his cheeks. He looked out the driver-side window, paused a moment, then held his right hand up to his mouth and coughed a dry cough. I sat back against the bench seat and breathed out.

"How we going to eat?" I asked, waited for Daddy to answer.

He breathed through his teeth. "We could dine and ditch." Daddy looked over at me with a smile, begging for approval, some alternating reciprocation to his spark. I reached my hand in my pocket and pulled the bill from my pants. A twenty-dollar bill. I thought about Margaret's hand, pulling on the fabric and it made giving the bill up justifiable. She'd also offered something more.

"You holding out?" Daddy looked far more interested in what I pulled from my pocket than the road in front of him. He squinted, and his brow furrowed.

"Somebody gave it to me—as a tip." Daddy's look of concern faded.

"Well damn, son! That's free money. Let's eat!"

Daddy drove us to the Olde Time Country Buffet and while we stood at the register, the only thing between us and rows of all-you-can-eat, Daddy said, "Two adults." He looked down at me and winked. We paid the full $7.99 each out of my twenty-dollar bill. I stood my full height and pulled my shoulders back. The word *adult* bounced around in my head, and I whispered it to myself as Daddy pocketed the change. He slapped me on the shoulder and handed me a plate.

"Should we get one for Mama?"

13

LITTLE

"You bet against him?" Mama was in the house, back for something she forgot. She walked through quickly. I already knew the truth, had known for a while. I heard Daddy backpedaling through the house, Mama on his toes. There was a crash and a rattle, and the thin walls shook. I took a spin through the possibilities of what could be left to break in the house and knew it had to be the camping chair. Wondered where I would sit in the living room with the camp chair broken, then remembered that I'd never sat in the chair. That was where Daddy sat when he got too unsteady to balance on his gone leg.

Daddy had tried for a comeback post-leg. I heard the whispers about him, about his time back, like he was some kind of haunted house. When we walked through Dollar General folks would whisper: *Just didn't have the same feel for the car. Lost that con-fi-dence. Timid for the pass. Stopped shootin' for the gaps. Hugged the inside.*

That's the story I collected.

His comeback in the morning's argument with Mama was even weaker. There wasn't hardly one at all.

"Can't do this no more, Wild." The walls were so thin, when they argued it sounded like I was listening through a blown speaker.

"He won," Daddy said, dragging out the O like he was learning to read. "Can't you see some good in that?"

"You traded away your goddamn mower for a chance to win—and bet against it anyway," she shouted. "Don't you see the stupid in that?"

I sat up in bed, waited for the reckoning. I shook my head

and it blurred their voices. I touched my knees, my shins, my feet. Everything was still there. With all my parts, I was pretty sure I could do it all over again. Maybe save his ass in the process.

"We'll win again. We got the check here to bet on the next one," Daddy whined from the den.

"But you won't win. You never win. You're gonna lose your ownself every single goddamn time." I had seen the arguments play out enough to be able to imagine the looks on their faces. I knew where they stood in the house, Daddy's slumping and leaning; Mama's left arm across her body and her other holding up a finger in Daddy's face. "I'm done. Figure your own shit out."

The last line was new, and I sat up to listen. I stayed that way till I heard Daddy walking back toward the bedrooms. I didn't want to see the look on his face. What would it have been? Disappointment? Embarrassment? Those looks had come to my door enough, so I flopped down and rolled over when I heard his steps come closer to the room. There was a knock and the door opened.

"You got school today. Better get cracking."

I sat up and pretended to yawn, covered my mouth in the most unconvincing way, then gave up the act.

"Mama gone?"

Daddy looked down at his shoe. He sucked in through his teeth.

"Mama's gone."

"For good?"

"Could be." He turned to leave. Daddy tapped the door frame lightly as he did. "Go on now, get your clothes on. You're already late."

I rolled out of bed. My stomach was heavy from the glories of the previous night's buffet. The laundry pile smelled stale, and I checked the armpits of my shirts to find the least offensive one. When I walked out of my room, I found Daddy in the living room, trying to piece together the broken plastic of the camp chair. Each time he'd get it standing again, it would hold there for a moment, then fall back onto the floor. Daddy looked up at me when I bent down to pick up a book of matches off the floor.

"Don't know what happened to this thing. Must've sat down wrong," he said.

"I'm gonna win again," I replied. "Car runs too good not to."

"I know it. She was sounding pretty angry, huh?" Daddy asked. I stood there a second, pretended to think about his question, but I just stared at the gold pack of matches in my hand, not sure how to answer. "'Specially when you got her up in the 7,000 RPMs."

I was glad I'd taken a beat to answer. Daddy couldn't shake his head off thinking about racing. He'd already moved on from thinking about Mama. "For sure," I said. Mama had sounded angrier than the car. The matches had an ape behind bars and music notes floating up from its mouth like it was singing. Between the notes it read, *Monkey Palace.*

Daddy dropped me at school. "I'm headed to the bank. Going to get us some cash and we'll be rolling," Daddy said. I could hear him slap, then rub his hands together like he did. He couldn't see my chin shaking.

I got out and closed the door without looking back, then hustled along under the oaks toward the front circle of the school. I passed the windows of other classrooms along the front of the building and glanced in. The other kids sat at their desks, backpacks hung along the walls, and I walked faster, attempting to beat the second bell. Right when I got up under the covered drop-off, the bell echoed under the steel roof, and I slowed my pace in defeat. I opened the doors to the school and changed my course, headed to the office instead of homeroom. When I got to the counter in the office, the secretary didn't even look up. I reached for the pen and signed in as *late.*

"Good morning, William," the lady behind the counter finally said. "Sister Theresa's wanting to talk to you." I stopped moving the pen and looked up. Her eyes were right there wait-ing. "You can go on in. Think she's waiting on you." I looked over to the right, saw that Sister Theresa's door was closed and looked back to the secretary. "Go on and knock," she said, nodding me over.

I let the pen drop and took a deep breath as I approached the dark wooden door. Felt like slow motion when I reached out a fist and knocked.

"Who?" asked Sister Theresa.

"William," I cleared my throat. "William Lemon."

I heard her chair creak through the door. "Come in."

I turned the knob and cracked the door, looking in first, an essential order of operations I'd picked up at home. Sister Theresa looked over the rim of her glasses at me, those black holes yanked on my gravity and I felt like I might tumble over the edge. Her hands were folded in front of her on the desk. She released her grip and pointed a finger at me, curled it slow and creaking to beckon me closer. She looked at the clock on the wall.

"You're late," she said. I looked at the clock and nodded. "I've been waiting." She paused. "Well?" She motioned for me to sit in one of the straight-backed chairs, hard with flat dark-red cushions tied off with tassels, like some sort of celebration of discomfort. I took off my backpack, dropped it on the floor, and sat.

"Sorry."

"Who's sorry?" She cupped her hand to her ear and leaned toward me.

"I'm sorry."

"For what?" She kept her hand to her ear.

"I'm late."

"Yes. You are. And what else?"

I thought for a second. She didn't move her hand. "For knocking George's teeth out."

"Ah." She nodded. "George." Sister Theresa sat back in her chair. She folded her hands again, as if about to pray. "You know—" She tipped her head back and looked at the ceiling. The skin of her neck rumbled and quaked while she thought. "George's mother came in to make sure that you would be back." Sister Theresa held both hands up, palms glowing in the light of the single lamp bulb. My feet went numb. The room smelled like the woods did right before the sun went down and they were covered in dew. Sister Theresa continued. "She offered grace. I must add that I am confounded by her willingness to offer forgiveness so willingly, but I am not here to question inspiration. I only hope that she has felt led to forgiveness through the love of Christ. She said that she would be praying for your peace." Sister Theresa put her hands down and leaned forward, her eyes fixed on me. I shifted around, squirmed in the chair and wrestled the thought that I might be in trouble, might have stumbled into some improprieties not of my own making—that just maybe I'd walked into a trap.

"I believe that you should write her a thank you note."

With that, Sister Theresa stood and shooed me out of the room. I kicked my heels against the rungs of the chair, and tried to make sure my feet were awake, then stood and grabbed my backpack.

"She was quite the advocate for you," Sister said, when I was on my way out. "Really impressive—for a Baptist," she added.

I was out the door. I didn't look back, and didn't finish signing in either. Instead, I powerwalked down the hallway to class. When I got there, I didn't bother to knock, just opened the door and kept pace toward my desk. Heard the snickers from the class and Mrs. Florence paused at the board. She looked over her shoulder at me and then to the door, which I'd left open. She didn't move again till I got up and walked back over to the door. "Sorry," I said, shuffling back to my desk and feeling the cold, waxed floor through the holes in my Pumas.

George turned around and watched me too. My middle knuckle had bent his front teeth in. I felt his stare, knew that with every mouth-breathing blow through the new gap in the front of his teeth, he created a wind tunnel of hate.

I set my backpack down and started to get settled in my desk when I noticed that my seat was covered in dirt. The toes of Tom's feet were propped in my seat just as they surely had been in my absence. I pulled my desk forward at the cost of my own legroom until Tom's feet slid from the back, then brushed the dirt back in his general direction.

"Billy just threw dirt on my pants," Tom whined, grinning at me and the floor. My back was to Mrs. Florence, and I tensed when I saw Tom's grin quickly shift to a grimace. It meant she was looking. The class was quiet and I heard her blow out a breath of exasperation in having not finished the word she was scribbling on the board.

"William, don't start your day like this. Clean it up and take your seat."

I knew not to argue. "Yes, ma'am," I said, not turning around. As I went to get the broom, Sedy smiled and mouthed, *Welcome back*. I nodded but didn't dare move my mouth or make a noise. I swept and kept my head down to stay unnoticed. I could see from the corner of my eye that Mrs. Florence continued to watch me. Sedy looked down and smiled. I noticed.

At recess, I walked down the green grass slope to the playground under the oaks. It was like a plunge down to some promised land of escape. We were all too big for the swings and slides. Most played a pick-up game of soccer. I sat down behind a large oak, out of view. The roots of the oak trees were like alligator tails, lazy and stretched out. I reflected on my morning. Dirt from Tom, menacing glances from George, thoughts of Sedy. I pulled the matchbook from my pocket. Daddy had been back to the Monkey Palace. It was a brand-new book. I tore out the matches one at a time, struck each one, and let it fly. I aimed for a large anthill, and watched as the flaming matches sizzled out when they landed in the sand. Across the playground, George sat by himself watching the game of soccer but not playing. He looked over at me, and then got up and started walking toward me. I eyed him all the way and contemplated what to do if he attacked. I was afraid that none of my ideas would work.

George hooked his thumbs through the loops of his pants as he walked up. "Good race the other night," he said.

I waited for the punchline. Didn't seem like there was one coming. I braced myself for a sudden move and watched his thumbs to make sure they stayed put in his belt loops.

"Sorry about your teeth," I said.

"Getting 'm fixed." His lisp was hard to miss.

"Why aren't you playing?" I pointed over to the soccer game, knowing that he hadn't been asked to play. The other kids, stumbling toward adulthood, yelled till their voices broke in their relish of the game.

"They're kind of treating me like shit. Think it's the teeth and all." He pointed to his mouth. "Besides, my mom said to tell you, 'Hi.'" I froze, and George continued. "I don't know." I looked over my shoulder, checked the trees behind me, then looked back at George. He pinched the bridge of his nose between his fingers, then sniffed abruptly. "Guess I'm s'posed to hang with you some."

My hands were cold. I was an ice cube, tumbled around the flopping tongue of George's mother. Margaret. Margaret's hand on my pants, brushing the denim on my jeans. I took a second to think about the offer. Having friends had ended for me with kindergarten. It was a foreign concept and the feeling in my stomach was the same as the one that came with the jerk of the steering wheel, a cold fear that tightened my neck. And—Margaret. "Now?"

"Nah," he said. "Sometime."

"Sure. I guess," I replied.

George looked back over at the game. Someone waved to him. He waved back and ran away.

I sat motionless and completely confused. I struck another match at the ant bed. The match rolled down the side before it burned out. The ants looked at the charred and smoking stick, walked around it, and kept about their business.

"What are you doing?" a sweeter voice asked. It dripped behind me and sounded smooth to my ears. Sedy appeared from behind the tree, held a hand on the trunk, balanced on a large, knotted root.

"Nothing." I pulled another match from the book. "You?"

"Nothing." She sat down next to me. She smelled like a perfume that hadn't gotten the ingredients ironed out yet. I could still pick them out. This one's a flower. This one's some smell-good. "Can I sit with you?" she asked, a little late. I nodded. She scooted closer. Her legs poked out from under her standard plaid skirt, two popsicle sticks at the beginning of breaking from their flattened form. I flicked another match at the ant bed. "I'm glad you're back," she said.

A scoff came from somewhere in my throat, exited my nose as a snort. It wasn't the noise I'd meant to make. "Thanks," I said.

She smiled at me, thankfully dismissing the snort, and scooted a little closer. She was getting awfully close to my arm.

"What are you doing this weekend?"

"Nothing, I guess. Racing probably." I pulled another match from the book, desperate for something to do to look busy.

"I heard you won."

"I did." My face felt flushed but I smiled and looked over at her while I pushed the match against the pad. It struck but the head stuck to my thumb. "Ow—shit!" I shook my hand and the match flung off flaring. I could see it change colors, heard it sizzle, and watched it taste air for the first time, gulping and flaming—straight into Sedy's hair. Sedy jerked up from the stump, both hands to her head like she was having a fit. She shook her hair and the tangle of curls offered their first puffs of smoke. She patted the back of her head and I sat glued to that log, unable to speak or move. Her hair flamed up like our Christmas trees when we used to get one, when Daddy forgot to water them and they died and caught fire in the backyard.

Sedy screamed.

"Little! My hair!" She slapped at the back of her head. "The hairspray!"

I jumped up, caught her by the flaming hair and slapped

at the puff of burning curls. Sedy dropped to her knees, then rolled on the ground and I rambled through memories of my brief time in Scouts. I cupped my hands and picked up scoops of sand and dirt and dumped them on her head. I was desperate to save her pretty face. She rolled and the flames went out, but Sedy's golden tangles were charred like the stumps of a wildfire. Tears streaked her face through the smears of dirt. I brushed a few ants from her cheeks and neck—travelers caught in the dirt. The smell of her hair hung over the playground, and I coughed.

"Little," she sobbed.

"I'm so sorry." I choked up too. "I'm so sorry, Sedy." I brushed another ant from her face, gently. "You all right?"

"Think so," she said. "Missing some hair." She reached a hand up to point; her hair was still warm and smoked a little. I couldn't help but feel that I'd just smeared the paint on the prettiest picture I'd ever seen.

Sedy turned to look up the hill. I looked too. It took a lot to get the teachers up from their lawn chairs. They usually just blew a whistle and yelled if something was up. But sure enough, every one of them was up and stomping toward us.

"Little, I think you might be in a lot of trouble." Sedy held her hair and tried to roll it up, to hide it. There wasn't even enough to tuck in the collar of her shirt.

"Yeah. I think so."

"I'm sorry," she said. Her chin shook a little.

"Me too."

"Should you run?" she asked.

We both kneeled there in the dirt. Me right there next to Sedy and we looked at the wall of teachers approaching. Sedy leaned into me and I could smell the tangle of perfume and smoke as she kissed me on the cheek. I would have held that kiss on my face forever if I could've, framed it and hung it someplace if I had the wall to do it. She moved to my mouth and briefly touched her lips to mine, closing her eyes, but I couldn't close my own. I wanted to own all of that moment. I looked at her closed eyes and saw the tracks of tears through the dirt on her cheeks and I hoped they weren't from pain. I pulled away and ran from the playground to the street, to the sidewalk, to the alleys, and didn't stop running until the arches of my feet ached inside my flat Pumas.

14

WILD

The breeze from my cracked window fanned my pocket—a bellows on the wad of cash and, believe me, I could feel it burning. It grew warmer while I drove the streets. I rode the yellow lines, the walls of sober barely pinning me in, and felt that I was drying a little too quickly. The sign ahead might as well have been neon. It was a lighthouse beacon at the edge of a cool sea. I was anxious to dive in and put out the flames in my pocket. I pulled into the parking lot of the Fountain Liquors and Lotto and nearly ripped the door off the hinges when I yanked on that handle. The clerk barely looked up.

"Hey, Wild," he said. The *Off Road* magazine in front of him had these giant breasts of tires, cleavage of tread, and shining tail-ends on curvy trucks. They crushed little cars and were tattooed with pinstripes and exotic paintjobs. He couldn't be disturbed and believe me, I understood why. Things were hot.

"Jimmy," I said, looking out on the colorful bottles of booze. "Need me something special—for the win." I thought for a second and looked over at the *born before this date* calendar. "Big one last night." I clapped my hands together and nodded, then grabbed a basket.

"Okay," Jimmy said. "There's some flavors over there above the normal shelf." He pointed up to the pints without looking.

"Need something more," I said. "Something special for the win." Jimmy pointed again, this time out into the store. His finger could have aimed at the giant inflatable cartoon shark smiling as it flew through the football goalpost, or the lady in the sombrero bent over and gently prodded by a curiously peeking cactus. I knew where he meant and walked there on a line. Straight and narrow just like I do. The shelves seemed lower and totally within my reach. "You hear about it?" I called to Jimmy at the front of the store.

"What'd you say?" Jimmy asked. He glanced at me through one of the angled mirrors in a corner of the store.

I found the vodka section—fifths, liters, half-gallons. They all looked wet and would do the job to get me running right. I prodded the plastic bottles on the bottom shelf with my gone leg. The jugs glugged and giggled. I was moving on from all them cartoon bottles. Just above my usual shelf were all the shiny, bold-colored fancy jugs covered in pictures of fruit from faraway places. They were *fancy*. I was surrounded by a native tribe of women with slices of fruit covering their titties. The volcano on the display throbbed and I swear smoke started to puff, just a little, out the top of that thing. Smoke rings floated in the clouds and then the voice in the lava said, *Pick me*. So, I did.

"Got to buy it to drink it," Jimmy called from up front, still not looking up. He'd caught me in my dreaming before, accidentally walking out with a bottle or two.

I chose me a bottle with two orange slices like twin giant suns and a banana like a strung hammock underneath them—a bottle with eyes and a smile to look back at me while I drank it down. I showed Jimmy every bill in my pocket, fanned them, as I paid.

"Wow. You have money today," Jimmy said while he slid the bottle in a brown bag and wrapped the top so the cap poked out. He knew that the cap wouldn't stay on all the way to the car. He swept up the caps outside the door every evening.

"What happens when you win. When you are a win—ner." I pronounced the word for him like he'd never heard it before, like *really* heard it from somebody who'd done it.

15

LITTLE

My lungs burned from running and the arches of my feet hurt from slapping concrete. I knew I was hungry, but I was always hungry. On top of hungry, I stacked tired and sad. I had to cross four lanes of cracked concrete, dead animals in the gutters, and the railroad tracks to reach our house. I was winded. With every engine whine, I expected to hear sirens crank up, either fire or cops, or even Sister Theresa coming to collect me up. The fire I was running from was the one I'd set. Sedy. She could still be on fire, like when Daddy threw a cigarette in the trashcan, and it never quite went all the way out.

Behind me, an engine shifted into low gear and I knew I'd been had. I didn't turn to look until the horn blew a low groan. When I did turn, it was to face Senior's truck. He stopped in the right lane, not even bothering to pull onto the shoulder. Traffic slowed behind him.

"Get in, boy," he said through the open passenger window. It was not a question, and I didn't mistake it to be either. I got in the cab. The interior glowed with lights that reflected off the gray leather seats. "What the hell you doing walking down the side of the road?" Senior looked at his watch, a large piece of steel strapped to his wrist with a shining metal strap. "Isn't it school time?"

I nodded and wiped the sweat off my face with the back of my arm.

"Watch where you put that arm." Senior motioned to the leather seats. "Calfskin." He put the truck in gear and watched his side mirror for a gap in traffic. "What are you doing out here?"

Running had seemed like the right thing to do at the moment. I remembered the kiss. It played on a loop in my mind and made it real hard for me to think of an answer, much less the repercussions of fleeing the scene.

"Look like that daddy of yours out there wandering down the street playing hooky. Good way to get picked up for truancy. Matter of fact, pretty sure that was the first time I had to pick Junior up from the police." He laughed to himself, and I saw him look in the rearview mirror before he looked over at me. "Dumb son of a bitch." I couldn't be sure who Senior was referring to. "Taking you back?" This time it was a question. I ran through scenarios in my head.

We pulled away from the curb. A horn blared, muffled behind the thick-tinted windows, which Senior rolled down as he held up his third finger to the cars behind him.

"I'll get you dropped off," Senior said. "First, let's take us a ride." We rode in quiet for a few blocks. The world was darker from inside the truck. The glare of the sun tried to break through the tint, and it looked like an eclipse outside the windshield, helpless and small. I traced it and knew by the way we were following it that we were headed west.

Senior looked over at me. "How's school? You getting smart yet?"

"Think so," I said.

"You *think* so?" Senior grinned. "That seems to be about two steps ahead of your daddy. Must get your smarts from that ghost of a mama you got."

The leather creaked as I squirmed, and I thought of the baby cow whose skin I was rubbing against.

"I got something to show you." Senior laughed.

We drove toward the edge of town, brushing on the fringe of the county line, then falling off it entirely. Finally, the neon words *Monkey Palace* burned through the tint. Senior pulled into the lot and then drove around back.

"You know where we are?"

"Yessir," I said.

"You bet you do. Finest establishment in this corner of hell." Senior cut the engine and stepped down from the truck. "Come on, boy," he said. I tried the door handle but couldn't get it to open. Senior slapped the hood of the truck and the pounding sounded like thick thuds from inside the cab. "Come on!" His voice was muffled and he waved to me emphatically. I pulled hard on the handle, but the door didn't move. Senior came around to the passenger door and slapped the glass; his rings on his fingers made a sharp cracking noise as they hit the glass, and I sat back for fear that the window would shatter. "You coming?" Senior called from outside, louder still.

I felt tears rim my eyes. I pulled on the handle again with a yank. Nothing. My throat knotted and my cheeks quavered. Senior pulled the handle from outside, gently, and the door opened. He stood there grinning behind the dark of his glasses. The sunlight outside was blinding, disorienting me. "Child locks." Senior chuckled knowingly. "What's wrong with you? Know I'm just messing. Get on out." Senior grabbed me by the arm and kicked the door closed with his boot. "Come on. Got something to show you."

He walked out past the edge of the oyster-shell parking lot, and I followed a few steps behind. A small, rutted road cut between two rows of pines, then opened into a field. There were broken plates all over the road that crunched underneath his heels. "Target practice," he said. In the middle of the freshly mowed field sat a crumpled car. The rusted shell was grown through with weeds. Even still, I could make out the front left quarter panel and caved-in driver's door, the source of the car's demise.

"I save this for your daddy," Senior said, smiling. He kicked a rock toward the wreck and it cracked off the flaking bumper. "Like to think maybe he comes out here to see it every now and then. Revisit his glory. This car predicts futures." He paused. "That boy wrecked everything I ever gave him." Senior spit. It landed on the hood of the car and ran down the steeply slanted bend of metal. He turned to walk back to the lot. "What do you say?"

Rust cracked the paint like a road map. The number on the side was a faded pale blue. The car had a better drawn pair of lemons than mine, but they were coated in dust. *Wild Bill* was still scrawled in cursive under them. It was forever Daddy's car.

"Come on, boy," Senior called. "I can always get another car. Maybe get another driver for my team." He winked at me. "It's easy to drop a loser."

I followed him back to the bar. Inside, the building pulsed and the windows rattled. It was dark but for the glow of the bottles behind the bar and the lights in the monkey cages. They screeched and pounded on the plexiglass, looked like they pounded the air to the beat of the music. Senior held up two fingers to the bartender. She quickly placed two sweating, topless bottles on the counter. Senior grabbed both and handed me one. He tapped the neck of his bottle to mine, then drank. He waved a hand at me to do the same, and I did. It bubbled in my throat like a Co-Cola and I coughed a little but didn't dare spit it out.

"One more thing to show you," Senior yelled over the honky tonk. He walked toward one of the glowing cages. The monkey behind it held both hands over its ears until it noticed our approach. Then it pounded on the plexiglass, banging both fists and baring its teeth. Its eyes were stretched beyond wide and I could see all the veins in their corners, a roadmap of frustration. Senior pointed his bottle at the glass. "Look at these ones." Senior pointed at the monkeys. "They never learn," he said. "No way out unless I feel like tossing them out in the field back there for target practice." He laughed. "Just kidding, of course." His smile faded, but he kept staring into the light of the cage as he pondered. He tapped his ring on the glass. The sharp noise could be heard over the music. "Only place for an animal that don't learn is in a cage."

Senior drove me back and didn't say a word. The tinted windows grew darker as the sun faded in the deep afternoon. The sun bounced behind the tops of the pines and then dipped below them. Senior pulled into the parking lot of ProCreations and into the fire lane. "Had a good time?" he asked.

"Yessir." I nodded, looking away from the dark glasses. "Think so." I rubbed my sweaty palms on my pants.

"We'll do it again," Senior said. "Maybe I'll have some new apes to show you." I had never thought of his words as a threat before then. "Soon." Senior smiled and his teeth glowed in the dashboard lights. "Child lock's off."

I reached for the handle and opened the door, slid down from the seat, and listened to the calfskin squeak. It sounded like a cry for help. I closed the door and stood to the side as Senior drove off. I coughed through the diesel and watched the smoke drip from his pipes.

I walked up to the automatic door of the store and realized I was shaky. I'd skipped breakfast and missed lunch. I'd only had a beer and it soured my breath. The doors spread like jaws and I walked inside. The lights buzzed overhead and everything was washed in white light. The air smelled of piss and woodchips washed in bleach. The AC was cranked and the store was freezing. One of the cashiers looked up when I walked in.

"Welcome to ProCreations," she said, then looked back down.

I wandered the aisles. Another woman pushed a broom down rows, while resting her chin on the top of the handle. She hit an end cap and swallowed hard before she continued to push in her malaise. I walked past a cage with a heat lamp beaming into it where eggs shuddered and rocked. Hamsters humped in the cage above. The whining of a dog broke me from my stare. An announcement came over the loudspeaker. It was Mama's voice, "Attention ProCreations shoppers—copulation on aisle twelve. Dogs." An old man pushed a shopping cart toward the far aisle, his cane the only occupant of his buggy.

He wheezed as he passed. I followed him down the rows and turned behind him.

At the end of the row, Mama held what appeared to be a floor lamp with no shade. She explained the act occurring in the cage.

"The male canine first nips the female on her hind quarters repeatedly, preparing her for the intercourse."

I stepped in closer. The old man was behind several other folks and bumped a young child with his cart in order to get it to move. His breathing was labored. I walked toward the small crowd.

"The female—she just kind of takes it, puts up with it—in this case. It's not like the spiders I showed you a little bit ago." Her voice waned, as if she needed to be wound up again. She skipped a few steps, trying to get through the presentation before the act was over. "The male puts his ears back. It's aggressive, but if he's really into it, he might draw blood." Her mouth stayed open after the last word. She and the small crowd watched the act as they would *Jeopardy* or the commercials between re-runs. It was on and was happening.

The water bowl sloshed with each heavy thrust, and Mama broke her gaze when she saw my reflection in it. She turned and looked at me. "Oh, hey, Little," she said, not breaking from her monotone. Mama pointed the light at me, still giving a demonstration. Her name badge read, *Nanny*. "Y'all, that's my boy."

"You been through this?" the old man asked; he motioned to the dogs, who panted. The female looked tired and bored.

"Sure have," Mama said, staring at the dogs. She still held the light at me and looked like she could fall asleep standing up. I wondered for a second if she had until she swung the light back to the cage.

"This pair is on sale right now. The bitch might already be pregnant." She looked down at a laminated sales sheet. "Just think." She waved her hand with the notecard, then looked back at it again, briefly losing her place. "These two just met, so you could get in at the honeymoon level." She looked over at me, then read the fine print. The words ran together. "This is a limited time offer, exclusions apply, frequent buyer cardholders get an additional 3,500 *Baby Bucks* for purchase during fall and winter months as defined on the Gregorian calendar."

The male dog released his mate, then flopped drunkenly over on his side. His tongue hung from his mouth. The female didn't move. She stayed frozen as she had been throughout the show. Mama turned off the lamp. The shoppers walked away in silence. I stood against the side of the aisle as they passed by and waited on Mama.

"Little, what're you doing in here?" she asked, not looking up from the dog cage. "Y'all dead or what?" Both dogs were still. She nudged the cage with her foot and the female put her tail down. The male blinked and released a slow stream of gas. Mama stared. "Just like y'all do."

"Got out a little earlier than usual."

"Hm," she said. "What you needing?"

"A ride, I guess." My stomach rumbled, reminding me of my neglect as if on cue. "You got anything to eat?"

"There's some jerky we keep up front. Usually feed it to the dogs. It's expired, but that stuff never goes bad. Sharon up there eats it all the time."

I followed her toward the cashiers.

"How was demo?" said the woman behind the counter that had greeted me earlier. She sat on her stool with a long flap of brown jerky hanging from her lips.

"Good. Girl is probably knocked-up."

"She still a puppy? Need some dog condoms around here. That dude's been running through all our inventory. It's like we're always starting over with the puppies." Sharon chewed the jerky an inch at a time like she was sucking in a noodle. "Who's this?"

"This is my Little."

"Your little what?"

"Little, my boy."

"Huh." She finished the streak of jerky, chewing with her mouth open. Sharon lifted a large bag of jerky with both hands, then shook it at me. She continued to chew. Her jaws were the most toned part of her body. I took a handful of jerky and it smelled like Mama's hands did most of the time.

I held up the jerky, nodded to her, and asked, "What kind?" while she chewed and dropped the bag back to the shelf under her register.

"Thanks. I try to be kind. Sometimes it gets hard around here, though."

We chewed.

A heavy whine broke the stale, meaty air.

"Got another demo," Mama said. "You can sit over here." When Mama came back, she had scratches on her arms and noticed me watching as she rubbed hand sanitizer on the cuts. "Got aggressive." Her arms shined slick. She picked up the black phone again, dialed, and sandwiched the receiver between her shoulder and her ear. She continued to rub on the sanitizer and let the phone ring until she got tired of balancing it. "Okay, come on, Little." Mama's Tercel was a kaleidoscope of off-whites pieced together from years of other Tercels. Each panel was a different shade of eggshell or tooth, a veritable rag doll of paints and materials.

"It's unlocked," she said, and I knew this from the missing door lock on the passenger side. I climbed in and smelled cigarettes. A ball-pit of fast food bags were crumpled on the floor. The passenger seat sat all the way back, nearly reclined, and I rested my feet in the trash. Mama drove through McDonalds, and I feasted all the way home.

Mama pulled into the front yard, nearly nudging the front steps with the bumper. She left the car running with the lights on and walked through the unlocked front door. I was close behind. Inside, the lights were off and Daddy was passed out on the floor of the living room. He lay across the remains of the camp chair. A bottle of vodka still sat snuggled in the cup holder of the armrest.

"Wild. You piece of shit," she said, keeping her voice low.

"You staying, Mama?" I asked, as she circled around Daddy's snoring body.

"Just picking up the last of my stuff," she said.

"Want to help me get him up?" I stood over Daddy but watched Mama. Her eyes glazed over. Any feelings she'd ever had for the animal sprawled on the floor were long gone.

"Not my stuff anymore," she said. "Let him be."

Mama turned tail and walked back to the bedroom. I heard her pulling out drawers and rattling coat hangers. I just stood there, surveying the still life of home. It was all uninterrupted angles. Mama came back out of the bedroom and barely had enough of her things to fill two hands.

"This is it," she said and sniffed. "Listen, Little. I'm trying to get a place. Been saving what I can, but it might take a minute." She looked down at Wild; he snorted. "I know what's right. I swear. This ain't it, but there's nothing else. Not yet." She walked by me, touched my shoulder with a handful of stuff, but I knew underneath it was warm. "I gotta go," she said and walked out the door, and then she was gone.

I laid down on the floor next to Daddy. The front door was still open and I thought that I should close it, but the temperature outside was the same as in. I pushed my hands into the pocket of my hoodie, looked up at the tiny dots of the white popcorn ceiling, and pondered them as an astronomer might, looking for connections and constellations. I saw Sedy, goddess-like and giving out blessings on the heads of monkeys, arms interlinked and flailing still, and flames that touched everything the sun grazed. The eyes of an engine flared, blinking pistons in its head, wore a habit and settled on the body of Sister Theresa, blessing itself with holy water. It saw me and opened its maw, gobbled air as I ran. The stars blazed brighter and burned toward their finale.

16

LITTLE

The car had me pinned to the wall. It was cold and the hit felt much harder than the usual bump and grind on the track. The force took my breath away and I couldn't snag another one from the thin air. I looked out the windshield into the night sky and watched the stars shoot and streak through constellations, a marksman firing a bow at a giant lion while a scorpion's tail swatted away arrows and stepped on planets. I'd been hunted and felt my bones roll side to side. When I opened my eyes, Daddy was staring out the other windshield, right at me and flexing every finger on the wheel. But I wasn't shivering on the track. I was on the living room floor. Daddy had pushed me over on my side and rolled me back and forth. I groaned and looked out into the empty room. The constellations were replaced by popcorn ceiling, and Daddy sat next to me on the floor. My body ached from a night sleeping on my back, and the rear of my skull held a dull ache from rubbing the floor. I kept my cheek on the ground.

"You were snoring."

"So was you," I said.

"Got to get up." Daddy rolled over to the wall and began to pull himself up. His hands and knee and hips cracked. He paused with each pop on his way up. "Least you're already dressed." It was the same thing I'd worn the day before. It smelled like smoked hair and sweat.

I thought back to the previous day with Mama and Senior. Then I remembered Sedy and school and I was immediately terrified at the thought of returning. I stopped breathing for a second.

"What's your deal?" Daddy asked.

"Nothing," I said, and took a breath through my nose. But I couldn't think of an out from my suspect behavior at school. I rolled over to my stomach and pushed up onto my knees. My head throbbed as the blood rushed forward and my eyes hurt.

"Well, come on then." Daddy pulled the bottle of vodka from the camp chair's cup holder. "Got to go." He tipped the bottle back and swished the last sip around in his mouth, passed it through his teeth as he walked to the door. I thought he might spit, but he kept it.

"Lemme brush my teeth," I said.

I rushed through my bathroom routine, rinsed my hands under the faucet, then ran my fingers through my hair. I took my shirt off while I brushed my teeth, then flapped out the shirt a few times, shaking the stink off yesterday. I threw the shirt back on, spit and hustled to the truck, then wondered why I hurried at all.

At the end of our block, we drove by the armadillo roadkill, narrowly missing its head. The meat had disappeared, but the shell rolled slightly in the gutter, a ball of organic decay. Daddy ran the stop sign and swung an arc onto the main road, using every available lane. What was left of the tires squealed along, but there was no traffic coming.

"You in a hurry?" I asked. Daddy pushed the gas and I pressed into the bench seat.

"Sign-ups are today," Daddy said. "Got to get to the track by noon."

"You got a few hours, right?"

"Listen, man." Daddy looked over at me. "You were holding out on me the other night. Had you some cash." He pushed the pedal harder. "And how'd you get home yesterday? I had some missed calls from Nanny's shop."

On the shoulder a man in a sandwich board shuffled slowly. The sign rocked on his body. His heels hung out from the backs of his shoes. I squinted at the sign as we passed. It read, *Repent*

for the Jesus now! He waved at us like he was telling Daddy to slow
down.

"Mama gave me a ride home." I pulled at the broken strap
of my backpack. "I told you where that money came from." I
looked back at Daddy, who rubbed a hand down his face, pulling the skin of his mouth as it passed. It made for a protracted
frown.

"You too good to wait for me now?"

"No—" I started.

Daddy slapped the steering wheel with the palm of his hand.
"I need you on *my* team."

"You didn't pick me up," I said. I considered that I had fit a
lot into my day. "Where were you?"

"I was there," Daddy said. He paused and sniffed at the
question, then looked out the window. "Trying to keep our family together." Daddy motioned with his index finger back and
forth between us. The sentiment was there, but the substance
of the gesture was lacking. The receipts of his afternoon were
crumpled up in the ashtray. The edges flapped in the breeze
from his cracked window. I was sure he'd spent the day cashing
in my winnings and relishing in the selection of glowing bottles.

I let it go. Daddy nodded and we pulled through the drop-
off circle of St. Francis. I was late enough to be the only car in
the circle.

Sister Theresa stepped from the shadow of the overhang
and walked toward the truck. I kept my head down and instead
watched her feet and wondered how she balanced on such
twisted digits. She slowly made her way toward us.

"What's that old bag wanting?" Daddy said. He avoided
moving his mouth as much as possible and tossed a cigarette
butt out the crack of his window, like he was going to get caught.
I grabbed my backpack from the floor. Then, in a moment of
brilliance, I remembered the matches in my pocket. I wedged
them in the crack of the seat.

Sister Theresa knocked on my window and motioned for me
to roll it down.

I sat up to see her face.

"It don't work," I said, mouthing the words for her. She tapped again, then turned her hand over and motioned with one finger for me to get out. I opened the door.

"Both of you," she said. Daddy pointed to himself, and she nodded.

"What'd you do, man?" Daddy said. "And hurry up on telling." He tried again to keep his mouth from moving.

"My hearing is just fine," Sister Theresa said, as I slid down from the truck and onto the sidewalk. "I'll take that to mean that you have not spoken with your father regarding yesterday's events." She put a hand on my shoulder. It was too much pressure, like she thought I might run if not contained. "I attempted to leave a message by phone. It seems your phone has been disconnected."

"Fire lane," Daddy said, pointing to the spot where he'd pulled up on the curb.

"Where's the fire, Mr. Lemons?"

"Mr. Lemons was my daddy. You can call me Wild. 'Sides, you never know," Daddy said.

"I do," she replied. "Come. Let me tell you about it."

Daddy turned off the truck and left it in the lane to join us. "What now?" He straightened his pants.

"Indeed," she replied. Then looked down at me. "Join me in my office."

Sister Theresa held the door open for Daddy. She did this while never taking her hand from my shoulder. In her office, she led me to the chair furthest from the door like she didn't want me escaping, then walked to her own as Daddy took a seat.

"You going to tell us now?" Daddy asked. His eyes swept around the room, wall to wall, from me to Sister Theresa. He was cagey and frazzled. I wondered if Daddy was in trouble. Sister leaned toward Daddy to address him.

"Mr. Lemon," she began. Sister folded her hands. She stared

at Daddy for a moment and waited for him to realize that she was speaking to him.

"Wild."

She ignored him. "One of William's classmates lost most of her hair yesterday in a blaze on the playground." I could still smell the smoke in my nostrils. I tried not to sniff too deep 'cause it would be noisy and might give me away, so I held the breath I already had.

"What was this, a goddamn wildfire?" Daddy asked. He blinked repeatedly, trying to get his eyes to adjust to the low lighting. Sister Theresa disregarded his question and cleared her throat. She closed her eyes and nodded, presumedly, at his use of language. Her lips moved silently for a moment. Daddy leaned forward and turned an ear to her to try to listen. He looked over at me and motioned his confusion. I mouthed, *Praying*, to Daddy and clasped my hands together. She opened her eyes and Daddy quickly sat back. Sister continued.

"She has implicated herself, but I have my suspicions." Sister fixed her gaze on me. "And why would I have suspicions, William?"

I had my head down. "Because—" I began.

"Don't know, smokey. You planning on telling us?" Daddy asked. He smiled and winked at me. I hung my head again.

Sister Theresa digested the dynamic of the room and looked back to me for an answer. She cleared her throat.

"'Cause I ran away," I volunteered, anxious to get the interrogation over with.

"'Cause you ran away," she repeated. "That's right. And are you aware that leaving school grounds without permission is a punishable offense?" She waited for my nod. "Why *did* you run away?"

"'Cause I was scared," I said.

"'Cause you were scared," she repeated.

"Her hair was on fire," I said, eyes wide.

Sister sat back. "The teachers say it was out when they

walked up. Sedona said that you put it out." I held my breath. "My trouble is that she couldn't produce the matches—that they simply disappeared. Like you did." Her chair creaked as she leaned. "Where did the matches go, William?"

All eyes searched me.

"Don't have them," I said. I was happy to tell the truth.

"But you did have matches yesterday?"

"No."

"No, ma'am," she corrected. We sat in a stalemate.

"Well, this was fun." Daddy stood. He pulled the pin on her *Take a Number* grenade, then—realizing he couldn't replace it—set it down next to the benign bomb. "We done?"

Sister motioned to me with her index finger. "You may go. Sign in for your tardiness and report to room 214 for in-school suspension. Close the door behind you."

I stood and followed Daddy out of the room. He pulled the door and it shook the wood-paneled walls as it shut.

"What the hell was that?" Daddy asked, eyes more open than I'd seen in years and still trying to keep his mouth from moving. I signed in on the front office notepad.

"Don't know," I said.

"You set some girl's hair on fire and runned away?" Daddy asked in an attempt to piece together the morning.

I looked around quickly. The secretary wasn't at her desk. I didn't answer. Didn't really have the notion in my gut that I needed to anymore. We were even, somehow.

"Good god, boy. You tell Nanny?"

"I got to get," I said.

"All right then. Get on. Be waiting for you."

"Awesome," I replied.

I headed down the hall and watched Daddy over my shoulder. He turned a few times, attempting to get his bearings, then walked toward the exit.

When I walked into the room, I saw that Sedy's hair was short all over, cut to be true and even in length where possible. The effort was there, but the hair wasn't. I ached to smell her perfume, but all I got a whiff of was smoke from my own nose.

"Hey, Sedy," I said.

"Shh," a monitor hissed from the corner. "No talking."

Sedy smiled and put her hand to her head.

I'm sorry, I mouthed to her.

She looked over at the monitor, who read a magazine.

I know, Sedona mouthed back.

"Thank you." I restrained myself to a whisper.

"Of course." She turned to the front of the room and swallowed.

We sat in silence and the comfort of proximity. I finally breathed again, and the day passed like we were sitting by a stream.

When Sedy's mother came to pick her up from ISS, she glared at me and made small talk with the monitor. I was dismissed after her and walked outside and waited at the usual spot under the old grumpy oaks. They creaked and strained under a cool breeze. Daddy pulled up in the truck with the trailer still attached. He walked the tires onto the curb and they squeaked in their displeasure. I climbed in, but Daddy didn't speak. I set my backpack on the floor and Daddy began to pull away from the curb before I could even close my door.

"Geez," I said, pulling the door closed and looking up from the floor at Daddy. "What's that all about?" Daddy flicked a cigarette out the window. A fresh pack bulged in his shirt pocket. I could see the red of the Marlboro logo through a small hole in the pocket.

"You ain't telling me much. Letting me come across things as surprises." Daddy looked over at me and held the wheel at six o'clock with his right hand. The smell of vodka and smoke was fresh and bright in the car, a scent I was accustomed to. The left side of Daddy's face was dark. A bruise. "Don't need to walk on no more land mines." Daddy pointed to his leg with a finger held out from the wheel, like the loss of it had come from a foreign war. "Going to your mama, lighting chicks' hairs on fire. Beers with Senior—you even going to tell me about that?"

I didn't own a response. I'd learned to fib from Daddy, and was normally pretty quick with one, but I felt empty—my brain somehow hollowed and burned out. The effect of a morning full of getting caught up, a day full of silence. But Daddy had plenty to say. I couldn't process it, just found a spot to watch on the windshield, a crescent-shaped crack.

"Caught me on the side of the road." I owned up. "Didn't have much choice."

"Always a choice." Daddy winced. He dropped the cigarette out the window, then pulled a pint bottle from between the seats. The matches were still sandwiched there too. The bottle was icy and Daddy held it to his face for a second before he took the top off and drank. He burped and blew out the chemical-coconut smell through the cab of the truck.

"Senior stopped by the house today." He put the bottle back. "House calls catch me off." Daddy looked over at me. "Weren't good." He smiled, but only half of his face moved, like he was melting in all the heat of things crashing and burning around him. "Had him a friend with him."

"Sorry," I said and tried to see Daddy's reflection in the driver-side mirror. I couldn't catch the extent of the bruise and gave up, knowing that I'd have time to see it, but the urgency remained in Daddy's voice.

"When you going to shoot straight with me? Don't feel like I can get a real thing from you the last couple days."

I'd felt that way before—anytime that Mama left. Without Nanny to fight, Daddy needed a new sparring partner. I didn't respond.

"Need to get your shit together, boy. Know who's on your team." Daddy pointed to himself. We pulled up to the house. The moss-draped oak trees bent heavy. Daddy turned off the truck and I grabbed my backpack. Daddy picked up the pint bottle and the matchbook from between the seats. We walked toward the empty house and a scrub palm near the front door rattled like a paper bag.

Me and Sedy spent the week in punishment. On Friday I walked outside into the light. I tried to follow the trail of Sedy to celebrate our freedom by talking above a whisper. I was sure that I never wanted to go back to my regular class. I would sit with Sedy in quiet and peaceful meditation for the remainder of middle school. I lost her in the crowd of students and parent cars; I lost her, but I ran into George and his mama.

Margaret elbowed George, then flipped her hair back.

"Hey, Billy," George said. Margaret sat on the hood of her car, parked nose in in the *Teacher of the Month* spot. I wondered what the lesson was. George stood next to her with his hand over his mouth, and I tried to build a wall between them when I blinked.

"Hey, George," I said, walked up and stood. The pair took up most of the sidewalk. The bumper of Margaret's BMW was pulled up over the walkway by a foot or two and there was no way to get around the two of them without stopping and waiting for her to move an outstretched leg. She was wearing pants that I imagined would look similar if a horse's legs were packed into some stretch denim and it was slapped on the butt with the command to trot. She had tassels on her boots. George looked around like he was ready to skitter off. I stared at Margaret. My imagination had me parked on the farthest points of her tight sweater and I flushed with sweat. My desire, as a destination, might as well have been the surface of the moon.

"How's class?" she said.

"I heard you set Sedona's hair on fire," George answered.

"Who's Sedona?" Margaret asked, sitting up with an involuntary groan. "She sounds pretty."

"Not now her hair's all burned off." George chuckled. I cringed and Margaret smiled.

"Why don't you invite your friend here over?" Margaret said to George. She looked at me and winked.

"Billy, I guess you can come over if you want," George said, wiping his nose with his thumb.

"Sure. I guess."

George, whose face had been exercised to the point of soreness during the momentary pause, could hold it no longer. His facial protest was mostly involuntary. Margaret slapped him on the back of the head and his face contorted with pain.

She winked again at me. "Well, come on then."

I looked briefly at the empty curb where Daddy would park and wait, then back to the doors of the school. Sister Theresa stood, arms crossed, hawking over me. Finally, I looked back to Margaret who waved to me with a hand as gentle as if teased by a breeze.

At George's house, he settled into a video game in his bedroom, racing stock cars in stereo. The noise was louder than the engines on race nights. His eyes glazed over and he forgot about my existence. I was yet to have a turn, and instead walked through their house. It was cavernous, arches and hollow fiber-woods led room to room. It was three times bigger than our house. I snooped, pushing buttons and looking out through Palladian windows, lost and ignored as I drifted through the space.

"Hey, Billy," Margaret's voice came from the living room sofa. *Judge Judy* blasted through the den. Margaret lay sprawled, legs propped on what seemed to be a thousand pillows, monogrammed and stuffed fat. She had a bright red slushie drink in her hand and the room smelled like strawberries and Daddy's truck. "Come hang a minute."

I looked back over my shoulder, sure that she'd spoken to somebody behind me. The sounds of car racing were distant. Judge Judy berated an offender, threatened punishments. Someone needed to pay up. She slapped the gavel and shouted down the offender. Margaret made space for me on the couch, patted a cushion, waved me over with the green flag of her hand. I followed the peaks and valleys of her body, then settled into the cushions as she lifted her legs. Margaret pushed her fingers through my hair. I couldn't remember the last time I'd washed it and pulled back, suddenly self-conscious. I glanced at the closed door of George's room. She turned my head back.

"But—"

"He's glued," she said.

I pushed and Margaret pulled, met my resistance with force, nails, lips, the punch of her tongue, the removal of my shirt and pants, and then I was a car traveling the curves, braking as I approached the bends only to accelerate at the moment of entry, pedal down and leaning into the crooks and turns. Funny what my body did automatic. Things I didn't know it would do.

"Slow down," she said, but her breath was sweet like candy, and I searched her mouth for cavities. I dove and explored, dwelled in the spaces I found and looked for a place to belong. I tried to keep time with the vrooms and squeals of the car in stereo sound, realized I paused too long, and took a breath. It was a track I'd never traveled, and I'd relied on instinct for direction. Margaret held my head, pushed me back for a moment.

"You're doing it wrong," she said. She scowled in confusion, then smiled a piteous grin at me, took over and drove. Margaret directed my youth and shifted, rode clench-jawed and sweated a closed-eyed focus on her own desperate chase. The trip was short, and she rode hard and fast, like she ran out of track when the race was over. I knew there was no way to cover the distance back.

I'd hoped to crumble into the cradle of her arms.

"Get up," she said.

I wiped my mouth.

I picked up my pants from the floor. They smelled like smoke and my ankles were cold. *Judge Judy* ended. George stayed in his room, content with his racing game. He didn't say good-bye when I left. Didn't even crack his door. Margaret drove me through Wendy's, then home. The ruts in our front yard were empty. When I looked back to her car, I couldn't see in the windows, but waved anyway.

17

WILD

Waited at the school for damn near at least half an hour. I knew this because generally when I passed out a snooze, a half-hour was about how long I slept. I woke up 'cause the window was down and cold air blew in. My goddamn jean jacket barely cut the breeze, but the air kept the pint of vodka chilled on the seat. It was fresh. I stirred and looked around the playground. Little normally woke me up when I conked. I took a long drink to wake up my mouth.

"Messing." I took another drink. "Messing, messing, messing." I shook my head and gave a think. The boy just kept on messing. I looked around the schoolyard again, then put my head on the steering wheel for a second and the cool rubber pressed into the thin skin of my forehead. My mouth hung open and I burped some coconut breeze, then looked up again to try to see if Little was hiding out somewhere in the empty lot. I saw some old codger cracking the blinds of a classroom, watching my ass, and I just looked at him harder, focusing for real. Somebody was watching me. "Messing." I pointed at 'em. "Messers messing." The blinds closed real quick.

I turned the truck on and drove that shit on the curb a sec just to show them what's up. The empty trailer behind me bounced off the curb and rattled. I'd forgot it was even on there. Left that school and watched the ground in front of me get wavy, like some big-ass tongue lapping up my truck like it was hungry. I chose a center lane on the main road, and coasted, pressing the gas here and there. I stopped by the house, and looked at it, making sure it didn't move too much. I took a few drinks and half-assed tried to look through the windows. No boy.

Kept the truck running and revved the engine now and again to express myself. My frustration. I drank and tallied up who messed the most, could count on my fingers to three or so on each hand, then decided that my left hand was best. I'd named that hand "Nanny" a long time ago, but then decided when I'd finished eeny, meeny, miny that I'd somehow landed on, "Senior." There would for sure be some new ruts in the driveway. I pulled away from the house and drove, this time pressing the gas pedal the whole drive, 'cause who gave a shit?

The ground thumped as I walked through the crushed-shell parking lot. Steadied myself on *Big Bill's* trucks, all lined up for the end of the season, and made my way to the front door, held on to the handle for a moment, and tried to get space to stop spinning—tried to catch hold of some gravity. A burp blew out of my nose and it burned. The bars on the windows bounced out with the give of their screws. A baby monkey was hand-cuffed to a single piece of outdoor furniture and a sandwich board hung around its neck that read, *Bouncer.* Couldn't scare me, no-how.

I opened that door and steamed into the room blind as my eyes adjusted to the dim heat. The hose-woman (I couldn't remember her name, or nobody else's for real, worth a shit) be-hind the bar was picking up on my pissed-ness and frustration and put her hand on the sawed-off shotgun under the bar top. Like I didn't know where that thing was at. She kept her other hand on the speed rail, ready to pour my ass another drink.

"Wild," she said, all smooth. I think she was thinking back to times when she called my name louder.

"Where's Senior," I said. "Where's my Little?"

She nodded to the back booth and I winked, then stepped and slid my leg across the piss and beer on the floor toward the booth. I went on and picked up a chair from a neighboring table, but Senior's ass was ready. He stood up real quick and put his knuckles right on my nose and I swear when it popped it blew up just like a ripe cherry. I'll be damned if I didn't flop down under my own chair, looking up at the bottom of my own weapon.

"You want me to finish your face, Junior?" Senior said. "Drunk motherfucker." I groaned out from under the chair. "I can go on and darken up that other side of your face—make it even. You dumb sonofabitch." I looked out from under that chair, my eyes watering. Senior held his own hand, massaged the knuckles and adjusted the rings. "Come clean this shit up," he yelled across the room at the hose-lady bartender. She took her hand off the shotgun and grabbed a bar towel, came prancing over. Senior settled back down in the booth. "And grab me a beer before you get over here," he added to the order. She'd just about nearly reached me on the floor and turned back to the bar. "Junior, I just can't really imagine that what you were coming in here, all hot and drunk, was worth fucking up your nose. You going to enlighten me, or just roll around down there in the piss and spills?"

I tried a little harder to roll on my side, took a swallow of thick blood from my nose and gagged when the backs of my arms stuck to the floor.

"You going to make even more mess down there?" Senior whistled at the bartender as she walked toward me with the beer and towels. "Get a bucket too." She turned again. "No. Leave me that beer and get the bucket." She came back.

I spit the mess from my mouth, decorated the floor and tried to see what I could make out of the picture I painted.

"You couldn't wait on the bucket? Just asked her for one." Senior took a drink off his beer. "You're like to piss me off all over again."

"Where's my boy?" I said out from under the chair. I realized I still had my truck keys in my hand, looped around my middle finger, and jingled them once.

"I don't keep up with him. That's your job." Senior laughed. "Ain't too good at it, seems like."

"Fuck you," I said.

"No, Junior." He laughed. Senior stood again and kicked the

bottom of my broke leg. "You are all sorts of fucked." Old hosey-hose walked up again. "What took you so long?" Daddy was pointing down at me under that chair. "Somebody made a fucking mess on my floor. Look at this shit leaking all over the place." He pointed to the spray of spit, flecks of red all over the yellowed linoleum. She took a dry towel to the outer expanse first, a belt of thin dots, and worked in toward the source, but it all smeared.

"You fucked up my galaxy," I said, and jingled my keys again, enjoying the sound and my moment of being a speedbump.

"Get up, boy." Senior kicked at me again.

"Lost *my* boy," I said, spitting again. I lifted the chair from below and moved it to the side. It fell over as I sat up. The room swirled and I felt seasick, then gagged a stream in the bucket.

"I was using that," Hosey said. She leaned away, with her back against the base of a booth. In my blurred vision, I tried to get a look up her shorts. Can't remember much. She threw the wet bar towel at my face. I remembered the pain of my nose, held it, and moaned again. It smelled like bleach, and I rolled to my side to shake it.

"Bet you did lose that boy of yours," Senior said. "If I was you, I'd be checking with his mama instead of coming around here messing with my furniture." Senior sat back down and drank some of his beer. "You're gonna lose a lot more."

The bartender walked away. I put my weight on another chair from the table and got to my knees. I was wet and sticky, breathed heavy for a second, then put a hand on the tabletop and got to one foot.

"Let yourself out, Junior," Senior said.

I walked slowly, propping myself on furniture, and attempted to hold my nose to keep it from dripping anymore. Drops fell into my cupped hand and rolled out onto the floor. The bartender didn't come back out from behind the bar. She shook her head. I wiped my hand along the bar and got close to the door. I pushed on the glass and made a handprint, some evidence to know that I existed.

18

NANNY

There was a rumor in the store that a small boy dog was on the loose. It was a rumor, and it made him a ghost, a phantom that was maybe caught on the cameras when the light of the exit sign illuminated his figure in zone two. The ladies up front chewed jerky and told ghost stories.

"He was up near Nanny's office."

"No stopping him. Can see it dangling when he trots."

"You seen him trot? Which video?" I heard them say. I hustled to my office and pretended to sneeze a few times, nearly burst into tears.

"You don't want that ghost dog, do you?" My chin quavered and I looked down into Lady's eyes, searched her little dog soul for the purity I knew she'd need to fight to maintain in her short life. I'd seen the signs of claw marks at the door. "Has he already had you?" I fought the thought out of my mind, an unholy ghost weaseling his way like Casper through the cracks in my door. Surely not. Her head shook. Surely Lady's belly bulged as the result of my prayers to some cosmic spirit. I sat on the floor in front of her cage and let Lady lick my fingers. We needed rebirth control. I closed my eyes and prayed again for an immaculate conception, that any swimmers, real or unholy-ghostly, would drown in lieu of something more formally god-like and female.

19

LITTLE

Margaret fed me so much, including all I could ever want from Wendy's. The steam from the fried chicken spun in cords, swirling, and I held my face over each sandwich hoping to soak some of that smell into my pores. I knew that the next time I broke a sweat, I'd lick my lips and try to taste it all over again. Margaret had driven through and gotten me a bag full of spicy chicken sandwiches and large fries. I could have easily eaten all of it. I was starved. Daddy would have smelled it when he walked through the door. I sat on the floor of the living room with the bag between my legs.

I heard the truck door slam in the front yard and looked up. The sounds of Daddy's curses and nose-blowing came next. Like a zombie. Daddy fit the bill when he stumbled in. His face was swollen all over. Each step shook just enough of his swollen jowls to pull on the skin of his nose and he grunted.

"You just leaving me out to dry?" Daddy moaned at me. I wasn't real sure if I should run or call an ambulance. "Weren't at school. Weren't at the house. Know that for a fact. Just 'cause you're here now don't mean nothing. Playing tricks," he said. "Mess-sing."

I'd seen Daddy rough before. His benders usually included a finale—the cousin's wedding, the nudity, the swinging housecat, the falling from a tree. But none of these had ever quite left him in this shape. His eyes were swollen and his breathing was hard work. I could tell that he was in no shape to talk, much less carry an argument.

"Where you been?" Daddy asked, getting loud. He put his hands on his knees. He blew a snot rocket of blood, both nostrils at once, on the floor, then pinched the bridge of his nose and pushed in, a failed attempt to put it back in place. "Goddamn." He sniffed and shook his hand out. His eyes watered. "You leaving me too?"

"Still here," I said, and rolled the top of the Wendy's bag. "I went to a friend's house."

Daddy propped himself against the wall. His head hung. "Know that's a lie." He paused. "I'm the only friend you got."

I stood up, Wendy's bag in hand, stepped toward Daddy, who looked up and flinched. I hadn't seen him flinch before. I was as tall as Daddy in his hunched state—even taller. It was the first time I'd noticed it, think it was the first he had. "Got us some food," I said. I pushed the bag toward Daddy, who sandwiched the bag between his arm and his stomach. "Saved this for you." I heard my own voice off the walls. It was deeper in the empty room.

I turned and walked back to my bedroom. Left Daddy standing there with the bag. That bag was cold and I'd fought the devil not to eat that last sandwich. I hoped he knew it. I heard that bag rattle and him grunting and knew he could give a shit less.

I sat on my bed and took off my Pumas, stretched my feet, and felt that they'd grown again.

Daddy walked in and stood in the doorway.

"Thanks," he said, and I absorbed the word.

"No problem. What happened to you?" I motioned to his face.

"Had a accident." He swallowed, looked toward the window of the room, then cleared his throat.

"One hell of an accident." I tossed my shoes toward the closet. "The truck okay?"

"Truck's okay. Gotta make sure the car's good for tomorrow." Daddy held his septum and breathed as deep as he could.

"You pay the entry?" I held my breath.

"Did." Daddy nodded as best he could. His face looked like it wagged when he moved, like there were no bones.

"We have anything left over?"

"A little. Enough to bet on a win." Daddy pulled cash from his pocket, there were still enough bills to be considered a wad. He looked at me. "Where'd you get the money for that Wendy's?"

"Friend's mama."

"Not your mama?"

"Not my mama."

"She got anymore?"

"Don't know about that." I thought about what I'd done to get the bag of Wendy's, and decided in that moment to take a shower before bed. "Maybe?"

"I'll be straight with you." Daddy paused and shifted his weight with a grunt. "Needing a win." He smiled and his eyes squinted shut.

"Yup." I nodded. "You needing a doctor?"

"I'll be good." Daddy paused. "I ever tell you about the wallpaper?"

"You did."

"Pineapples everywhere. I wanted pineapple the whole time I was in the hospital because of the wallpaper. When I slept, I dreamed about my leg. When I was awake it was always pineapple. They only ever served me turkey." He laughed, and his nose trickled blood. "Been worse. Think it can always get worse."

"Guess so," I said. I had my arms around my knees, my shoes on the bed.

"Always does. I'll be outside." Daddy slapped the doorframe. "Need to feed the beast." I laid back on my bed and thought of Margaret and wished for Sedy. My thoughts were interrupted with the sound of the car roaring to life. It shook the windows, first at the back of the house, then the noise screamed through the empty halls and rolled off the ceiling until it found its way to my bed. Even with my eyes closed, I heard the carburetor suck air, not only from the immediate space around it, but also from the very air that I needed for my own lungs. It was the feeling I'd felt in the last race, holding on to my breath to keep the engine from taking more than its share. It pulled through the venturi and fired through cylinders and flamed out through broken, barely hanging tailpipes.

I got up and walked to the shower to rinse off my day and the feeling of being hexed.

Daddy worked long into the night. The neighbors' dogs barked with every dropped wrench. He fine-tuned and tuned again, until the clicks and clacks were sharp and the sparks timed to absolute top dead center. Finally, I heard him drop the hood closed.

"You trying to bite?" he yelped.

20

LITTLE

We pulled up to the paddock and I climbed out of the truck and walked around to the back of the trailer without a word. The gate lowered with a creak, slowly at first, then dropped the tail for the last few feet of free-fall. The back end of the car looked dormant, almost peaceful as it sat in the dark of the trailer. The dust kicked up by the tailgate settled in a layer and the track lights behind me reflected in the last bit of speckled chrome on the bumper.

I wished that I could walk away. The week had taken too much out of me, and I was exhausted and hungry and my mind wandered. Daddy hadn't let us eat all day to preserve as much cash for betting as possible. Daddy took a drink, the last of his current bottle, then stepped from the truck and walked around back to help roll the Lemon Party II out of the trailer.

"You all right?" Daddy asked.

"I'm all right. You?"

Daddy climbed into the trailer, grunted around the car, and let the straps loose in the trailer. "I'm all right," he said. I watched his face, and it was looking a bit better than the day before. The swelling had gone down a bit. Daddy had held a cold bottle to his cheeks and nose for most of the day. He drank them before they got too warm. "Help me get this last one." Daddy reached down to the bottom hook, a half-assed effort, and I walked up and unhooked the strap. The car rolled. "Shit," Daddy said. It ran over the tip of his prosthetic and I stepped back out of the way as the car moved down the ramp. It stopped when it bumped one of the bleacher supports. I walked over to it.

"Got my gone leg," Daddy called as he looked down. "Good thing, I guess."

"No joke," I said.

"Thing just started moving," he said. "Not even sure I touched it." Daddy held his hands up. They vibrated a tremor.

I put my hand on the hood and the matte paint felt warm like skin.

"All right?" Daddy called.

I walked around to the back. There was a dent in the steel column, but the bumper was unscathed. "Looks like it," I replied.

"Want to move it up? Keys are in it."

I pulled the car to the line-up. I had pole position, a fortune that was totally foreign to me. I took the keys, and then walked back to the truck. Daddy was closing the tailgate.

"Let's walk," he said.

We made our way up the sidewalk, toward the glow of the dots, the cigarettes and bodies crowded around the rail. As we walked up, there was a rumble in the silhouettes. The cigarettes fell in a shower to the dirt and patches of grass below. They came for Daddy and handed him beers.

"What's the bet, Wild?"

"That a fluke, or what?"

"That boy know how to drive?"

I got a pat or two on the shoulder. I walked toward the railing and looked for Margaret. Instead, Sedy sat on the ledge waiting to meet me.

"Hey, Little," she said. She gave a small wave, bent her fingers toward me, then put her hand in her back pocket.

"Hey, Sedy."

"Good luck tonight," she said. She wore jeans and a sweater, a windbreaker on top of that, and a knit cap, crocheted by some relative, topped off with a bow. No hair hung out from under it, but the bottoms of her ears did. Her earrings reflected the light of the concession stand.

"Thanks," I said, unsure of where we existed on the evolutionary chart of child to adult. Sedy gave me a peck on the cheek. I watched her walk away, then turned to Daddy while he fended off questions.

"That was cute. Save some for me?" A voice came from behind me. I looked over my shoulder and saw Margaret walking slowly toward me. I forced a laugh and let my hair hang over my eyes, held my helmet in my hand. She brushed her hand along the back of my pants, then stepped out of the light and into the shadow of the stands.

Daddy walked up.

"You ready?"

"Ready. You?" I squeaked. My heart raced. It could've easily outpaced the cars on the track. I looked at Daddy's hands, a beer in each of them. Daddy took a drink from his right.

"Couldn't be more ready." He laughed. "Give 'em a show, boy."

I cranked the engine and it breathed, rumbled, groaned— stretched as I pressed the pedal to feed it. It took great helpings of air and gas, gulping and belching as it fired exhaust into the cars behind me. The black smoke hovered above the ground, the ghost of consumed gasoline, a remnant to choke the living.

The view from the front of the pack was clear and empty. A groomed track sat waiting for the violations of tires and laps. I had only ever felt grooves and grew nervous at the responsibility of creating them. I questioned what I was to do, as leader rather than follower.

Like he sensed what I was thinking, the official walked up to the Lemon Party II with his headphones on and yelled, "Rolling start, okay? Keep the formation, okay? Warm your tires up, okay? But keep it slow, okay? When I wave this flag, it's go time." He pulled the green flag from the back of his pants. I heard engines behind me rev at the sight, a conditioned response. "Okay?"

I nodded, squeezed the wheel, and tried to breathe deep.

The official waved us out onto the track, and we left the

feeder road two by two, with me a bit ahead of the car flanking me. I wiggled the wheel and wagged the back end of the car to warm the tires. The cars behind me did the same. I gave the engine some gas, just fed it a little bit and could feel it smile; its stomach warmed and the black smoke blew. I wanted to hang on to the warm-up lap, but the start approached. The official pulled the flag again and dangled it in front of the stack. I hit the pedal and held my breath. The roar from my engine led me in a streak across the clay.

The track opened wide, spread out in front of me like some peaceful meadow that I was driving through alone. The engine drowned out the world, the lights, the people, and it was just me. The only way I knew I wasn't alone was when I looked in the sideview. I'd made a gap between me and the pack. The cars behind me were a flock of confusion. They watched while my tires gripped and I flew away. I felt the car cycle through every reciprocation—the spark toward ignition, the balance of cylinders firing in opposition, and the gears freeing then catching as the wheels flew faster—but as I came to the turn I realized I had to slow. When I tried to downshift I lost my wheels. The steel guardrail was dead ahead and I knew it would be unforgiving at my speed. I slid and time slowed, I blew out, tried to breathe, and all I tasted was exhaust. My oxygen left. Particles replaced it, pumped and flew from my mouth and nose. My heart had wings and fluttered in a breeze of carbon and hydrogen, a thousand beats per minute, a spark at top dead center, in exothermic frustration, the watery by-product combined with the mud of my own slinging, my own mess, and tapered clay from the corners of my eyes. The engine was so thirsty. The wheel turned in spite of my grip. The engine rumbled like a laugh, like I was never in control from the start. The tires bit, chewed on the clay, and the car turned, swung its tail to the side, a wild animal in a harness, and drifted through the turn. I kept my hands on the wheel but eased my grip. The gas pedal moved under my foot, but I didn't touch the brakes. The engine breathed and fired and controlled, burned up the track. I was on a ride, and finished the race without remembering what I'd done to take the checkered flag.

I pulled to the side and waited as the rest of the pack finished their final lap. I had to be patient, but I could've been patient forever. I stared at my hands on the wheel, motionless, useless. When everybody finally filtered through the checkered flag, I pushed my head and shoulders through the window. Daddy was there to pull me the rest of the way out. I stood there on the clay, feeling the wet earth through the hole in my shoe. Legs shaky as a foal. Sweat dripped from the rim of my chin strap. Daddy slapped me on the back of the helmet and I nearly fell over.

"Hells yes, boy!" he slurred. "We done did it now!" Daddy poured his beer over my head, helmet and all. The beer crept down my back and I couldn't help but feel a chill as I looked back at the car, now quiet and peaceful. "I bet for you, boy! Gonna get paid!" Daddy cheered and pointed at the crowd. I looked up at the stands in the lights. A couple hundred empty faces, dark spots for eyes and void of emotion. "We gonna get paid," Daddy yelled up to the stands. The folks were still stunned by the magnitude of the defeat, the surprise that my last win was no fluke, that I was no longer a joke. The official walked down the steps and brought me the trophy. I put it on the hood of the car, then shook hands with the official as he gave me a check. My hand shook and the check shimmied like a flag.

Daddy howled. He screamed into the lights and I watched his celebration. The stands emptied. I drove the car—tame now—toward the paddock with Daddy on the hood, kicking his leg in the air still shouting into the night.

I pulled the car behind the trailer and Daddy slid down the hood to the ground.

"Hang on a second. Used to always do this," he called. Daddy held up a finger behind him and step-slid toward the truck as fast as I'd ever seen him move. As I climbed out of the window Daddy rattled around under the driver's seat, eventually pulling

out two beers. He walked back and cracked both on the hood
of the car, then poured them into the bowl of the trophy. Daddy held it and drank. "Oh shit," he said, then held it up in front
of my face. He nodded at me. "Drink you some. We won."

I took the trophy with both hands and took a small sip, then
held my breath while I tipped the trophy. I made an exaggerat-
ed, "Ah," then handed the trophy back to Daddy and wiped my
face with the back of my gloved hand.

"No fun," Daddy said. He looked into the trophy and
watched the waves of beer slosh off the sides of the gold-
colored plastic. He rode a high that crossed time and injury. He
opened his mouth and chugged the rest in one gulp. He turned
the trophy over onto the hood of the car, and not a single drip
ran down the matte black paint. When I picked up the trophy,
there wasn't even a wet ring where the beer had been.

"I knew it would be worth it." Daddy waved a finger at me
and the trophy. "Knew it."

"What?"

"The engine. That's what."

Daddy cracked another beer and poured it in before walking
toward the ticket window, trophy in hand, to collect.

I was still lost in the race and ticked through the frames of
what I could remember. It had been such a blur. I remembered
breathing as I ran flat out into the turn, toward the wall, then
felt short of breath. I felt it again when I saw the headlights of
Margaret's BMW bounce and flash through a pothole as she
pulled up next to me. The window lowered and I looked inside.
Margaret wore a white tank top. It was cold out.

"Get in," she said. "I'm here to collect my winnings." I
looked around, then to the trailer. "History's any judge," she
said, detecting my worry, "we won't be long." She smiled, then
reached out toward the pocket of my race suit. I stumbled
around to the passenger side and got in. "You're sweaty," she
said. Margaret wrinkled her nose, but then drove us around the
corner behind a wall of old tires.

Margaret was right. It didn't take long. It was only a few minutes, but just long enough for Daddy to come back to the truck. I walked back and found him passed out in the cab, head resting on the steering wheel. My knees were weak and with my racing suit now open in a V, the cold night air blew across my skin. Margaret had bitten me a whole bunch of times, and I felt like I'd been mauled by a wild animal and hoped that the small welts popping up on my chest would benefit from the cold. I could see my own breath and was happy to still have it. "Hey, Little," came a familiar voice behind the car. Sedy leaned on the roof. Her head was propped on her mittened hands.

"Hey, Sedy," I said, still a bit stunned. I looked back over my shoulder toward the tire wall.

"Saw you win."

"You did?" I asked, unsure what else to say. Just then, Margaret drove out from behind the tires, hitting the gas hard and making the ass-end of the BMW wiggle over the grass as it hit the pavement. Her windows were down and she blasted some Twisted Sister butt-rock anthem. Sedy watched her drive away. It was hard not to. She turned back toward me.

"I did," Sedy said. "Never seen anything like it." I saw that Sedy had streaks down her face. "You like her?"

I felt my heart fall into my stomach, flop down into the emptiness. I didn't own anything, never won anything much to lose, much less the affection of a girl so right. Regret was an abstract term, reserved for the well-off. I walked around to the other side of the car and sat on a curb. My big toe pushed almost entirely outside of the sole of my shoe.

"I don't think so."

"Isn't that George's mama?"

"Think so," I said. I pulled my shirt closed and tried to zip the suit against the cold and the realization that my welts were showing. The zipper was broken, so I held my shirt together with one hand.

Sedy stood on the curb next to me. "She has a nice car, huh?"

There was a small space left between us. I shook.

"You cold, or just embarrassed?" Sedy asked. She pulled her windbreaker closed.

"Both, maybe." My hand fell asleep from holding my shirt so tight. The bottom fell out of my stomach and through the trapdoor went any appropriate words. "You seen my daddy?" I asked, trying to change course.

"I did." She sniffed. "He's sleeping in the truck." She pointed ahead of the trailer with a mitten. "Must've been tired."

"Always is," I said.

"You liked me, right?"

I kept nodding, then held my chin to my chest, wiped my eyes with my fingertips and rubbed them up through my hair.

"I'm sorry, Sedy." My chin quivered. I felt choked in the throat, then the pressure again around my eyes.

"Not yours to be sorry for," she said.

"Sedy," her mama called from up on the hill. "Sedy-Jane!" her mama called again, but Sedy was looking at me. There was no sparkle of blue, or the reassurance I totally depended on. I looked deeper, hoping to see a glimmer, but her eyes were dim. "Little, you own you." She turned and started up the hill.

I felt the last bit of air leave my lungs in a vacuum. My chest collapsed in heaves. Sedy was gone. I sat there on the curb, arms around my knees and head down. I tried to take inventory of what I had left but came up empty.

From the truck came the rumble of snoring. I walked past the driver's side and saw the end result of Daddy's celebration. His head hung over the steering wheel. I bumped the front of the truck as I passed, but Daddy didn't stir. The track lights blinked out and cast darkness over the park except for the glow of the concession lights on the hill.

I climbed in and scooted onto the cold seat, sat for a moment, and cleared my throat. I elbowed Daddy in the ribs. He snorted and stirred.

"How much you win?" I asked.

"Monies," he said, "many monies." His head fell back from the wheel, toward the window. It bounced off the glass with a meaty thud.

I opened Daddy's door slowly, careful not to let him fall out. As it opened I caught Daddy's head with one hand and pushed him back into the cab. I forced a hand into Daddy's pocket, grabbing the wad of cash. I slipped a couple of bills from the wad and pocketed them, then stuck the fold of money back in Daddy's tight jeans. Daddy moaned, then giggled. His face was bruised but he had a smile on it. I understood something he'd felt forever. Winning after losing was warmer than a fire. Losing after winning would make a person feel cold through and through.

I closed the door and climbed into Lemon Party II. I cranked it and rolled it into the cave of the trailer. I cut the engine so I wouldn't choke in the exhaust, then pulled myself out the window. The car seemed tame, satisfied with the win, ready to rest. I strapped the wheels down with the ties Daddy had left in a tangle earlier. I brushed my hand along the tail end of the car. Even in the cool of the night, the car stayed warm. I dealt with the confusion of Margaret and Sedy with the simplest thought I could muster. I had my car, and I had my win.

21

LITTLE

I drove home after the race, and the next morning, when I opened the door, I saw the gray morning punctuated with the bug of my daddy rolling on his back in the front yard. His legs flailed in the air. His prosthetic was bent out of sorts and his shoe had a tire track across it. Daddy had slept in the truck, because he was too drunk and heavy for me to carry, and the truck's windows were all fogged up. At first I thought he was pissed, then I realized what he was shouting. "I won," he howled, and wiped his mouth off with his shirt sleeve. "I won!" He reached his hand into his pocket and pulled the wad of bills out. He rolled around and tried to stand, but his leg buckled under the weight and he landed back on his elbows, cash still in hand.

"What are you doing?" I asked.

"I won!" Daddy replied, holding the bills up for me to see.

"You told me," I said. "Every time I tried to move you last night." Daddy squeezed the cash back into his pocket. Somewhere down the block a dog barked, loud and pitched, leashed.

"We can get a new dog," Daddy proclaimed. He laid on his back and stopped rolling, his leg still out of place. "We can get a yard full of them if you want."

"I don't know," I said, and walked down the steps through a fog of my own breath. "I could go for some breakfast." Daddy rolled to his knees and pushed himself up to his foot. This time he tried to balance on the front bumper of the truck. He began to topple again and I caught him under the arm and helped him over to the front steps.

"Shit, it's cold," Daddy said, sitting on the concrete. He

buckled his leg in place. "Got to piss like a racehorse before we go off and do anything." He stood again and walked into the middle of the front yard and unleashed a steaming stream on the yard. "Good fucking morning, neighborhood!" he called. His breath came out in a fog. More dogs barked. "Got yourself a winner." Daddy shook himself. The neighbor across the street cracked their blinds and closed them quickly. "And some wiener!" He looked over his shoulder at me and laughed. He zipped up, then stumbled toward the steps. Daddy grabbed me by the sleeve. "Come on, boy, let's get us some breakfast."

"Got to get my shoes first." I broke Daddy's grip, nearly toppling him, and walked back inside. In the bedroom, I slid my feet into my Pumas. Outside, Daddy was already in the truck, attempting to light a cigarette. I got in and Daddy looked down at my feet.

"Look at those shitty things," he said, talking about my Pumas. "It's a wonder you can even drive."

I looked down and wiggled my toe through the bottom of the sole. "All I got," I said.

Daddy put the truck in drive and rolled through the yard, the trailer still in tow. The cigarette hung from his lips, still unlit. "Won," he said. He drove down the road, using his knee to steer, and finally caught the cigarette with the flame of the lighter. "Win-ner," he said, and huffed.

"Everybody thought you were a fluke." Daddy pointed at me, cigarette in hand. "I hustled too," Daddy began. He laughed, high pitched and manic. "Told 'em that we didn't change a thing in the car before the last race." Daddy waved the cigarette and swirled rings of smoke like magic. "*They* thought there was just *no* way." He grinned at me, and it looked like the corners of his mouth might connect to his eyes.

"But—the engine," I offered, without another thought. I immediately regretted interrupting the happiest I'd seen Daddy, and wished I could catch the words by the tail, but they floated right through the smoke rings.

"They bet against us. Dumb sonsabitches." Daddy slapped

the wheel. "Don't you get it?" The smile held, but in the pained way it did when it wasn't real. Daddy wiped his hand down his face and pressed on his eyes. The cab of the truck filled with smoke, then he tipped the cigarette ash out the window. "Some of those folks were pissed." Spit speckled the window from his emphasis on the letter P. "All right by me. They've been taking my money long enough." Daddy pointed to his chest. "I got us paid."

"Do you even—" Daddy began but broke off when he noticed a man walking down the shoulder of the road through all the empty bottles cast off from Saturday late-night drives, the filth of broken garbage bags, and the last gray remnants of cotton bolls blown from the backs of trucks en route from farm to market. He wore a sandwich board that read:

ONLY THE BEGINNING
OF THE END

I followed Daddy's gaze and looked over his shoulder to catch the other side. The back side of the board was taken from a "Cash 4 Gold" sign. Gold was scratched out and the word "SOULS" replaced it. There was also an equation:

redemption = yours

Daddy shook his head and looked back at the road ahead. "Didn't do his math right."

My stomach rumbled. I watched the shoulder carefully, looking for any other signs that walked on two legs. Daddy laughed a nervous snort and then pointed at the billboard with the arrow to the Waffle House, the only place open on Sunday. The yellow blocks surrounding black letters meant warmth and food.

"There's our turn," Daddy said.

We ordered and ordered, running the waitress and short order cook until they united and stepped outside for a smoke break. Daddy slowly came down. We filled our stomachs until we struggled to move. We huffed waves of our contents back and forth across the table, laughing at the fact that we barely made a dent in the stack of bills in Daddy's pocket. The waitress dropped our check and Daddy even left a couple of singles for her.

"Got to take care of our people," Daddy instructed, feeling that he'd done the waitress right. "Hey, man," he called over to the cook. The man looked back over the noise of the exhaust fan and the sizzling grease of the grill. Daddy gave him a thumbs-up and rubbed his belly for effect.

The man waved back with his spatula and shook his head. "Gone have the shits," he muttered.

"We even impressed the cook," Daddy said. "Man said we're the shit. Cook says that, you know you done right." Daddy paid at the register and we walked back to the truck. "How you feel about winning now?" he asked.

I nodded, lacking words. I felt tired—full and warm, even though cold wind blew across the parking lot and through my worn-out hoodie.

"I got errands to run," Daddy said, acting like the memory of a to-do list reconstituted in his brain with the nourishment of a proper meal. "Probably gonna be pretty boring. You wanting to ride? Anything you're needing to do?" Daddy tried to soft-sell me out of his day. I knew all the dots on his map.

"I'm good," I said, wilting against the side of the door. "You can drop me."

The ride was quiet except for our churning stomachs. The rays of the sun filtered through the waving glass of the truck. The warmth on my face made my eyes heavy. Daddy pulled through the front yard then backed to the carport.

"Help me get this thing off of here," he said, pointing to the trailer.

"Whole trailer?"

"Nah. Don't even know if that'll come off the hitch at this point. Car is just feeling heavy in there is all." Daddy pretended to think for a second. "Mind washing that thing while it's out?"

I groaned and pushed myself off the door and sat up. "Don't be moaning. Not like you've done it in a minute. Pretty sure I washed it last."

Daddy left the truck running while I unhitched the tailgate and unstrapped the Lemon Party II. It carried globs of mud from the previous night, now glued to the sides of the car in gray streaks and pockets of cemented clay. It rolled easily from the back of the trailer, and nearly parked itself on the concrete pad of the carport. I felt that I'd barely pushed. I put up the tailgate and locked it.

The car sat idly on the oil-stained cement pad. There was no fresh oil on the concrete. It was unscathed from its exercise the night before, metal skin stretched tight and fresh. The old dents looked intentional, for aerodynamics and a more angular and mean composition.

"That you driving last night?" I asked. I walked around the car, timidly, looking for it to come to life—afraid that it might. I'd seen it happen in a movie.

I turned on the hose. The water was near freezing, and I started on the back. Chunks of gray mud fell to the floor, and I would swear that water steamed as it hit the car.

22

WILD

I went and paid Jimmy another visit. I could hear the drums pounding, big old *boom, boom, booms* before I ever even stepped a foot in there. The glass might as well've been shaking. Jimmy didn't seem to notice, but all the greenery I was crawling through, the goddamn jungle, to get back to my volcano god and the native ladies was giving me rug burns. Jimmy finally came over there and yanked my ass up off the floor.

"Do you hear it?" I was talking pretty loud, I guess.

"What the hell do you want, Wild?"

"Look!" I pointed at the wall where the ladies were dancing, swaying their hips and pointing at the coconut bottle tower, gleaming handles sparkling.

"I know, Wild. I put up the display yesterday. Very exciting."

I pulled a bottle by the handle from the second shelf and Jimmy caught the bottle from the top, when it tried to topple. "Like a volcano," I said. I cradled the handle in my arms, just about the size of a big heavy baby and thought back about Little when they'd finally let me hold him. He didn't have coconut covered titties, but I sure felt like I liked him back then. I looked over at Jimmy. "I won *again*," I said, and could hear my own voice booming like the volcano god. Maybe my eyes spun like pinwheels of fruit. I sure hope they did. I paid for that bottle in cash, carried it out of the store, and spoke out to the sidewalk of folks in the morning light. "Behold!" I held it up for them all to see and praise, shook it and watched the bubbles jiggle and pop.

I tipped that bottle back as I drove to the Ross Dress for Less. Little needed some shoes, and I was gonna get him some.

There were dinosaurs in damn near every color in the kids' section. They did tricks on skateboards and poked each other with crayons like they weren't already bright enough. I looked for my island ladies in all the colors hanging from the ceiling but wasn't seeing them so I drank some more out of my bottle, imagined all that island music, and hunted me a pair of Pumas for Little to drive in. Red stickers dotted the boxes of mismatched pairs strung together with bungees and I grabbed some off the shelf. Sat myself down on one of the shoe-sitting benches where you try on the shoes and stuck my bottle between my legs, held my arms out there stretched in front of me and blew through my lips, driving me a car. Flew down a straightaway and pushed hard through a turn while I stuck the front half of my foot in one of those shoes, testing it out till I needed me another sip and the kid next to me was crying, annoying as hell and sticking his face in his mama's boobies right where I wanted to be.

On the way out I picked up a gold-colored watch, bigger and brighter than Senior's and with a couple extra dials that I was pretty sure did things like time fast racecars. Next, I stopped at the Texas Roadhouse and ate a steak lunch with a glowing martini off their *All Business* menu. They brought me two endless baskets of rolls that I promptly stuffed in my pockets and down my pants till my pants swolled and they brought the manager, who told me they were totally out of bread.

"But you know I won? You ain't never served you a winner yet like this one here!" I pointed at my pants, bumped up with dinner rolls, tried to grab a name badge off "Steve" right before they carried me out. "Put me in a plastic bag to go, you sonsabitches," I said, but they didn't. Didn't know what to do with the winner.

Back in the truck, the bottle smiled at me. I smiled back at it, thought of my native ladies as I tipped it back. We had a dance, they played little guitars and had hips that wiggled big and wide. I drove two parking lots over, rattling the truck and empty trailer over curbs and sets of speed bumps, to ProCreations. I held the handle on the sliding door as it opened a couple times, then me and my bottle moved real fast and dodged it the next time and walked inside to the big lights and puppy dog squeals.

"Where Nanny?" I called. I tried another S, just standing there blowing, but that shit was broke. My Ss were all caught up and bunched on my teeth and I checked them with my fingers to make sure I hadn't chipped one on the drive over the curbs. "Where Nanny?"

The ladies of ProCreations had them another language, some "code words" they thought I hadn't quite picked up. But I knew their language. I was a *code breaker*. When I came in and they was thinking I was drunk they said things like "puddle-puddle." When I peed at the entrance, it was "piddle-piddle." For me getting locked out of the house they called, "tail down at the entry," and for any time I was trying for making up they stopped their chewing on the jerky long enough to say, "Pet-pet—pet-pet." By the time I got in, the cashier had the microphone in her hand, finger on the button, and was squinting at me, trying to get me figured out.

"Pet-pet—pet-pet, Nanny," she called, judging me. I turned and looked over at her.

"Where Nanny?" I said. I started shuffling my way over toward that cashier and she decided that she had announced the wrong code. She keyed that mic again.

"Correction. Puddle-puddle. Nanny, puddle-puddle."

Nanny walked up.

I turned to her, focused real hard. She stood there with her arms crossed over her chest, her nametag hanging over them. "You can come home now," I said, real assertive-like, and pointed at her.

"Oh yeah?" she asked. "Why's that?"

"Lookie here what I got." I held up my bottle.

"Bigger than usual," she said.

"Damn right." I took a drink. "I can afford these now." I held the bottle up for the cashier to see as well. She squinted, then ate her a bite of jerky.

"Really, Wild? How? You sold every piece of your business. Your lawnmower, the edger, weed-whacker, blower. What'd you sell now? Your truck?"

"No, woman. I *won*. O-N-E." I wrote the letters in the air for her with my finger.

"What? A scratch-off? Only thing you ever won at is spending money you don't got."

"The race," I said. "Won the race." I was still smiling. She just wasn't getting it. "You go on and come back to the house now. I won."

"You didn't win nothing," she said.

"I did."

"You didn't. You sold your living for *our boy* to win a race."

"Two." I held up two fingers. "I'm a win-ner." I held up the bottle in my other hand for her to see the smiling fruit. Bright, big oranges and a happy banana. An offer. My ladies might've made her jealous. She got like that.

"I'm dry, you dumb sonofabitch. You'd been paying attention you'd know." She slapped my two fingers down. "Get straight, Wild."

23

NANNY

I patted my pockets for ChapStick. There was something about the flavor of cherry ChapStick that let me start over fresh. My mama bought them for me at the market. I still grabbed a couple and stuck them in my pockets when I breezed through. She always put it on fresh before she let my dad have a piece of her mind. If I saw Wild, had to hear him talking his nonsense and carrying on, I reached for my tinted ChapStick and put it on, rubbed my lips together, felt them come back to life. The tube probably got washed with some of Little's racing stuff, because it was a little crusty. I swear, everything in my life was crusted with dirt. I couldn't avoid it. Everything was a reminder of the fact that my life was getting dragged through the mud and had been for years.

Wild was still talking. He's drunker than I could think possible if I hadn't been there myself so recent. He looked like a pot of water boiling over with its lid off balance, wobbling back and forth when the steam bubbled out, like it all might just spill out at any second and we'd have to mop his ass up right here at the front of the store. Somewhere down in the bubbling, behind all that steam, there was still Wild. A baby Wild was swimming, drowning down there underneath all that water. But it wasn't water. It was vodka. That baby drowned in the booze. I put on the ChapStick and waited, waited for when it was time for me to talk or to have his dumb ass dragged out of the store still bubbling.

I watched his eyes roll around in his head like marble-painted bowling balls cosmically fucked up and tumbling into the universe, a galaxy outside of my own, and I wanted to push my fingers into his eyes sockets and roll his goddamn head out into the parking lot. Maybe it would have bounced and busted out the windshield of his truck I was so tired of seeing. Every time I saw that truck my hands went numb, and I started running through my head on how I could best escape. I'd get a strike after giving so many spares.

I found the ghost dog we were looking for at ProCreations. I brought him to my car and named him Stewart. I'm pretty sure that's what my dad's name was when Mama wasn't calling him "asshole." The bitches Stewart was leaving behind in the store weren't good for much anyway. Besides, I knew Lady, my experiment, would need to be strong enough on her own before she could hold down a dog like Stewart. It didn't matter anyway. Lady already had a bowling ball in her belly, conceived off my prayers.

24

WILD

I tripped out past the dark windows of the empty box of the store next door, down one more storefront to Henry's Outdoors and More. I unbuttoned my pants and stuffed the bottle of vodka down the front of my jeans, then struggled to breathe as I walked inside. I pushed a cart through the toy aisle, made some small talk with some electronic fish and stuffed elk and shit, made me a couple of selections, then consulted a taxidermy deer with an arrow holding a directory to its breast. I followed the sign to the home section and found a new camp chair. Got it pulled out in the aisle and tested the cup holder for my fruit ladies. The bottle was too big, less I flipped it over, so I got me a camp mug too.

At the checkout I fanned the wad of cash at the clerk, some teenager hot thang smacking on gum. She had her a belly button ring that hung out from under her shirt and I thought about pulling on that thing to see if it was real. She said, "Dang," when I unfolded the bills and I just couldn't help but smile.

"Like your watch," she said.

The bottle of vodka swished.

Back in the truck, I got to feeling that I'd gained a net zero on the day. I'd lost a woman, but gained a new camp chair. I swam through some more of that bottle and pondered my mower, then realized I needed to tell a couple more folks of my winning ways. I was willing and able to pay for some redemption and I drove out to the Monkey Palace. I watched the shoulders for additional signs while me and the truck floated along the main drag, then swam all the way to the county line.

Pulled the truck behind the building and the trailer slid when

I braked hard in the oyster shells to let everybody know I'd *arrived*. Yanked the door and stomped into the bar. There was a table of two sitting in the middle of the room eating a plate of french fries and picking the last bit of chicken from a pile of wing bones. Other than that, a lonely old man sat on a stool at the end of the bar nursing a beer. The monkeys were quiet, and the music was turned way down. I walked to the bar and the hose-lady bartender held her hand on the shotgun.

"Bud Light," I said, grinning like a possum. "And I'm buying me a round for everybody!" I turned and pointed to the room. "I won!"

The bartender set my beer on the counter and about that time I saw Senior walking across the room and the cook split the double doors of the kitchen. I turned back to the bartender and I'll be damned if I didn't knock my bottle back over the counter and behind the bar. That bottle exploded and sprayed all on her. I was bummed, but laughed as she held the expression of surprise and a foam beard on her face. She looked funny.

"What in the actual fuck?" she said.

"I'll get me another one. That one's busted," I said, and pointed to the cooler. I pulled out my wad of bills and put it on the counter.

"Nope. You won't," said Senior. The cook wiped his hands on his apron and walked around behind me like I didn't see him. I felt him back there lurking like some big old grizzly bear. He wasn't there to clean up the spill. I turned to him.

"Why don't you go on now and get me something to eat," I said.

Senior took another step toward me. "I'll give you some-thing to eat." He snatched my money off the bar, and when I went after him the cook wrapped me up from behind. Senior walked toward the back, through the kitchen doors, and that old grizzly cook dragged me like a goddamn sack of potatoes. I was looking at that table of diners and they didn't even bother to watch. The cook dragged me through the kitchen, and the bright lights burned my eyes. I covered them to adjust, but I barely had time 'cause Senior kicked open the back door and there we were, out in the parking lot.

"Hold that sonofabitch down," Senior said, and motioned to the cook to pin me, but he didn't put me down gently. He flopped my ass on the ground hard, and then stood on my arms. The broken shells pushed up into my skin and only hurt worse when I tried to move. I saw that man's kitchen shoes, caked in grease and dust from the parking lot, the ash of cigarette breaks, and flour from fry batter. Any other time, it would've made me hungry.

"I'm tired of hearing your mouth. Nobody in there wants to hear it." Senior held up the wad of cash. "You say you're hungry?" Senior leaned down, cut the stack in half. "My cut." He pocketed his cut, then tried to stuff the wad of bills in my mouth, but I snapped at him. Senior stuck his fingers up my goddamn nostrils and waited on me to breathe. "Let me go on and get you stuffed." I held my breath about as long as I could, till I felt warm and started to lose my color vision, then I gasped. Senior stuffed the wad of bills in my mouth till they touched the back of my throat and I gagged. Senior looked to the cook. "Got anything else you want to stuff in there?"

"Nah, baby. I get that enough at home," he replied. I moaned on the ground. Thought maybe I'd caught my own tail. I sprayed puke from around the sides of the wad of money. Tried to get it on their shoes.

"Should've taken my cut out of there," Senior said. He motioned for the cook to let me loose. He stepped off my arms and I rolled to my side. I pulled the bills from my mouth and heaved.

Senior put a foot on my back and pushed me over on my stomach. "Don't bring your dumb ass back out here until you done being a loser."

"I won," I said from the ground.

"Can't win till you're not a piece of shit. Besides—boy won the race." Senior and the cook walked away. The backs of my arms were tore up and bled on the bleached-out shells below.

I picked up my money and wiped my steak lunch off the bills, then stuffed them back in my jeans. I stumbled as I walked out toward the row of tall pines and out into the field. There was a breeze and the tops of the trees waved like my ladies had just a little while earlier and the sparklers in my vision looked just like exploding stars. Now they were out of reach. I sat down in the clearing and stared at my car, remembered the sounds, the flash of light, the months of rehab, and those fucking pineapples in the hospital. I lost it all and motherfuckers were still trying to take my wins. I remembered Nanny, pregnant and having a baby in the room behind me while I laid there flat on a bed, helpless like some goddamn bug.

"I am re-deemed."

I parked in the front yard and walked through the house. I held myself up along the wall with both hands and my face and left greasy streaks on the shitty paint. I stepped through Little's bedroom door. "Got you something," I said. I stuffed my arm into a large plastic bag and held out a red Puma box to the boy. A worn-out *Deep Discount* sticker fluttered to the floor as Little took the box. Little's face lit up as he popped the top off and pulled a brand-new shoe from it. The shoes were held together with an elastic band and the other followed it and came out too. Little's smile faded. He tried to put on the left shoe but couldn't fit his foot in. He pulled his foot out and looked in at the tag.

"Dang. Haven't worn a size six in at least two years. Worth a shot, though," the boy said.

I did everything, gave everything, lost everything. "I'm supposed to keep track of all y'all's sizes?" I asked. My face was burning up and I snatched the shoes out of Little's hands. He flinched, then watched me stuff the shoes back in the box. I struggled to slap the lid on, but it got there. Stuck the box under my arm and reached into the large bag again. "You're so grown up now." I threw the big-ass stuffed camouflage bear on his bed. "So grown up."

25

LITTLE

The new bear wore Realtree camo overalls and lay face down on the bed, hidden in the sheets. I grabbed it up by its arms and held it out in front of me. It had a limp fabric rifle stitched to its hands and played "Goin' on a Bear Hunt" in a series of beeps and boops from a speaker in the crack of its pants. I stared into its face, its nearly human eyes. It was the same size, maybe even the same series of bear, as the Valentine's bear that had ended up in Fast Rabbit's pawn. I wondered what holiday this one celebrated and how long I would have it to celebrate with.

By midweek, the high tide of emotions and excitement from the win had all but dropped to a dead low. I could still poke my toes through the sole of my shoes, and I felt more and more of my world's spin and wobble. Daddy drove me to school, fussing with his phone and a cigarette, same as ever. He hummed in short bursts, cleared his throat, and acted like he might say something every now and then, but the words didn't come. Sedy was out sick. Gave me plenty of time to consider my screw-up and even less to look forward to when I got in the classroom. I came up with lots of lines to try to say. None of them were right.

There were a bunch of rumors that floated through the classroom. We'd been having health class once a week. Someone had seen Sedy give me a peck on the cheek pre-race and spread the word that she was for sure dying of some strange disease. This gave me all sorts of worries. I would have picked it up from Margaret. I had nothing left to waste away, and why wasn't I dying? I held my breath every day when I approached my class, hopeful that Sedy's desk would be occupied, hopeful for a chance to apologize again, to make things right, but it was empty for three days.

There were mixed fortunes in the classroom, but no congratulations or recognition for me. George seemed to make the biggest gain with his new braces. They were bright and shiny, a mouth full of guardrails, mismatched with his gray, Co-Cola-stained teeth. But the whistle was gone and the fact that the braces were there was enough to allow George back into the fold. He was welcomed back, invited to play soccer by the other kids on the playground. I would've asked George if he was thankful for the braces if I hadn't caused them in the first place. Tom and George taunted me, teased me with the disastrous things that could happen to my car, and to my body, on the track. On Monday, Tom threw a rock at me. Tuesday, a boiled gray hotdog held over from lunch and rolled up in a napkin found its way down the back of my pants. Wednesday, when I walked out the side door, racing to find Daddy's truck, a McDonald's cup filled with day-old Sprite rained down on my back. I could have changed it all with a few words. But when I thought about what those words would have cost me—Sedy—I I knew I couldn't afford it.

26

NANNY

"Nanny had a little lamb—checkout, Nanny had a little lamb—checkout."

I'd had enough visitors. Didn't think I could handle another. "Hold that thought." I held up a finger to Lady and pleaded for her patience. She was getting bigger. Her little belly was swollen from the Lord and the baby growing in there. I walked to the register.

I looked around and didn't recognize a soul. Just one girl, near being a lady, stood there at the cashwrap holding her hand out to turn down the offer of beef jerky.

"Not who I was 'specting."

The girl looked at me, stood there, eyes sparkling in the fluorescent lighting like she might let loose some tears.

"You pregnant?" I asked.

"No, ma'am. Not that I'm thinking. Wouldn't be possible."

"Anything's possible," I said. Believed it too. "Whatchu needing?"

"Talk if you can."

"I can. You're hearing it."

"Yes, ma'am."

"What's it about?" I asked.

"Little."

"Come on, then." I waved her on to follow me and she did. "What's your name?"

"Sedona. Get called Sedy a lot."

"Hi, Sedy. I'm Nanny. People call me Nanny. But you know that if you're here looking." We walked into my office. Lady was rolling around in her cage, trying to get comfortable. She was probably getting kicked in her belly. Should've told her to get ready for the rest of her life.

"Aw, look at the puppy," Sedy said.

"You can pet her if you want."

"What's her name?"

"Name's Lady."

"Is she pregnant?"

"She's big, huh?"

"Yeah. She looks wobbly. Kinda uncomfortable too."

"That's what getting knocked-up will do. She's gassy too. Don't know if you smell that."

"Store kinda smells that way."

She was young. Her nose couldn't pick up the nuance. The layers of smell in ProCreations.

"So, what's this about Little?"

27

LITTLE

I watched the clock all week, urging the minutes to move faster. I waited every afternoon for Daddy at the curb, hopeful for his ride, but every day I ended up walking home. Daddy spent his days blazing a trail between the house, Wine Time, and the Dollar General. At Dollar General he filled up bags with olives, paint sets, Vienna Sausages, tortillas and Easy Cheese, and paint—splurges that had, in the past, been difficult to justify, as they weren't considered mood leveling. When I came home, he'd painted watercolor pictures of racecars, often the same race car, until he ran out of paints, then he hung them on the walls and celebrated his accomplishment. In the late afternoons he paced the house, waiting for the next race day to redeem the wad of bills that shrank in his pocket, to make it feel whole again.

At night, Daddy passed out in his new camp chair, bright citrus fruit paintings peeking over the edge of the cup holder. I used needle-nose pliers to pull the dwindling wad of money from Daddy's pocket and snuck a few dollars, here and there, from the shrinking stack. I stashed them away, and every morning Daddy complained about the money situation.

On Thursday I walked into the classroom and found Sedy sitting in her chair. My head got real warm and I walked just about as fast as I could over to my desk. Sedy didn't look back right away, but she noticed me a minute later and smiled politely when she saw me staring. She looked skinnier, and she punctuated her smile with a quick nod my way.

"Hey," she said.

168C.H. HOOKS

"Sedy. You okay?"

"Stomach flu." She put her hand over her stomach. "I'm good."

"I heard you were dying?"

"Not the first person to say that this morning. Not how things work, Little."

The class was quickly called to attention with a series of announcements over the intercom: there was another fundraiser coming up, a reminder from the lunch ladies to "take all you want, but eat all you get," 'cause they'd noticed food being rolled up in napkins and pocketed, and a note that Spirit Day was approaching quickly. Finally, Sister Theresa neared the end of the dailies and made a special announcement.

"It has come to my attention that students are spreading both STDs and rumors. The timing of this couldn't be more of a divine convergence. For those of you experiencing the temptation of desire, abstinence training will begin next week. We will steel your young bodies to temptation and stop this potentially rampant proliferation with the spirit of prayer and a shot of celibacy." She paused. "For those of you spreading rumors and uncertainties—three Hail Mary's and an Our Father." The mic was still keyed, and she allowed the students time. Her chair creaked over the intercom and my neck grew cold.

The Catholic students pulled their rosaries from their bags and began whispering intently. The rest of us folded our hands and faced ahead. I looked to Sedy as she moved the beads between her fingers. She was gentle in the simplest task. She caught me with a quick glance from the corner of her eye but faced forward. After the contrition, Sister Theresa cleared her throat over the intercom, then led us through the Pledge of Allegiance.

I watched the clock on the wall, counted seconds and willed the minute hand to move. I would swear the hands shook, bounced backward with every tick. PE was two hours away. It was when I would be able to talk to Sedy. My jaw clenched with impatience and sweat dotted my worksheets. When the break finally came, we lined up in the halls and walked single file to the gym.

We played Death Ball at least twice a week. It was an opportunity to take out the aggressions of our middling hormonal bodies, our minor rages for minor slights. I stood against a wall, waiting to play in the next round while the dwindling teams threw rubber balls at each other across the middle line of the gym. Sedy had been the first to get tagged. I had let myself get tagged as well. We'd been on opposite teams, but now stood next to each other on the padded walls of the gym.

"I'm glad you're back." I had searched for the right words for days. Error proof ones that couldn't leak or run or be misconstrued.

"You missed me?" she asked.

"Yeah," I replied. "Only friend I got."

"Friend?" she asked. Sedy turned and bent over to get a drink from the water fountain. She blushed, like perhaps it had been real. I would have held her laugh if I could, cradled it and protected it, saved it, and never dropped it.

The air around us split in perfect aerodynamic streams and made a hissing noise as the tiny bumps of rubber grip fanned through space. With speed, the projectile achieved lift, like a minie ball, and tagged its unwitting target—Sedy. Her feet elevated from the ground, and she hovered level for an instant, as if she'd levitated. The throw came from Tom. A spray of red flecked in a stream from her nose and created an arc in the air as she lifted and finally settled directly in front of me. She was a creature of beauty now splayed on the floor, red in the face and struggling to come to after hitting the ground with the back of her head. She blinked her eyes and they crossed as she attempted to focus.

"Ow," she moaned. I stood, confused and helpless over her. She had a bloody mustache from the spring of her nose. She heaved, then cried. I knelt and moved my hands around her, frantic to help but totally useless. The gym teacher moved me out of the way with a push as she scooted in, towel in hand. She lifted Sedy's head and pushed the towel into her face. "Get ice," she grumbled at me. I ran for the cafeteria, shoes slapping the gym floor. When I got to the double doors, I looked back at Sedy.

"*Sorry.*" Tom sang the word out of obligation and self-preservation. He stood with another ball under his arm, insurance in case he'd missed with the first. George stood with him. Tom never strayed from his claims of the throw being an accident. He knew the potential ramifications of an intentional facial, but the throw had been so hard, so catastrophic that it knocked her blue-tinted contacts out. I found them on the floor later and put them in my pocket.

The rest of the day was quiet. A dark mood hung over the class. Most of them had never seen so much blood, much less coming from a person's nose. I'd grown up with Daddy. Nearing the end of the day, I started to get my stuff together, readying myself for my after-school scramble.

"In a hurry, Billy?" Tom whispered as he leaned in, just behind my neck. "My aim's been pretty on today."

"Fuck you, Tom," I whispered.

"Hard to get anywhere fast when you're always waiting on that piece-of-shit daddy of yours."

I turned quickly, but Tom sat back, arms folded across his chest and eyes to the front of the room.

"William," Mrs. Florence said. "Is there a problem?"

I turned back around, fuming. Sedy's desk sat there empty all over again.

I had a plan. I would skip waiting on Daddy and try to make it to the corner before Tom could catch me.

I couldn't take any more of Tom, so when the day's final announcements and prayers over the loudspeaker were polished off, I broke for the door, ignoring the bruises on my feet from my earlier sprint. I nearly ran over Sedy in the hallway. She held her head tipped back, a ball of tissue crammed in each nostril. The school nurse held her by the arm, and her eyes were swollen from crying. She waved a hand behind her back at me, but I was squeezed between the nurse and the wall.

"You okay?" I asked, but the nurse kept pulling her along, and tipped her head back further when she tried to turn. I felt a familiar boiling anger in my throat, then remembered that I was still being pursued. I raced out to the playground and headed toward the curb, just in case Daddy had pulled himself from the camp chair. But he hadn't. Instead, a different car waited at the spot—Mama's. I looked in both directions as I walked up, to make sure that Tom's daddy's truck wasn't headed my way. I looked in the windows of the Tercel, still unsure of whether it was really her. The windows were fogged from the heat, but as I got closer I saw Mama, sure enough, sitting in the driver's seat, circling pictures in an ad paper for office furniture with a Sharpie. I opened the passenger door.

"Mama?" She looked up. The paper had nearly every item on the page circled. "What're you doing?"

"Just reading some news," she said. She rolled up the ad and stuffed it between her seats.

"Okay, but what're you doing here?" I asked.

"Come to maybe pick you up." She wiped her nose. The veins in the whites of her eyes throbbed and she blinked them wet again. "What are you doing?" she asked, making small talk.

"Trying to get home," I said.

"Kind of what I wanted to talk to you about," Mama said. She patted the seat next to her, but I froze, confused, and missed the invitation. "Seeing if you're wanting to come live with me." The car door gave a bit more and bounced under my grip.

"When?" I asked. The conversation was familiar. The thought had been kicked around for years, anytime things around the house heated up. I was a cotter pin holding together all their rust.

"Now," she said. "Like—today." She pointed to the seat

again. This time I really noticed, then looked around. "Got my own place. Signed for it today." The carpool line thinned. I turned back to the car and Mama.

"We're winning, though." I leaned into the car. It was warm, and I tried to keep myself both in and out. "You could come home."

Mama shook her head.

"Think things could be getting better." It wasn't true and I knew it. The words felt stale when I spoke them. Like I'd recycled them from Daddy and Mama after hearing them about a million times. She looked ahead at the fogged windshield, then waved with her hand. She wasn't motioning me in.

"Letting all the heat out, Little," Mama said, her chin wrinkling as she talked. Her eyes got shiny. I closed the door and watched as she wiped a spot clean on the windshield with her shirtsleeve. She didn't wave or look at me when she made a U-turn in the street and bumped her tires over the curb on the other side and drove away.

I looked over to the carpool line and noticed Tom's truck as it lurched and left the lane. I ran across the street, and kept my head down as I walked the back-alleys all the way home.

I didn't mention the conversation with Mama to Daddy. Daddy wrenched on the car in the carport. We ate at Taco Bell, where Daddy ordered for me without asking me what I wanted. We were back on bean burritos, ordering from the dollar menu, limp bags of burritos, eaten slowly, not knowing when the next meal would come.

The next morning, Daddy drank from his bottle through a straw as he drove me to school. I noticed that the straw rested in the gap of a missing tooth. Daddy didn't return my look.

"You know, I used to feel bad in the mornings sometimes? I've got tricks up my sleeves for life!" he said. He stopped making sense to me. I ate the leftovers of my previous night's bean burrito I'd left on the seat of the truck to stay cold. On the right, we passed a man in a sandwich board. The board had a picture of a white Jesus in a crown of thorns and Daddy grabbed the wheel tight. "Such a good picture," he said. "I'ma get me one of those boards next time I win. Tell the whole goddamn town 'bout my winning ways."

Daddy stopped the truck, still a block away from the school, perhaps forgetting where he was going, but I understood to get out. I watched him as he drove away to another galaxy, another void of thought.

It was only a couple minutes before Margaret pulled up in her BMW. I froze in my confusion. She was slick and I knew where to sit in her car, how to fold into the seat and disappear in the tan leather. She'd taught me. I felt totally unprepared to talk. I hadn't learned proper technique for saying no. There was a large scrape down the side of the car. The passenger side mirror was held on by its wires and shook from the vibrations of a song I didn't know. She rolled down the window and slowly turned down the music as I approached the car. Her eyes were wide and white dribbled from one nostril. She snorted and swallowed.

"Where you been at?" she asked, still talking too loud from the deafening noise. I'd seen her gyrating and singing at stoplights before.

"Going to school," I answered and pointed over my shoulder.

"Let's go skip," she said.

"What are you skipping?" I asked.

She pointed at the school. "Duh."

"Don't think I can," I replied.

"Come on now." She smiled.

I looked back toward the school. "Can't."

"This about your little girlfriend? I got ears and eyes." She pointed to her face and gritted her teeth. The grinding was loud. "I pick winners. Thought you might be able to hang on a little better than your daddy." She leaned forward and let her arms rest on the wheel. "There'll always be the next young thing." A wave of skin popped between her shorts and her T-shirt. "I can promise you, she ain't got what I got."

I considered yesterday's announcements and contrition. I thought of Sedy, her body floating in space and time, a cloud of red. I watched the cloud of my own breath equalize with the cold of the air around me. Margaret pushed a button and started rolling up the window and I pulled my hand away. She hit the gas hard, not realizing the car was still in park, then put it in gear while it revved. The car lurched and crunched through its transmission as it limped away.

28

WILD

A race car's got a cage. My cage is home. It spins faster than the earth can twirl. Earth hasn't hit a wall yet that I know of, but a car sure can, and when it did I was always so damn happy to be in my cage. I walked to the carport. The car was there, all mean and black and comfy looking with its cage inside. I orbited it a full couple of times. Orbiting? That's the word, right? I poked at it here and there, seeing if it might come to life, wake up growling at me like one of Nanny's old-ass dogs we let out in the neighborhood when they got too mean.

I'd asked Little to get the car prepped. Just a couple things to do for the race, but it seemed like these days the boy couldn't be bothered to follow through. Boy had become a mystery of not doing shit. I knew about the girls and the *hormones* and the *burning loins* and all the things I'd got chased out of windows and beds for. Still bothered me to see Little getting uppity and such.

I slid through the car window like a slip 'n' slide, into the cage until my ass bounced on the old seat springs. Just a driver's seat. Room for one. The work of moving muscles, flexing and bouncing, squeezed a throb up from my neck and into my head and I knew for sure a drink would fix it. I wrapped my fingers over the wheel, one at a time, like I was sneaking up on it. The padding felt small and thin in my hands since I wasn't wearing any gloves. Never had a feel for the wheel when I was wearing gloves. Same for me and Nanny or any other lady. That's how we ended up with Little. I grabbed the gearshift, tipped it through the tree of gears, not like any tree I seen. Branches off that thing looked like it was laying down dead. I let the shifter settle in neutral, then cranked the Lemon Party II, revved it a few times and watched the cloud of smoking exhaust, burned oil and floating carbon, blow from behind. It poofed a heavy coat on the dirt yard. Nanny's dogs had run ruts around a post, chained and chasing each other for a bite of a paw or some nook. Shit was worn out from their running and running and chasing.

I was still revving the engine, watching that ticker tickle the redline and wagging that tail. My Lemon Party was better, cleaner, faster. I let off the clutch slow, slow, slow. The vibrating of the engine was shaking my knee through my gone leg, and I gave a push on the gas. Balance, perfect goddamn balance. The car rocked, just loose enough to have a little play, just tight enough to get up and go. It pulled on its reins like any good animal, like Senior had told me. I watched my thoughts fall out of my head and drift off to where busted thoughts go when they stop being useful.

I let the car go, and it rolled up into the back of the trailer, into the dark, dark, dark, pushed the clutch and the brake and the car settled back to resting potential. If there was stars, this would've been space. I'd be tumbling through the dark, maybe find some big ol' god hanging out near the ceiling. I'd find the end of space at the end of the bottle. I held the bottle up to my lips, tipped it back, finished it, and looked through the bottom like a kaleidoscope. I spun that thing and looked through the mouth. I thought about my comeback. My goddamn triumph. That night I took my usual walk up toward the orange glowing dots, little stars and suns, but instead of two good legs, I hobbled on my shit-fitting gone leg. I'd stuffed an old T-shirt around my joint to make it snug and bit my lip through every bit of sharp pain, defying gravity, so the crowd could see me walking normal-like.

People held their cigarettes between their teeth and slapped me on the back and I held on tight, struggling to keep upright. I'd practiced walking for months. Watched myself in the mirror. Walked back and forth and back and forth and back and forth and back and forth and wore out a strip of carpet and had that shit down to a science, but still winced with every step. That crowd stood and clapped for me and I felt a wave, not a wave of arms and big bellies bobbing doing standing sit-ups, but a wave of warmth and relief that I was back doing what I did. I stalled the car on my first shift. I couldn't feel the pedal. I came in last place that night. It was dark when the lights went out. Darker than the trailer, darker than the room with the lights out and off when I didn't pay the bill 'cause the sponsors bailed, and the fans bailed, and the money ran out. Don't I know it when they laugh?

My pocket felt light as could be when I climbed out, but my jeans were tighter than ever. I swung my legs around and slid into the space between the wall of the trailer and the car, tightened up the orange straps around the wheels, then grabbed the bottle with the smiling fruit. I stepped out of the trailer, onto the tailgate ramp, and found Little standing there.

29

LITTLE

"Heard the engine," I said.

"Yeah?" Daddy replied. He snorted. I saw his eyes were glassy and he chose his words sparingly.

"Sorry," I said, and looked into the trailer. "Was gonna do that this morning."

Daddy looked down at the empty place on his arm where a watch should be. "Well, it's past noon now," he said.

"Sorry," I said again.

Daddy stepped off the tailgate and we both stopped to pick up a side.

"It's dark in that trailer."

"Yep," I said.

"Thing sure is noisy," Daddy said. "'Specially in there."

"Uh-huh." We lifted the tailgate shut.

"You ready for tonight?" Daddy asked.

"Think so. You?"

Daddy patted his pocket, involuntarily—a tick. His mouth was dry, and I knew he wanted a pull of the bottle, but I looked and it was empty. He paused for a second. "Think so." Daddy propped against the trailer. "Need another win." He took the weight off his gone leg. He looked at me. "You all right?" Seemed like he was trying to make a repair, like I was one of his tools.

"I'm all right."

"How's Sister treating you?"

"Haven't seen her." I leaned against the trailer as well. "Bunch of those guys are pieces of shit though."

"Always have been," Daddy said. He thought for a second.

"Just like their daddies." Daddy pushed off the back of the trailer and stood again. "Get 'em on the track." He pursed his lips and puffed out his cheeks. I thought he looked like a monkey. "Thanks for getting the tailgate."

"Uh-huh," I said.

Daddy walked around to the cab of the truck and grabbed a pint bottle. He took a long drink, then stuck it back between the seats. He watched through the passenger window as I walked back into the house.

The sign read *Welcome to I-17 Motor Speedway—Home of the Mudslinger Series*, and the truck bumped over the dirt and gravel leading up to the ticket booth and track. The windows were cracked, and the air blowing through the small break was just enough jet to vaporize the vodka from Daddy's breath. If he'd have tried to light a smoke, the cab would have blown up. We followed another car, a spectator who didn't pull a trailer. We were late, running behind for the paddock. Daddy pumped the brakes each time the sun blinked and flashed through the red reflectors of the car we followed; must've thought they were brake lights. Daddy looked over at me. I had my head against the cold window, even through the bumps, but saw him looking. He started moving his mouth like to say something, but no words came.

I looked at him for a second. I had my own question. "You ever feel like you weren't driving?"

"What you mean?" Daddy said. The car ahead turned to the public lot and we passed the ticket booth and circled the outside of the track.

"Like you weren't really controlling the car."

Daddy squinted. "Like in the ruts? The wheels'll kind of dig in their ownselves for sure." Daddy glanced back at me, then to the road.

"Nah, not the ruts. Like it's driving itself. The car, I mean."

Daddy clenched his jaw and the skin stretched tense. "Don't get spooked, boy. Last thing you want to do is get superstitious.

Don't be getting weird." Daddy reached down and knocked on
his gone leg. "'Sides, we need this win." Daddy put his hand
over his pocket, hopeful for another bump in his bottom line.
His stomach growled. "Just go on and shake that stuff out of
your head." He stopped the truck and turned to me. "For real."

"It's nothing," I said. I wiped my palms on my race pants
and nodded.

"Come on now," Daddy said. He shook his head like he was
shivering and then he smiled. He playfully slapped my leg with
the back of his hand. Too hard to be playing around. "You're
good, right?" I nodded. "Got plenty on the line." The track
lights were on. The days were short. At the beginning of the
season, it was still light out when we were done. Now, when the
race was over it was pitch dark. Daddy pulled into the paddock,
backed the trailer toward the pit, and then stopped. It was my
cue to jump out. I walked around to the back and unhitched the
gate, then let it drop with a squeak.

"You gonna let him up front?" I heard Daddy arguing with
the official.

"You're late, you lose pole. That's how it goes." The man
tapped his clipboard. "You know that, Wild."

The other cars were unloaded and stacked in place. Daddy
sat in the truck while I rolled the car from the trailer. Tom and
his father tweaked the throttle of their car, it screamed a high
pitch. George sat on the hood of his. The other racers milled
around the paddock.

I tossed the straps back in the trailer, then pushed up the
gate and walked around to the front of the truck.

"I'm gonna pull the truck around," he said. "Got a bet to
place." He winked at me and clicked his tongue. "You got it
from here?"

"Breaking tradition," I said, not realizing I cared.

"Get out of your head, boy." Daddy pointed to his temple.
"Seriously." I watched the side of his mouth sag as he pulled
away.

"Lost your pole, huh?" Tom asked as he watched me toss

my helmet in the car. I kept my head down and only looked up when I noticed Margaret walking by. She looked me up and down. Her short-shorts had worn a rash on her thigh and the denim explored the crevices of her body. She carried a hotdog and as she passed, she bit the end off in a way that made me flinch.

I climbed through the window of the car and cranked the engine. I pulled around to the back of the pack. I cycled through my situation. I would need to climb past seven cars to reach the front. Tom and George were a few cars ahead. I would need to continue to fend off Margaret's advances and somehow check on Sedy to see if she was okay. I revved the engine out of frustration and people in the paddock turned their heads. I let off and the engine sighed, like I had teased it. I held my breath with every rev, not wanting the engine to steal it.

30

WILD

Little was bumming and getting weird about tradition. Tradition. For real. Tra-di-tion. Never cared before. Now he's a winner and he needs to do winner things. I parked the truck, angled it in 'cause I didn't want nobody scratching the paint, and walked up to the betting booth. Not a single person came over to talk about betting. Not a soul! They were there. I saw 'em by the stars of their burning cigarettes. They bobbed and circled. I nodded and watched, waiting for them come over but the conversations continued. I gave them a minute, but they didn't come. Don't need them anyway. "I burn bright enough!" I pointed to my chest. "Well, fuck all y'all then." I waited until the final call for bets, then walked to the window. I made my big-dog bets on every dollar I got—bought fifty or so. Saved my monies by not eating and just drinking from the fruit bottle. I walked on under the bleachers, checked my hands and they were still there. I stepped into the light of the track and searched the sidewalk below for my shadow. I tried to step on it and catch it, but when I looked into the car window and saw my reflection, I damn near didn't recognize me. It was like I had disappeared, and if I'd disappeared, I didn't exist.

31

LITTLE

The race official walked through the paddock and checked numbers against positions. I didn't get a chance to pee before turning on the engine and the rumble vibrated my bladder. I shook my legs and my right knee tapped the keys. The keychain was shiny, chipping enamel, a flame that read, *Good Company*. I pushed in the clutch and fed the engine once more. The air around me waved from fumes and the heat radiating from the hoods. I felt the Lemon Party II pull at my grip, ready to go, but I kept my foot on the clutch. The stands were full. Ahead, the cars at the front of the pack pulled through the gate and onto the track.

I heard the wave of noise. It washed over row after row of cars until I tasted it and felt it wrap me up in sound. There was nothing else to hear. The crowd in the stands shook their arms and they clapped. I decided to maintain control; I would starve that engine and hold on to my presence, and I would do this for as long and as much of the race as possible. I took a deep breath and pressed the gas, felt that the cage was a bubble, then swam out onto the track. The line of cars already stretched beyond a quarter of the groomed dirt, nearly reaching the first turn by the time I entered. The lights flashed off my hood and the cars stuck to formation. We drove a full lap, weaving to warm up tires or simply out of impatience. The green flag waved, and the line of cars spilled out, spreading over the track.

I felt the car slide through my grip. I held tight and maintained even as I pressed the gas harder. I passed two cars quick, like they weren't moving on the same track, and felt that I had jumped to another plane, another track of my own. Tom and

George were also passing folks. They moved quickly along the outside to the front of the pack from their much better position. They were moving faster than the last race, which made me wonder what part they'd upgraded. When I pushed the accelerator harder, the resistance gave and the engine growled. A car slid from my left and I jerked the wheel to miss it. The engine gasped, chortled like it was pleased, then screamed to life. It relished in the moment of stealing my air. I felt it get sucked from me as I pushed back into the seat. My eyes watered, blurring the colors of the other cars. I held tight to the wheel, the pedal flexed beneath my foot, and I felt it grow hot through the hole in my shoe. I closed on George's car and passed it; I was well beyond him when I closed in on Tom.

I saw dirt—each individual drop of mud—as it flung from Tom's wheels. Seconds beat as the images flashed by. The warm bodies in the stands were a smudge as I rounded the turn. Tom swung wide, letting his car drift through, and slid smooth through the gray, oil-stained clay. I took the turn closer to the inside rail. The wheel heaved and I could hear the clunk of my steering as it reached its furthest point, but I kept my speed, and coming out of the turn, into the next straightaway, pulled even. Me and Tom both ran flat out for the finish line. The crowd roared, I know they did, but I couldn't hear it over the howls of our engines. I only heard the thump of compression, the sparking of fluids as they moved through my machine—pressed deep into the seat—and the combustion that forced fluids through my own veins.

I had the inside, and Tom leaned his car toward the point of the approaching turn to cut me off. Greedy Tom. I would need to give way or attempt to cut through the gap as Tom slid through. I saw him in my mind, his words, his attempts to embarrass me, how he'd hurt Sedy, made her levitate and broke her nose. My bumper rubbed steel. Then, I saw Tom spin three times on the track. I saw the shock on Tom's face, the determination to maintain control, and the flash of him each time his car rolled toward the steel of the outside guardrail. I pulled through the turn, and only slowed when the red flag was waved from the grandstand. The remainder of the pack was far behind, stopped at the scene of Tom's ragdoll flip over the barrier wall. Drivers had climbed from their cars and shouts carried through the night air.

I would swear that I attempted to pull my foot from the accelerator, that I didn't shoot the gap through the turn. It was dangerous, but legal, and the race was official—we'd put in the required laps. I was the winner. The official brought down the checkered flag and they took a photo of me holding it in front of the Lemon Party II. No one cheered. The stands were quiet. Behind me, Tom was removed from the wreckage and placed on a stretcher. He gave a thumbs-up as they wheeled him toward the ambulance. A clap broke out from the stands.

Daddy was the lone cheering voice.

"I won!"

32

LITTLE

Daddy's excitement was short lived.

"You explain to me how I'm not gonna get paid out more than that." He pushed his bet slip back under the cut out in the window. Donald looked at it again, then turned it around and slid it back at Wild.

"Those is the odds, Wild. Almost everybody bet a winner tonight. Your boy," Donald said, pointing over his shoulder at nowhere in particular, trying to find the spread. Daddy squinted and looked in that direction, "is a proven winner. He won tonight." Donald nodded at me. "You watching?" Donald took his hand off the ticket. "Just why in the hell is that gonna get you upset? Lucky you won anything. That other kid is pretty banged up. Still got the winning check." Daddy picked up the ticket and looked at it once more. "You want me to pay you out, or what?" Daddy looked over his shoulder. A line formed behind him. "I'm happy not to. Be glad to keep it." Daddy pushed the ticket back under the window and Donald pulled out a strap of bills. He pulled a couple off and slid them to Daddy, who snatched them up and held them up to the light, to take more time at the front of the line, to protest, to see if the bills were real. Then he flipped off Donald and walked by the others in the line.

A man slapped him on the shoulder. Slapped me on the shoulder too. "Thanks, boys! Got me paid," the man said. "Easiest bet they is!" Another bettor handed Daddy a beer.

"Cheers!" they said.

I heard the gravel crunching behind me, looked over my shoulder and saw Margaret. I didn't want to talk or anything, just wanted to work. She walked up behind me, reached around, and swiped between my legs while I latched the trailer door. The last thing I wanted was for Sedy to somehow see me around her again. When I turned, she flicked her tongue out at me. It was long and lizard-like, and I was sure that I saw it wrap under her chin.

"Heard Tom's pretty banged up," she said, entertained.

"Yeah, I think so," I replied. "Was an acci—"

"Got me a little excited, watching that race." She stepped in close and I flattened myself against the back of the trailer but felt the heat of her body. Her chest grazed me, and I turned my head as she brought her face toward mine and ran her tongue along the side of my face. It felt rough, like a cat's, and I think I groaned out loud. Through my squinted eyes, I saw George walking from the concession stand, down the path. He stopped when he caught sight of us. Me, pressed against the trailer, Margaret's tongue pressed against the side of my head, and her hand pressing and making vigorous motions on my racing suit.

My eyes widened in terror and Margaret turned and saw George. She pushed off me, then slapped me across the face. "Ew, you little fucker!" she squealed.

George came storming down the hill, but she caught him by the arm, intercepted him on his way to me. George glared at me over his shoulder as Margaret dragged him toward their car. She'd kept him off me for the night, but she couldn't do a thing about school on Monday.

"Damn it," I said.

I got the car in the trailer. Pretty sure Daddy was making me do it alone because of earlier. When I opened the passenger door, he'd already finished his beer. I kicked the dirt off my shoes and got in, then put my hot cheek against the cool window.

"Hey," he said.

"Hey." I watched Daddy from the corner of my eye. "How'd you make out?"

Daddy winced. He grabbed the wheel with both hands.

"That was stupid," he said. "What you done was dumb." The window grew warm from the heat of my face. "Look up and listen, boy! Now somebody goes on and gets hurt." Daddy pointed to his gone leg. I felt poorly enough. This wasn't the conversation I saw coming. Daddy started the truck. "How's the car?"

It was a question I could answer. "Barely scratched," I said.

"But scratched, huh?" Daddy replied. "Dumb." He pulled away from the paddock and threw his empty beer bottle out the window. Our stomachs growled at each other.

"We won," I reminded him. "Can we get that buffet tonight?" I kind of thought that maybe if we weren't human, we would surely eat one another.

"Not enough," Daddy said. "Everybody bet for you. Can't win much when that happens. Can't win with winning."

All Daddy'd ever wanted was another win, but even with my win, I realized there was no possibility for satisfaction, for even the simplicity of something slightly better. We drove through Taco Bell and Daddy picked from the dollar menu.

33

NANNY

I'd been standing around in Sister's office for at least ten minutes, just waiting. Didn't have time for waiting. I stopped by the house when I knew they were out racing. There was a stack of mail. Ads for Hardees and Rooms to Go. Right there at the bottom was a note from Sister Theresa asking me to come in and have a talk. So, I did.

When I heard the doorknob turning I turned to see what would come through it. Sister scooted through the cracked door like she didn't want the lamplight leaking out. Maybe she wasn't wanting the office light to come in.

"Have a seat," she said.

"Please?"

She neared her own chair and looked back at me. "Did you need something?"

I waited.

"Have a seat, please."

"Thank you," I said. I sat down.

"This should not be contentious. I believe that we have the same hope in our hearts." Sister reached down under her desk. I heard a little door open and she popped back up holding a Diet Coke. She held a small napkin under it and gestured to me.

"No, thanks. I quit."

She put the Diet Coke on the desk and a straw in the top.

I'm not gonna lie. My mouth watered.

"Your son and your husband were here recently."

"Not my husband."

"Oh?"

"We got engaged a long time ago. That's all over."

"Oh." Sister leaned back and her chair squeaked. She took a moment, then sat up slowly.

I got a look at her toes. Mine ain't the prettiest, look like Stewart's minus the polish, but shit. "You asked me to come in."

"Let me first make it clear—that I have my concerns," she pointed her old bony, crooked finger my way and continued. "But I would like to hear yours."

I sat back and let out a big old sigh through my nose. It whistled a little, but I pretended like it didn't happen. "Got years of them. Plenty. Why's that your business?"

She sat there a second and her jaw moved, clinched on and off and I could see the muscle through the thin skin of her cheeks, like she was chewing or maybe there was something crawling around in her mouth, words she just couldn't quite spit out. "Because your son will not be in school here much longer."

She jumped right in after that. Couldn't get her to stop even though there was a whole bunch of it I wasn't wanting to hear. She finally got all those words out that were crawling around. She left me with, "And then there's Margaret."

34

LITTLE

I was late for school on Mass Monday. We rolled into the gas station as the truck breathed its last fumes. I helped Daddy push the truck to the pump and considered us to be fortunate to have made it so close instead of like before, when I would have been walking to the nearest station with a gas can from the trailer.

Daddy went inside to pay while I stood with the gas nozzle in hand. I watched as he took his time in the store. He went to the coolers first, then walked the aisles, then finally to the register. My class would have left for Mass by then. I would have to get a note from the office and take my backpack with me to the chapel. It was my favorite day of the school month, free moments to think between standing and kneeling and sitting.

When he came back out, he waved at me to start pumping, then tossed an empty tall boy in the garbage before climbing back in the truck. The ticker made it around to four-fifty, then slowed as it approached five dollars—then stopped. I knocked on the glass.

"That it?" I asked Daddy, who stared down at his phone.

He looked up.

"Shake that thing real good. Lift the hose up too," he replied, and motioned an example of the operation. I did as I was told, then hung up the nozzle.

The truck shuddered and shook back to life and Daddy's phone rang again. I climbed in. The phone sat back in the ashtray and beeped. The number of the incoming caller was an 800 number.

"You going to pick up?" I asked. Daddy pursed his lips.

"Nope. Got no time for all that."

Daddy dropped me at the curb and I ran to the front entrance of the school while Daddy waited at the curb.

"Tardy," came the voice from behind the counter. "Get signed in." The school secretary tapped the pad, though I knew what to do. "Y'all are already in the chapel," she said, but I was already walking back out the door.

Students waited in alphabetical order in the back pews for confession. This was a routine experience for the Catholic students, but a great mystery for me. I normally sat in the pew through the entirety of my class's individual visits. As I entered the chapel the last girl from my class stepped from the booth, and my class moved in their line toward the front of the dim building, covered in the glowing stained-glass deaths of saints. I was considered absent and certainly not missed, so I stepped into the booth while my class walked away.

I sat on the short bench, my back against the wall, and waited. I continued to wait and began to wonder if somehow Father Dennis had stepped out through some hidden side door when I heard the rasp of light snoring. I knocked on the wood paneling.

"Bless you," Father Dennis said.

"Thanks," I replied.

"Good." Father yawned. Through the vented wall I heard him wiping his nose. It was a wet noise. "What brings you in? Ahem, how long's it been?"

"Last chapel," I lied.

"Okay, sounds about right." I heard Father Dennis scooting up, trying to get comfortable. "And what do you accuse yourself of?" I looked down at my shoes. "Have you honored your father and mother?"

"Honor," I whispered to myself. I repeated the word, rolling it back and forth.

"Sounds like you're stumped," Father Dennis said. He leaned forward. "Are you keeping modest thoughts?" I thought of Margaret, and wondered if she was included in honoring mothers and modesty.

"I think," I said.

"You think—of what?" Father replied.

"I think I do." I considered her off the table. I wasn't ready to surrender those thoughts no matter my level of confliction with them.

"Okay, that's good. Any strange gods?" Father asked. I'm pretty sure he sensed a holdout. He tried another angle.

I took a breath and thought of the engine. I'd lost control in the race. "Feels like something takes me over," I blurted.

Father Dennis was quiet. I heard him sit back. The bench creaked.

"Something? What is it that takes you over?"

I was unsure how to proceed. "Not sure. It steals my air. Makes me do stuff I'm not wanting to do."

"Like what?" Father asked. I sighed, considered Tom's face as it rotated and distorted with each flip. "Have you hurt someone?" Father asked, intently.

"I did," I answered. "I mean, it wasn't on purpose." My face flushed. I knew I wasn't making any sense, and thought for sure that Father Dennis was pressing some silent alarm on his side of the booth, that I'd surely be arrested.

"How did you hurt them?"

"Can't control the car," I said. "I tried to take my foot off the pedal, but nothing happened, like I'm not even there. Like it's living through me."

"The car?" Father Dennis asked. "Little?"

I heard the creak of the bench again, this time it sighed from the release of pressure. The door to the confessional opened. "You won, though." Father Dennis reached into the booth and pulled me out by the arm. "I heard a lot of folks made good money off you." He looked around.

My eyes adjusted back to the light of the sconces and pendant lights of the chapel. My feelings weren't released, just choked somewhere in my throat. "Tom's all right. He's got a broken arm and hand, and a concussion. We've been lifting him up to the Lord. Word is, he'll be back tomorrow." Father Dennis smiled. "Besides, you're Methodist, right?" He pushed me toward my class, who were seated at the front of the chapel. George sat in front of me.

George stuck close to me all week. When I rounded a corner, George was there, when I looked up, George's gaze was there to meet mine. The interactions were quiet. George was a ghost that haunted my space. Then the haunting became physical. I would be on the receiving end of George's shoulder. Doors swung open and bumped me. Anytime I sat, I could be sure that my chair would be shoved with one of George's hips. It happened at lunch and Sedy noticed. She sat across from me, the brightest spot with a broken nose.

"Think it's Tom?" she asked, referencing the accident. I shook my head. She chewed a bite with her mouth open, her hand covering it, then swallowed. "Knows, huh?" She spoke breathily. Her head tilted back, the bandage over her nose prevented her from using the voice that I loved, the one that I thought about when everything else seemed to lose its pieces. "Think he's upset." I nodded my agreement.

"Think so."

I watched George walk farther down the table and sit down by himself.

"Not good," she said.

"Not good," I agreed.

35

WILD

It was Thursday. My bottles tinkled around all empty and bounced into each other like they were excited or something, like I cared about them when they were empty. The music stopped. The volcano god stopped talking. I knocked the empties over on the floor and they made a sound like they might get broke. I creaked up from my camp chair and stepped to the kitchen sink and ran some water into the bottom of my empty fruit-ladies bottle. Drank that too, just in case I'd missed a sip. I cupped water from the faucet and splashed my face a few times. Felt the water find the cut on my nose. It was like a small ditch running from cheek to cheek. Remembered taking a net in the ditch back when I was a kid and catching all the mud-colored crawfish and their claws pinching. My nose stung a lot more than those pinches ever hurt so I let it loose and shook my face and when I stopped it was a dull throb in my head. I filled up my hands again and ran my fingers through my hair, pulling tangles. I slicked the bulk of it back, and tucked the rest behind my ears, put on my Goodyear hat, pulled it low, and breathed out. I looked at those empty bottles sitting there on the counter and stared into the pinwheels of fruit, thought of my native ladies and watched that bright fruit spin in the morning sunshine which hurt my eyes. I blinked, and the bottle grinned empty right back at me.

"Well, just look at you," I said. I adjusted my pants, resituated, and realized that Nanny had stayed gone a lot longer than usual. "Nan-nay," I called. "Nose hurts!" She'd been the one busting it before, so not real sure why I was needing to call her and tell her 'bout it now. "Nan-nay!" I walked around the floors of the house, creaking and making them talk to me. "Tell me something, creaking floors—where's my Nan-nay?" Walked those floors right out the door and got in the truck feeling about as fresh as I could or had in recent times.

I pulled the truck out of the drive and ran over the armadillo-goddamn-dinosaur in the gutter with a thump and watched the shell wobbling in the mirror. The tires on the trailer bumped up on the curb and I yelled, "Get back!" at the curb 'cause it jumped out, and I tried hard to keep the truck between the yellow lines and the other lines and the shoulder. I turned into the lot of ProCreations and might've took the turn a little early, jumped up on that curb, and hit the sign, which they'd planted damn near in the street. I helped move it out of the street. At least a piece of it or two.

The sign-spinning man, looked like it might've been a buddy of mine, was wearing some headphones and was dressed up looking like a wiener dog. He jumped out of my way. Shouldn't have been in the street anyhow. Dogman's tail was whipping super-fast. They had grass on the street, but never paid me to cut it, so I just thought I might go on and help them out 'cause it was looking tall. I lined up a little bit and pushed the gas and I might as well've had me a big old giant blade on the bottom of the truck. I made a pass on the grass and tried to line up the wheels like I did when I made marks on some fresh clippings, and I made me another pass, but it was all crisscrossed up and it got me thinking about how many times I had to tell Little to line it up, and line it up again, 'cause it's like the boy just didn't hear me and now he's a winner. Messing and winning, messing and winning. But I mowed that grass down flat like some pancake grass and it got me good and hungry. I saw water squirting up like a fountain and I knew I'd taken me out a sprinkler head. Entry to the strip mall needed it, a sprucing anyhow. Those motherfuckers got them a fountain.

I walked in the store and the speaker was squeaking and popping out calls: "Pet-pet—pet-pet, Nanny" from that ball of a cashier's jerky-filled mouth. It sounded more like putt-putt

and I walked straight over to her, slapped that bag from her lap
and jerky went skittering all over the floor. That smell made my
stomach do some tricks. Next thing I knew a big-assed parade
of dogs and cats and ferrets and shit from every corner of the
goddamn store came clawing and toenail tapping, goddamned
dancing in the aisles. Nanny came walking out like she'd been
watching the whole damn thing, arms crossed and pissed-off,
looking like I did some shit. Swear she was shoeing chinchillas
and rabbits with the toe of her shoes.

"Go," she said, and pointed to the door. I reached out and
tried to snatch the intercom mic from that cashier, who still
had it keyed and was talking some nonsense and babbling like
her jerky was an eee-mer-gen-cy. I got that microphone. I had
things to say.

"Let's do us a demo!" I said, and pointed at Nanny. She was
still pointing at the door. "Demo on aisle—" I was looking
around, looking for the aisle number where we were standing,
but I didn't see one so I said, "Here." I was showing these ladies
how we did it, thrusting toward Nanny, and that cashier wrestled at my hand and took it off the mic.

"You got to go, Wild," Nanny said. I was ready to do us a
show.

"Put them big spots on us. Let's—" I was thinking—*incubate*.
I put my hand down in my jeans pocket best I could. Had to
push a little 'cause it was tight. "Ouch." I might've grumbled
a bit. "Look here." I held up my big-assed wad of cash-ola. It
was a little thicker than it'd been, 'cause I had the change from
paying with a C-note at the Taco Bell. "Hang on." I weeded
out the receipt and left Little's check in the middle of the stack
for some volume. Then I pointed back at my wad. "You got
to come on back home now. Little's shacking up with Margaret, and I need me some winning tail. I'm a win-ner." I'll be
damned if Nanny didn't walk herself up real slow. Shouldn't've
ever trusted that woman no-how. Crazy woman snatched that
money out my hand. She walked brisk over toward the doors
and had me slipping when I tried to catch her. Nothing could've

got me up right and jerky-woman for sure wasn't. Nanny was out the door. I scrambled up on all fours and did me some skating across that floor and finally got back up when I was able to catch ahold of some lady's shopping cart. Had her dog in the baby seat and it nipped me on the sleeve, but I caught up to Nanny right about when she took that wad of bills and threw them out into the breeze that blew across the flat, wide-open parking lot, like big green leaves mixed up with dead ones. They blew off to the far corners and crooks of the lot, but I chased those bills, caught most of 'em and shoved each one back in my pocket. I turned back to Nanny.

"Nothing I want gets won," Nanny said. She walked her ass back inside.

36

NANNY

I'd heard Margaret's name enough lately. The white bubble of skin that swolled over the rim of her jean shorts looked like a balloon full of milk, one of those funny balloons the magician at the Chinese restaurant used to blow up with the bicycle pump and make into a hotdog or a hat. I'd never be able to look at a squeeze of toothpaste the same again.

She was full of herself and praise for Jesus. I could tell it in how she was walking. Her calf muscles shook and balled up above her wedges and she looked like a cowgirl. But when she chose my boy to ride, she chose the wrong horse.

"Hey, honey, you got a second," I said. She didn't stop walking, jiggle-clomp, jiggle-clomp. "I said, you got a second." A little louder that time. I had Stewart with me, and his collar jingled.

"I heard. And no," she called back over her shoulder, not even looking. She pushed the little clicker-button in her hand and her car lights lit up all happy, like it just couldn't wait for her butt to be in its seat.

"You must be thinking I was asking. I was telling."

Now she stopped and turned. I got a look at her face, dolled-up like she'd never known a moment when she wasn't on top. Wild and Little'd both seen her makeup dried up and broke.

I walked up to her, let the dog sniff her crotch and she frowned at me, scrunched up her face good and tight like the creases in her denim. Dog sneezed. She held the clicker in her hand like she might try to use it on Stewart. She had tips on her fingernails, long and white.

"Stewart here has better taste in bitches than the other two men in my life." Stewart sneezed again. I could smell her too. She smelled like a baby just got spanked with powder and the bag busted. Must be tough walking around all wet and oily all the time. "And by taste, I mean I'm going to let him get your scent, and if you so much as float near my boy again, I'm going to let Stewart gobble you up." I poked Stewart with the toe of my shoe, and he snarled at her. Her butt was on the hood of her car now and her ankles looked like they might roll around in her strappy shoes. I kicked the shit out of one of her headlights for good measure.

37

LITTLE

Tom came back to school with his arm in a cast and sling. I stared his way. Really didn't see too much damage until he turned. His face was bruised, the purple kind that looks black in the dark, but glows sick and yellow around the edges. His left ear was bandaged and the bandage was close to needing a change. I thought he was in relatively good shape for what I'd seen of the accident.

With Tom back, he and George were reunited, and I was on the receiving end of both their glares. My chair got bumped twice as often, and if I wasn't ducking a door as it opened, it was being shut in my face. George and Tom whispered and looked in my direction. Even if they weren't saying a thing, I was still feeling some heat. They gave me flat tires in the hallways. I stayed in the public spaces, and held my bladder during restroom breaks. But it wore on me. We sat in our homeroom in small circles, making collages of a wiseman or a shepherd or cattle.

Sedy tried to keep me happy by making me laugh, but it hurt the muscles of my stomach and my bladder ached. I winced at her attempts and I got a headache. Sedy colored a donkey, tilted her head back and brayed for me. I laughed.

"I guess I could've been a Christmas duck." Sedy kept her head back. The bandage looked like a duckbill.

I laughed and my bladder cramped. I felt a small trickle of warmth in my pants, then felt a chill down my back and immediately stopped laughing. I'd forgotten, only for a brief moment, my predicament. I held my shepherd over my pants, then lifted it slowly to reveal a small dot.

"Mrs. Florence," I called, my hand raised.

"Yes, William. What is it?" she replied, her own focus on cutting a star from a yellow piece of thick paper.

"Can I go to the bathroom?"

She looked up from her task, then up to the clock on the wall.

"Go ahead," she said, motioning with her scissors. I was already headed toward the door, shepherd still in hand.

I trembled with relief, and the pressure in my head lifted from my cheeks to the top of my hair. By the time I finished and opened the stall door, Tom and George were standing there in the bathroom with me. That pressure I felt was replaced with cold. I hadn't quite gotten my pants zipped and buttoned when I stepped out and George landed his fist against my left cheek. It felt flat and cold on my cheek, to the point of numb, and it carried enough force, enough pent-up pissed off, that it knocked me to the floor. I landed in the puddle that had formed through a day's use and misses in the boy's stall—right on my ass. The wet crept up through the back of my pants. I tried to stand but my shoes didn't have a lick of stick left on the bottom and they went right back out from under me. Before I could try to get to my feet again, George grabbed me by the cuffs of my pants. They were too long, a school hand-me-down, and the rolls on the cuffs made a perfect handle. I was dragged out of the stall while I grabbed at the slippery floor.

"Nice driving, fucker," Tom said and kicked me in the ribs. I heaved, but the breath didn't come. I saw it all like I was watching from the ceiling. "Bet that felt like getting T-boned." Tom laughed and looked at George and before I could catch my breath, he kicked me again. He leaned down close, his nose damn near mine. "You gonna pay for my car?" I felt tears come and puddle in the rims of my eyes. I was still stunned but tried to get to my elbows.

"You trying to get up?" George chimed. He leaned down to me, spit from his words speckled my face. "Why you trying to get up on my mama?" he asked. George grabbed me by the hair.

"Want me to get after your mama's titties?" George and Tom laughed, and though one was high and one was low, the sounds chased each other around the room, bouncing off the painted concrete-block walls and reaching me there on the floor, where I ached and wheezed. I couldn't speak. I'd never thought of my situation and George's being the same. I did have a mother. She worked at ProCreations. She did not live with me. I saw her sometimes. She was a ghost. She was a person once. She floated away from home. I floated away from home. I floated. I could see my own head, resting on my elbows on the boys' bathroom floor. Then George wound up and punted my face. If my head were a football, it would have traveled far, instead it snapped back as if on a swivel. I kept my eyes closed, felt the burn of his laces on my cheeks, and my head spun like the papier-mâché planets that hung from the ceiling of my classroom. I was on my elbows but my head was in deep space. I heard another voice and I think I saw the words pass by, a strange locomotive of strung-together letters happily bouncing toward an exit from the cosmos of my head, spilling from a mouth I realized was my own. I couldn't catch them before the vacuum of the outside world sucked them out.

"Not like your daddies are getting after your mamas," I said. A long string of spit and blood spilled on the bathroom floor. A puddle formed and ran into the cracks of the tiles like thin arteries or rivers seeking low ground. "Pretty nice too." I opened my eyes and the light burned, but I registered the look of shock on George's face. He stepped on my lower back and stooped to talk at me.

"What'd you say?" He didn't wait on a response. "My parents got divorced two years ago." George took his foot off my back, then stomped the other foot on the back of my head. It hit the puddle and bounced off the tile floor before it settled in the mess, a hard relief. "'Cause of your daddy," he called.

Another noise, and I realized that it was the door opening and shutting. The smell of the urine-slicked floor burned through my nostrils like smelling salts. The quiet was interrupted by a thump coming from the floor, then the walls, then from my head, and finally my own chest. It pushed through my arms and my stomach, out into my hands. Every hair on my head screamed.

Two boys appeared. "What the hell happened to you?"

I tried to close my eyes, to go back to the dark and the planets, to see if I could watch another train of letters pass by, but I had to open my eyes. The boys asked more questions and I had to conjure an answer.

"I slipped."

They didn't dare touch me. They used hand sanitizer after looking at me. I crawled, palms slipping and knees aching, smearing a trail of blood behind me as I crawled into the hallway. Sedy stood in the girls' line and caught sight of me first, or maybe she was the only one who cared. She scrambled over and held me under an arm, tried to support me.

"Don't," I said. "I stink."

I thought she laughed, but when I looked, her face pursed, her chin quivered, and tears rolled down her cheeks.

"Billy?" she said.

I couldn't catch a train of letters to respond.

Mrs. Florence didn't try to stop Sedy from helping me to the nurse's office. She didn't want to touch me herself. I was on my feet somehow. She walked me slowly and I was amazed at how strong she was.

38

WILD

I drove hard. Light poles flicked past my windows and the
screaming of the truck's engine hit my ears like a mosquito,
made me swat at my head till I pressed the pedal of the truck
harder, hit a new gear, got the groans a little lower and watched
the gas gauge wobble toward the E. My palms and knees were
bruised and aching, all scratched up from skidding around the
parking lot chasing my own dollars. I passed the strip centers
where some losers my age, other drivers from my history, spun
signs advertising and screaming *Going Out of Business* blowouts.
Flew by the stripping clubs with their kinda full parking lots.
I squinted and shook my head hard a couple times, focusing,
keeping the yellow lines from dancing around too much like
jump ropes, and broke through to the end of the four-lane road.
Pushed the pedal again like it was a final lap. The two lanes tumbled into the piney woods and that gave out to the marshlands.
Pulled on to Early's road, made tracks again through the ditch,
drove out to the covered cement pad and pushed the brakes,
sliding a little further than I meant to. Cut off the truck and
stepped out onto the pine straw covering the ground. It was
slippery on the wet pine straw for my gone leg and I took some
care when I walked toward the carport. I'd spent enough time
on the ground for the day. Sounded like a billion rattlesnakes
rattling, maybe cicadas, don't know, didn't matter 'cause it all
announced me being there

The engine lift stood there just like we'd left it. So did my
lawnmower. It looked just like it did the day I got it. Damned
thing was a promise and a threat, rainbow and a curse. When

I'd traded it, I thought I'd doubled down for a promise that was a curse.

Screen door slapped the wood frame and I squinted toward the back of the house. Wasn't real sure what I was going to do when I got to the mower, maybe steal it, but I hadn't got that far ahead in my head. Early walked over toward me, licking his fingers and lips like some fucked-up housecat.

"Hey, Wild, what you doing?"

"Nothing." I looked back at my mower, then around at wrenches and a hammer sitting there on some white, grease-stained towel on the ground.

"Fancy surprise seeing you wheel in here. You in a hurry?" Early wiped his fingers, freshly licked, on his work pants. Left some orange stains in strips.

"How I drive. You know that."

"Guess so." Early walked up and stuck his hand out for a shake. I held mine out, took a look at my own palm, lava running out and burning in the stream with scrapes and dotted with holes all bloodied from the parking lot. Early looked at my palm too and put his own back down to his side. Wiped his fingers on his pants again. "What can I do you for?"

I kinda walked around the covered area, holding my own self up on the posts and such. Poked around the tools and broken machines. "Things are getting weird."

"You're winning, right? That's what you were wanting."

"Losing some too. Need it." I pointed at the mower. "Need my mower back." Sat down on the seat of the mower.

"What're you gonna do with it? You gonna take a cruise around here?" Early laughed at something I wasn't finding all that funny.

"Need it," I said again.

Sss came a hissing in the straw, calling to mind old no-shoulders and I shivered a little, checked the ground around. Looked like that orange pine straw was moving and it made me check my legs, put my hands on my knees and feel for some solid ground.

"Don't know the difference between want and need, do you? Funny how you come out here when you're wanting something." He didn't know how much I was needing things back to normal, what I was willing to do to get it that way.

"I'm taking it, Early. Don't be getting in my way."

Ooo, came the call from an owl in the tall pines, whistling in my ears like a train whistle.

"You're good, Wild." Early chuckled again. "You was thinking that was payment somehow?" Early pointed to the mower. I saw it fresh, but it still looked better to me than the scratches and dents and half-flat tires all cracked and dried-out rubber and such. "Surprised that thing even runs. But I wouldn't know. Haven't even needed to try it."

Early pointed around his place, his property, what he owned. The whole damn place was covered in pine straw and it all glowed like the ground was burning. Not a blade of grass poked through. "Just straw and snakes out here. Home sweet goddamn home." I pushed up and took a step toward the mower. Early stepped aside. He put a hand out as if to show off a door-prize. I stopped and looked at him there all sweating and greasy, glowing teeth and blacked-out eyes.

"You're good," Early said, gently and more quiet, trying to coach me like some wild animal. "Take it if you really want it." I struggled to focus on his words, tried to catch them and step on 'em like busted smoke, figure out what he was trying to do and pin it down, wrap my own head around it. "Just don't come back looking for anything else. Not real good about trading back the good stuff. You know?"

U-u-ulllll, bleated out the goat lurking over in the shadow of the carport.

Early bent a little at the gut and waved an arm toward the sad machine. "Got everything I ever needed from you."

39

LITTLE

The nurse shoved cotton balls up my nose, felt like it was breaking all over again. She wiped my lips with iodine and pushed on my stomach to check my ribs, which were sore as hell, but still there.

"You fell?"

"I fell," I said, wheezing as she pushed.

"You fell?"

"Really far." I nodded my head.

"What did you hit on the way down?" she asked.

I was silent.

"I'm going to call your folks."

Daddy pulled up, kind of on time, said he'd been an hour early. He missed every phone call from the nurse. My face had stopped bleeding. I pulled my hoodie tight, attempting to hold my ribs and organs steady, took shallow breaths and walked through the fog I breathed out with each one, like puffs from a train. I chugged with each step toward the waiting truck and was relatively happy to see it, even happier to not walk home. I pulled my hand from the pocket of my hoodie to open the door. Daddy had the window open when I walked up.

"Guess what I got?" Daddy whistled a burp through his teeth.

"I can't," I said, straining on the words. I coughed and choked a taste of blood into the back of my throat. I hocked it to the front of my mouth and spit on the curb, staining it.

"Got the mower back." Daddy motioned behind him.

"Right back there in the trailer. We," Daddy pointed back and forth between the two of us, "are redeemed."

The pain in my stomach eclipsed the pain in my face. My split lips throbbed. We hadn't mowed in weeks. We hadn't kept up with the accounts we had left. The landscape, browned and dried, cracked with my steps.

"Won't believe this," he called.

I was hunched and my backpack weighed about a thousand pounds, had me leaning on my busted ribs. Daddy didn't notice. Started making engine noises, babbling about the lawn mower. He pointed to the trailer, and I put my bag down, held my stomach and walked around back where the mower was sitting.

"Great," I said, then gagged up a stream of puke and blood.

"What's wrong with you?" Daddy yelled. "Don't you see?" He pointed at the mower. "I got it back! We're back in business!" I looked up to see his eyes all streaked like some fireworks blew off on the whites, flash blasts of red lines, yellow creeping in from the edges.

"It's winter," I said.

Daddy celebrated by drinking a bottle of vodka in the cab of the truck. He waited for me to climb in and it took a minute. Took just about everything I had to get my bag to the floor of the passenger side. The car smelled like the nurse's office. Like rubbing alcohol, with the addition of cigarettes and stale, broken leather and oil. Even with the window down, the smell of the booze was trapped. It made me gag a few times. We sat there and watched as the other parents picked up their kids. They wore sportswear and balanced large SUVs and broken relationships, yanked children around by their arms and loaded them into cars more expensive than years' worth of our work.

Daddy smiled at me.

"You're looking like me," he said.

I attempted a smile back, but not because it was that funny. Instead, I had the odd thought that this was what it meant to become an adult: this was what was handed down—this inheritance of broke. That the experience of being beaten would never end. That I could have stayed on the bathroom floor and never gotten up and that perhaps it would have ended there, in a puddle of my blood and urine, that perhaps it would end there anyway, just another time and another place.

At home, Daddy sat in his camp chair. I had taken a shower, let the water run on my burgeoning bruises and rattle off my bones. I rinsed off the dried blood, but I still couldn't shake the smell. I'd pilfered through a pile on my floor for some relatively clean clothes and then laid down.

"You sure?" Daddy held his new smiling bottle out to me. The fruit spun like the spokes on wheels. "Sure you don't want a sip?" Daddy swirled the bottle by the neck. "Could help. Been such a buzzkill." He raised his eyebrows, and I watched his eyes roll loose in their sockets. In the dim light, he looked like a flap of bruised skin draped on a skeleton. Even through the pain in my ribs, I heard my stomach growl. I'd checked the pockets of my pants and found a dime.

"You ever cash the check?" I asked, looking over at Daddy, unblinking.

He reached into his pocket to show that he'd only blown the cash winnings so far. He pulled out two singles and a white piece of paper, folded and crumpled. Daddy unfolded the white paper with force enough to make a snapping sound as it pulled flat. I squinted toward the paper in Daddy's hand, then looked harder.

"Not the check," I said.

Daddy held the receipt from Wine Time and turned it. He also squinted at it, then dropped it on the floor and reached real quick back into his pocket where he found nothing.

"Come on, boy," Daddy said, getting to his feet and swaying. I watched, not knowing what to make of him getting real spastic. "Come on!" Daddy screamed. "Get up!" He walked over to me and pushed me with his gone leg. I rolled onto my back and groaned. Daddy stood in the room, pulling his hair back. "Shit, shit," he spit the words around the room, still pulling on his hair. "Shit!" he yelled. I rolled to my knees and watched Daddy move around the room. I knew that he was looking for something to throw. But there was nothing left—just the camp chair, where his current bottle of vodka rested. Daddy pulled me the rest of the way to my feet.

"Where we going?" I finally asked, but Daddy said nothing in return. Outside, evening breeze blew cold and felt good on my face. The trees overhead swayed and the streetlights glowed with yellow halos. I climbed into the truck.

Daddy repeated, "Shit," all the way to the parking lot of ProCreations.

He pulled into the lot and all four tires squeaked when he braked. He left the truck running and jumped out, licked his finger and held it into the air to check the wind. It blew toward the highway at the far end of the parking lot. Leaves from some faraway trees mixed with the trash and blew as tumbleweeds through the night. Daddy got back in the truck and pulled it toward the gutters at the far end of the lot, then turned it off.

"Your mama," Daddy stammered and cleared his throat. His eyes watered. "She fucked us, man." Daddy pulled his hair back, then slapped the steering wheel with both hands. "Totally fucked us," he said, then shook his head. "Get out," he said. "Get out, get out, get out!" he shouted and pointed to the parking lot.

"What?" I was doubled over in the seat.

"We got to find the check. Your mama threw it out here." He motioned around the lot. "She's your mama. Go find it!" I knew not to argue. I couldn't. I opened the truck door, held my stomach through the pocket of my hoodie. I stepped to the asphalt and started looking down at the rolling piles of leaves and trash. I made my way along the gutter, stooping and checking each receipt I found, gasping with my aches and still not understanding just what the hell was going on. I looked back as Daddy wheeled the mower from the trailer. He cranked it, then putted through the lot, inspecting garbage and running over piles as he left them glittering in the air. Employees of the strip of stores pressed against the glass and watched us, me spitting blood and Daddy mowing trash. Daddy drove by the storefront of ProCreations twice, holding up his middle finger both times for the employees to see. The animals inside didn't like the noise and howled tremendously.

I made it through the entire length of gutter when Daddy pulled alongside me.

"Find it?" he shouted.

"I would've told you." I raised my voice. It was all of the volume I could scrape together. I was hunched and tasted blood in the back of my mouth again. I spit.

"*Sure.*"

"Are you kidding? I would." I wasn't sure that I'd even made a noise.

"Okay," Daddy said. He looked out on the lot, let off the clutch a bit.

I gathered myself to speak again. "Did you?" I yelled.

"Nope." Daddy shook his head. He turned the mower off.

"I'm starving," I said, relieved. I gave the truest statement I could make, hoping for reciprocation. "How're we going to eat?" I slowly sat down on the curb.

Daddy sat quietly on the mower. The wind blew and the tiny pieces of trash and leaves blew through the air. I watched as the employees went back about their business. I hadn't seen Mama in the mix but had somehow hoped she would come outside, check on me, come to my rescue. Daddy came up with no answer, just sat looking off into the empty space of the lot.

It was Thursday. We were broke. Daddy'd lost the check. "We can go to Hungry World," I said. "It's Thursday. Might be open."

Daddy had me put the mower back in the trailer. My stomach cramped in the cold and it took me several tries before I was able to push the tailgate up and reach the latches.

Hungry World cast a dull neon glow onto the sidewalk. The line of people waiting for food in the cold slinked down the block.

As we passed by on the street, they stared at the body ahead of them, watching their backs as they shuffled along.

"We weren't supposed to have to do this again," I said.

"You hungry or not?" Daddy asked, he blinked hard, then shivered. We bounced over the curb and into the empty lot next door. We hobbled toward the double doors of Hungry World, me limping behind Daddy. We supported ourselves on the wall. The praise band played and sang, huddled in the cold on the sidewalk, all but Margaret, who sweated as she sang. She gave a thrust toward me to punctuate her line and my face throbbed in embarrassment for us both. The cold of my limbs and the stomach acid welling up in my stomach, unmet, unsatiated, and unsettled pushed on my eyelids, made my body heavy. I leaned into the wall.

The steam from the trays of food glowed in the neon. The volunteers handed us our plates. I supported mine on an arm as the workers scooped shepherd's pie. The plate grew heavy under the weight and I skipped the salad and walked inside where we were allowed to eat in the lobby. I sat on a carpeted step and the heat of the building was the most warmth I'd felt in days. Daddy slid down a wall, and sat on the floor, his legs in the way of anyone needing to walk by. They stepped over him like the space was empty.

"It's good," Daddy finally said.

I grunted a response, worked the food down with my swallows. My stomach cramped as I ate and I slowed. My plate was still full of food.

"You gonna eat that?" Daddy asked with his fork way too close to my plate. I didn't respond, but pulled my plate closer, putting it on the step next to me. Daddy mopped his plate with a roll, then looked over at me again and held his plate out. I didn't look up at him.

The volunteers opened the doors from the lobby into the theater, propping them open with wooden wedges. Daddy stood to go in—I did too—but threw away the rest of my plate of food. The shepherd's pie slid through the flimsy plastic bag

and thudded to the bottom. Daddy looked at me, but he didn't
argue. He didn't deserve what I threw away. Gray light filled the
room, and I followed Daddy to a row of seats near the back.
After a few moments of quiet, the double doors closed and the
reel spun, flashing frames on the screen.

The chariots raced around the track, giant wheels spun, and
bodies flung from the wooden crates. They were trampled underneath hooves and hardwood. Daddy shook his fist at the
screen. "Go on!" he yelled. "Step on it!" as he rooted for the
racers. The hero whipped his horse and circled the dirt loop,
eventually letting himself be crushed in a terrific pile-up. Daddy
booed and nearly stood. The hero's woman was a basket case.
She beat her chest and Daddy laughed.

"It doesn't go down like that," he whispered to me. I didn't
look at him. Daddy pulled a pint bottle from his jean jacket and
drank. The bottle swished and bubbles sparkled in the light.
Daddy set a silent burp free into the theater and I watched the
heads of others in the audience turn as they caught the whiffs
of vodka.

The villagers burned the hero's body. There was a lot of
weeping and the audio didn't line up with the actors' mouths
as they jabbered. I struggled to focus on the film. I looked
over my shoulders here and there, making sure that I wouldn't
get surprised by Margaret. I didn't sleep. Daddy didn't either.
I didn't eat enough to be full and I couldn't get comfortable
in the seat. The theater lights came on and I was surprised by
how fast the time had passed. I followed Daddy out of Hungry
World and into the cold.

"He could've won," Daddy said on the drive home. "No
reason for ditching like that. All he had to do was take the
outside. He could've backed off then, let his buddy pass. Nobody ever takes the outside. He had the speed. Just got to go."
Daddy slapped one palm over the other, mouthed *Zoom*. He
broke down the possibilities with the addition of racing theory.
I kept my head against the window. The cold felt good on my

throbbing head. I'd had a miserable headache for most of the day, and the flashing light of the movie had pushed me close to a migraine. The pressure made my head feel like it was in a balloon. "He was so stupid-close." Daddy finished the race in his head. "No redemption in that," he said. "What's he get for all that? Woman's left out there getting all sad and not laid. Got to finish it out for the win." He thrusted.

"But what's the point?" I asked. I'd had enough. I didn't want him to keep talking, and wished I wouldn't have asked.

"*My* point is—he wasn't a winner. He could've been, but he wasn't." Daddy held up his fingers and illustrated how close he'd come.

"He couldn't win," I said. "Wouldn't have been a movie."

"Still could've been a movie." Daddy shook his head. "That's dumb, man. Think you've got it all covered now that you won a couple races," he muttered. I thought he was kidding at first, and I forced a smile. But Daddy's expression was unchanged. He talked through his teeth. "Don't you start telling me a lesson about winning," Daddy said. He pushed the pedal and the truck sped up. Daddy pointed and looked over at me. "Been winning longer than you been alive."

"Not saying you didn't win," I protested. But it was too late.

"That's right you didn't." Daddy continued to point at me. His finger got closer to my face. "'Cause I don't stop!"

We pulled up in front of the house. Daddy missed the usual ruts and the truck felt oddly out of place. He kept the truck running and I opened the door. I stood there a minute, holding the door.

"You gonna close it or what?" Daddy asked still looking ahead.

"You coming in?" I replied.

"Nope. Too much night left. I'm going to go on and keep at my winning streak," he said. I shut the door and watched as Daddy drove away. The front yard pushed up through the hole in my shoe and the ground was hard and cold.

I walked to the carport and pulled the chain for the bulb overhead. It didn't come on, and I stood there alone in the dark, looking at the car in the light of the moon.

In my room, flopped down on the bed, I rolled side to side until I found a position that let me feel my bruises the least. I grabbed the camo bear and pulled it to my chest, then reached into the bear's pants and pulled out the wad of cash I'd been stashing away. I put the cash in my pocket, then let my heavy eyes close.

40

Nanny

Every time the wind blew, they chased those leaves like desperate ghosts. I couldn't escape the haunting. Little couldn't either. Maybe it made me desperate. Desperate to save what I could. I stood behind the locked automatic doors of ProCreations, watching Wild drive around the lot on the lawn mower, some beat up and lost fool, howling all angry, watching his soul jump out of his mouth in puffs while he smoked up the parking lot.

In my office, Lady moaned and whined. Her belly was swollen as could be. The moon was full and it pulled on baby, made her labor hard.

Stewart panted at the doors and fogged up a small patch of the glass. Out in the night, Little searched the lot like a kid would. Spooking like a dog when Wild got to yelling. He hopped from curb to curb like he was moving his marker in a board game. We wore out Candyland.

41

WILD

I could've drawn a better line down the road than the one that was out there, curvy like some drunk toddler'd drawn it. My wheels bounced between the curbs 'cause that line was all funky. The headlights of the cars in front of me helped me find my own lane. I drove on, into the dark of the highway, past the trees, and found the lights of the Monkey Palace. I slung gravel pulling into that parking lot. I drove past the line of "Big Bill's" work trucks and parked my truck across a few spots. I sat in the cab for a minute, reflecting, thinking, getting a little pissed and steaming some at the boy.

I crunched across the shells of dead animals. Some kind of life, lived out, then just ended up being some place for folks to drip their hot oil pans on top of when you're dead. I held onto the hoods of the parked cars to keep myself up, then walked into the light of the neon beer signs that glowed in the night sky like pretty stars.

The thumping bass shook my bowels and made me know I was empty, even though I'd eaten about all I could at Hungry World. I pulled on the door to the bar and noise spilled out into the lot, like I'd busted open a wound. The monkeys pounded their plexiglass cages and the room bounced and shook, gyrating, full of bodies. I couldn't be sure if it was my eyeballs shaking or if the room was really wiggling like that. "Bud Light," I said to the bartender, who wouldn't look me in the eye.

She looked around to see who might come out of the kitchen. I was still standing there just about not giving a shit, when Senior walked up and nodded at her. She put that bottle on the counter right there in front of me where I pointed. "Damn right," I said.

Senior stood next to me at the bar. "I feel like we've talked about this," he said. He took the beer from the counter before I could grab it. Senior drank my goddamn beer. "Get him one too," he said to the bartender. She pointed to herself like some other jackass was gonna do it, then pulled another beer from the cooler.

"'Cause I'm a winner," I said to her. I picked up the beer and drank about half. Senior watched. "Won again," I said, this time to Senior.

"You are one clueless sonofabitch, aren't you?" Senior said.

"Might be clueless, but ain't no loser."

"You driving the car?" he asked.

"Cash money," I said, putting two dollars on the bar. They might've been my last two, but I slapped them sonsabitches down with the conviction of a man with a pocketful.

"Your car's in the field out back," Senior said.

"Like I haven't seen it." I turned to Senior. "What now? What else you got to say?" I spread my arms, but sure enough, that bastard didn't do shit. The music boomed and bumped along. The bottles rattled behind the bar. A monkey banged both fists on its cage. Another one laid on its back, kicking the plexiglass with both feet.

Senior shook his head real slow. "Finish that," he said.

I was already tipping that thing back trying to suck it dry like the tits of some golden goddamned cow, some Bud Light god to bless my brains and keep my balance.

"Got something else to show you."

I finished that beer and set it down hard on the bar. Bartender grabbed the bottle to toss it in the trash, and I sniffed deep, stared at her. She looked back at me and froze a second like some raccoon caught stealing trash. Eyes deep searching for something good and finding me.

"You not done or something?" she asked.

"Oh, he's done," Senior said. "Come on." He waved at me, used his middle finger and wagged that sonofabitch at me like a goddamn pointer to get to following him; and I did, walked away from the bar, lights flashing from mirror-balls over the dance floor and strobing off the walls and triple-lacquered tables, like a shitty seafood restaurant for all the spills. My eyes were heavy and squinty and barely open and I tried hard to stay balanced with all the bass thumping and monkeys pounding. I was trying sober but playing pretend and the act could use a polish. I paused for a second and looked a woman on the dance floor up and down. She was wearing a halter-top, and a sparkling chain hung from her belly button and I wanted to jingle it, maybe blow on it like a wind chime. She bent and shimmied and I was damn near hypnotized, like she was some magic ninja. Senior grabbed me by the shirt and pulled me along. Had to follow in order not to lose balance, but I kept on watching that woman over my shoulder. Bet she was redeemed. Jingle, jingle. Walked the rest of the length of the bar to a door that said "'ployees Only."

The monkeys were loud as shit. Made my thinking not work. What I couldn't hear in the bar could be heard through the back door access to the cages. Every one of those panels behind the cages had a nameplate for the monkey. I looked over my shoulder, following Senior, passed *Ernest, Stevie, Bubba,* and a whole bunch of others. Senior walked along, tapping the backs of the cages where the apes were screeching and pounding on the plexiglass on the other side. Held my ears and my breath. The smell of live animals was both real familiar and offensive as shit. We walked to the end of that narrow hall and Senior tapped a wooden slat wall like the others we'd passed.

"Look here," Senior said. "This one's empty. For now." He pointed to the nameplate on the final cage.

It read, *Junior.*

I rolled in the cage of the car. The Lemon Party was always a good car, a safe car, the fastest goddamn car on the track and everybody knew it. The front quarter panel was crumpled around my leg; I could see it still there, good and broken and fresh as mine. It had gone numb from the crushed nerves. I'd become part of the car and couldn't ever escape. The cage was there for me, I was born into it, birthed into metal and hot gas and flaming combustion and blown rubber. There were screams from the stands. I pounded on the roof, and pounded on the door, but my leg was in the trap. Car bit me up in its teeth, some kind of revenge for mistreating a wild animal, and it wouldn't let go. I yelled at the top of my lungs but couldn't get a word out. Passed out and woke my ass up in the hospital, pulled from the car, my leg left behind, the price of escape.

"This one's for you. Looks pretty homey, don't it?" Senior pulled out the wood slat. The cage was made up with a small pad and a water dish. With the wall pulled out, I could see straight through the plexi, out into the bar. The view was wavy, the lights of the bar swirled and the plexi shook and the scene skewed. "Just waiting on you. Right here where you belong."

42

LITTLE

In my recurring dream, my wooden chariot raced on the dirt of the track. The ruts were far bigger than my wheels and I wobbled in and out of them and felt all of the cold through the slit of my robe. The back end of it flapped as I tried to keep up with the speeding cars. They slung mud that pelted me in the face and eyes until I went mud-blind. The lead car on the track pulled up behind, ready to lap me. I wiped the mud from my eyes and saw Daddy forcing the bumper of the Lemon Party toward my bare feet. His gone leg was a flopping hood ornament. The disembodied leg flexed its foot and pointed at me, a target. I cracked the reins of my horse, but the wood chariot's wheels slogged through the gray clay. I couldn't gain any speed, and I noticed that my horse was also missing a leg. Daddy bumped my chariot and the wood beneath my feet creaked. My chariot slid to the side, but Daddy wasn't content to pass. He revved the engine and tipped a bottle to his mouth. It was the smiling fruit bottle he kept in the truck. One of the orange slices caught the glare of the track lights and winked at me. Daddy revved the engine again and caught me in my chariot, mid-drift. This time the bumper cracked the wood harder, my axles wobbled, and the wheels rolled away without the chariot. Daddy drove me all the way into the wall and the hood ornament kicked me in the head.

I thought about confession and the movie and my current condition when I rolled from bed. The bruising was worse than the night before and I was stiff as I moved. My breathing was shallow, and every time I twisted or turned, I took a quick, sharp breath through my nose. The house was cold and I slid my feet into my cold Pumas. I'd slept in my clothes and my hoodie. I stood and walked into the den. Daddy was there, already passed out in the camp chair. The vodka bottle sat in the cup holder, but it didn't wink. It stared at me, and in the slices of citrus, my eyes found the spokes of wheels.

I walked outside into the night. The cold numbed my bruised face and woke me up. I pulled my hoodie close and walked to the carport. The car was dark but radiated warmth, like a body warming as it slept. I put one hand on the hood and then placed the other on the metal as well when I felt the warmth. I kept my palms on the car, sliding them along as I walked to the driver-side window. I pulled myself through the window and into the cage, and slid down into the seat. My ribs ached but sinking into the seat seemed to soothe my hurt.

43

WILD

When I woke up the light was pouring in and my jeans were cold and stiff. They were sticking to my skin and made my joints hurt. My gone leg was itching and I reached down to scratch it. The cold of the house made a whole bunch of static and when I touched the gone leg it shocked the shit out me, made my head hurt worse, and my eyes and teeth and jaws and such just a little bit tighter. The room hovered right near refrigerator temperatures, and I was happy for the cold when I pulled the vodka bottle from the cup holder.

"Little," I yelled. "Where you at?" The sun was way up, and I floated through the days of the week in my mind, settled on Friday, and was pretty sure I was right. I got up and walked through the house. My steps made noise! Creaked into the floor with a *tap, tap, tap* and echoed through the big empty. "Little?" I stepped into the hallway and looked around the corner into his room. It was empty but for the bed and the bear that lay on his pillow. The bear was there, the bear was there, the bear was there, and I might get to needing that bear. I kept on walking, room to room, and settled on the idea that maybe Little had gone off for school. Then I got a little frantic, scrambled to the door, and yanked the sonofabitch open to the outside to make sure Little hadn't taken my truck. It still sat there in the front yard, and I stood there staring at it for a minute before I heard the snoring that was rumbling out there, louder than the dogs and screaming and plates breaking and sirens in the quiet morning. I walked over to the carport and the morning sun glared on the windshield of the Lemon Party II. Little was huddled there in the car, his head tipped back and his waves of snores breaking in my ears. I poked his arm through the window and nudged him.

"Boy," I said, whispering at first. Thought I'd give some respect for sleep. He didn't budge. "Boy," I said louder, and poked him again.

"What?" Little asked, white crusts of dried spit painted in the cracks of his lips.

"School, man. You got school, right?" I was still a bit thrown. Usually, the boy got on up and got moving before I got out of the chair. "How'd you end up in here?" Little looked around the car. The sun hit him in the eyes. He started pulling himself out from the car all frantic.

"I'm late. Shit, I'm late." He grabbed the outside of the roof to pull up, scrunched up his face and slunk back down in there. I put my hands under his armpits and started pulling.

"Shit. It's cold out here. You cold?" I said, still pulling. Little swung his legs from the window and slid to the concrete floor. He sat there holding his side. "You all right?"

Little wiped his hand down his face, his eyes were still sleepy and fogged up. He held his stomach. "You hungry or something?"

"I'm all right." He hunched, then stood up all slow and looked at me. "You all right?"

"I'm all right." I blew out a crisp breath of vodka and whistled through my teeth. They were slick and cool. "You ready?"

Little looked down at himself. He looked all right, clean and such, 'cept for the streak of blood down the front of his hoodie. "Can be. Just got to brush my teeth."

44

LITTLE

Tardy again. I signed in and the secretary didn't speak. She typed intently and pretended not to see me. The door behind me opened and Sister Theresa walked by. She grimaced, and I was sure it was at my face, then opened the door to her office and walked in to begin the announcements. I set the pen down and turned to walk out. A poster with a lighthouse and a giant breaking wave hung behind glass on the wall, but I didn't read the words. In the blank white space of the wave, I caught a glimpse of my reflection. My lips were too big, and I had a dark line across my nose. I reached up to touch my face to make sure it was really mine. The pain was real, and so was the reflection.

I opened the door and stepped into the hallway. A line of kids stood along the wall outside the classroom. They held index fingers over their mouths but were still kinda noisy. My head hurt less, but my side ached. I walked down the hall, past the hanging artwork, and thought of the banners at the track— past season champions' names and years in bright colors. They would blow up toward the sky revealing bleachers and the legs of the crowd as the cars fanned by. Daddy's name was on a couple of them, so was Senior's. Mine was not, and I found myself examining the names scribbled on the artwork in the hallway, as if I would somehow see my own. I passed the last piece of colorful construction paper and made a left turn into the straightaway. Voices droned. Teachers speaking in various shades of monotone. I stretched to loosen up my side. In the windows of the classroom doors, I saw my classmates. I'd made it through each year, and then I considered my current one. It was the first time that I wasn't so sure I'd make it out.

I reached homeroom and when I opened the door, no one turned. Mrs. Florence didn't stop talking. She wrote with chalk on the board, clicking at the end of each letter and rubbing the billowy sleeve of her blouse through the dry dust of erased words. I moved slowly toward my seat. Tom rested the cast of his broken arm on the back of it. Sedy looked over at me and I attempted a smile, but couldn't keep her gaze. She put her hand over her mouth, teared up, and looked back to the front of the class. Tom moved his arm and I sat, the angle of my body causing more cramping. I couldn't get comfortable.

During our bathroom break, I stayed in the hall, by the water fountains with Sedy.

"I'm so sorry," she said. She motioned to her face, as if to mirror mine. She no longer had the bandage across her nose.

"Not yours to be sorry for," I said. My lips got in the way of my words.

"I'm so, so sorry," she said again. I wished that she would stop, and the wish was granted when Mrs. Florence held a finger to her lips.

"Shhhhh," she hissed.

Sedy mouthed a whisper in my direction. *Sorry.*

Tom and George walked out of the bathroom. George stuck out his bottom lip and made monkey-like movements with his arms and bowed legs. I turned away. So did Mrs. Florence.

Sedy left for a doctor's appointment before lunch. I looked at her empty chair, across from me in the lunchroom. The other students laughed and traded portions of their lunches. Tom and George and the rest of the class sat together, bunched in rows and talking.

A banner hung over the stage in the lunchroom. It had a picture of the school mascot and slogan, *Wise Owls are Winners!* The bell rang, and everybody stood from their tables. They dumped their trash in the cans and lined up. I stood last and moved slowly to join the line. I pretended to drop something in the garbage but had nothing left to give. The class walked out, leaving me behind. I wondered if I'd disappeared when I was beaten. What had brought me to this point? Things had been bad, but not unbearable. I had existed. I used to wonder what it would be like to win, and now I missed losing. I considered what I'd gained from winning, and now I'd gladly give it all back.

45

WILD

There was Little limping out of that school head down and grumbling and belly aching. I reached across the truck and popped the handle. Already had the door open when he got to the truck

"Hey, boy! Hop in," I said. I was slapping on the steering wheel like I had me a song in my head. Little climbed in, dropped his bag, and crawled up in the seat like a goddamn toddler. Sometimes I could still see the baby in his face. Thought he might cry any second. "Think we should drop the car off tonight. Get it there early," I said. "Don't want you losing pole again."

Little nodded and I pulled us away from the curb.

"Heard there's a decent purse tomorrow night." I slapped on the wheel again, made my palm hurt how hard I was trying to squeeze some excitement from that boy. "You get that one and we'll get us a blower *and* a leaf eater. We'll be back in business for good." I looked over at him, gave him a wink, looked at the road a second, looked back over there at the boy and checked in on just whether or not any of my words were landing. Thought I might have to give him another wink or a nudge or something. Boy just wasn't giving off nothing.

Truck bounced over the railroad tracks and there was a man standing there holding a sign.

ARE WE BLESSED?
WHAT HAVE YOU SEEN IN THE ABYSS?

Another one trying to make peace with the Lord. I threw my empty bottle at him and it broke on a railroad tie.

I pulled into the front yard and slid through the grass when I hit the brakes and slicked a track in the grass like we were water skiing. Didn't say anything to the boy; he was already opening the door and melting out of the truck. Watched him roll the mower out of the trailer, then heard the Lemon Party II cranking and firing as he pulled it up the ramp. Funny, when the car hopped up in the trailer, the whole truck bounced, like it was a big old whale that swallowed up the car.

Little got back in the truck, and we rolled on toward the track. The sun was still out and orange bounced through the lights, making them look like they were glowing even when they weren't lit. The sound of engines rolled through the truck and rumbled in my ears as we cruised up the gravel and dirt road.

I pulled us into the paddock, and Donald walked up on me like I couldn't see him from the sideview.

"Go on and get that car out," I whispered over to Little. He nodded and hopped out the door.

"Wild," Donald said, knocking on the side of the truck like he was the po-lice or something. "Y'all here to practice?" The tailgate dropped and I flinched a little at the noise. Donald looked over his shoulder to the trailer. "Know it costs money, right?"

"Just here to drop the car," I said and gave him a grin.

"You gonna pay the storage?" Donald asked.

"Go on and fuck off, Donald," I said. "It's one night." I was done grinning.

"You kidding, right?" Donald said. "Ought to make you pay to park your ass, right here and now."

"Wouldn't have the butts in your stands if it wasn't for me."

"Long-ass time ago, Wild."

Little rolled the car down the ramp and the truck lurched even with it in park.

"That's good right there," I hollered back at Little.

"Ain't good at all," Donald said. "This is the last time. I mean it." Donald was staring down his shiny nose at me and blew out his mouth. I held my breath and looked off through the windshield, listened to the engine noise and knew which turns the driver was cruising through. "I don't even want you around here. Not a damn single good thing has come from you. Your daddy was the last good thing out of your family." I felt my teeth grind, smooth white, squeaking slow like glaciers, and I clenched my jaw. Donald pointed over at Little. "You two bust up every fucking thing you touch."

"Don't you talk about my boy." I felt steam running out of my skin and flames from my fingertips.

"You gonna protect him now? You've damn near ruined him. Now you got him running people off the track."

I yanked the door handle ready to whup that man. Donald kicked it back closed. Probably put a dent in the door. Jammed up my wrist and I was stuck. "You want to park it here tonight or not? Might have to listen to some truth." I took my hand off the handle. I worked my wrist back and forth.

Donald walked away. A car drifted around the dirt and a cloud of dust blew in swirls, circles fighting and floating. Little got back in the truck.

"We good?" he asked.

"Till tomorrow," I said, but was about ten miles off. The engine screamed around the track and we pulled the empty trailer home.

46

LITTLE

I waited through Saturday morning. I kept busy with washing my race suit in the sink, then hung it outside to dry. I looked under the carport and the mower was gone from the same spot I'd left it the day before. Daddy's truck was gone, so was the trailer. Daddy'd always spent the entire race day at home. He would sit in the camp chair and vroom around the circles of his memories, telling stories to nobody in particular, breathing coconut to his ladies on the bottle.

I could finally move my jaw, so I ate the Taco Bell from the bag in the "tomorrow spot" on the counter. By the time mid-afternoon rolled around my race suit was cold and dry on the line. I pulled it down and put it on. I took my stash of wadded-up cash from my school pants and put it in my race pants' pocket. I looked around the room for the bear, but it wasn't sitting there. The feeling I had at its loss was something other than surprise.

I pulled the bunches of extra fabric from the waist of my racing suit and would swear that it had fit more snugly at some point. I scavenged the nooks and crannies of the house for a stash of food. In the bottom of the freezer, behind a bag of green peas, I found Mama's emergency carton of ice cream. It was a pint of vanilla and I opened the top. Freezer burn had claimed the ice cream and turned it all into broken white rocks. I used my fingers to dig in and cracked off pieces to suck on. I pulled the paper carton apart and ate up the last of the flavor from the container. The shreds of the empty carton was a reminder that Mama wasn't coming back. The clock on the stove said 3:33 p.m. I wasn't so sure Daddy was coming back either.

47

WILD

The woman across the pump from me was wearing one of those tank tops that crept up her middle-aged belly like she was hot stuff. She looked at her phone, then noticed me watching her. She stopped pumping all of a sudden and hung up the nozzle. "Excuse me. Can you not?" She pointed at me, and at her own eyes. I pointed to myself and my fingers smelled like gasoline.

"Gonna clean up," I said and looked down at the red plastic container, the one for the tools. I filled up the two-gallon tank and it overflowed a little bit. "Shit," I said, then looked over at the ticker on the pump. Held out my hand to the woman. She got into her car in a hurry. "Twenty-five cents," I said, but she didn't pay me no mind. She shut her door and started her car. "A quarter!" I yelled. "You cost me a quarter from your talking." But she drove away, tires squeaking when they hit the black top. "Don't know who I am, do you?" I said, standing up. I put my chest out like a goddamn rooster, followed her car with my eyes. I picked up the container and stuck it in the back of the truck. "Cleaning up," I said.

Next I drove to the AutoZone and passed the worker-man, who was on his way out.

"Be right with you," the man said. "Gotta check this battery out here."

"Hmph," I replied, but I wasn't giving two shits about that man's service. Took me a package of cheap blue shop rags from the shelf and shoved them in the front of my pants. They were itchy and hung out the top, but I walked out anyway.

"You good?" the clerk called from the hood of another car.

"Good?" I asked. I heard the drums of the volcano god, beating heavy on the sides of my world like a forty-gallon can. Maybe it was my heart in my head. I raised my arms. "Good!" He put his head back under the hood, never knowing the goodness of swimming in the grace and leisure of coconut faith.

48

LITTLE

I walked out the front door and left a note for Daddy on the back of my blank homework for school. *Race day!*

When I looked over my shoulder at the house I thought it looked unfamiliar, like it was somebody else's. Big. Empty. No shadows on the walls. No mold streaks, just mold. I stood in the trough of our muddy front yard like I was sinking. I walked the front path toward our street. My shoes were covered in mud from the ruts and I tried to shake them off with each step but couldn't. I walked toward the main road, passed the empty shell of the armadillo. It laid there in the leaves and didn't even stink anymore. I looked down the road. I had time to get to the race but would need a ride to the track. It was farther than I could make on foot.

Less than an hour and a half later I walked up the incline of the strip center parking lot and into the doors of ProCreations.

Mama took her fifteen, which she normally reserved for plowing through a couple of cigarettes and staring off into the infinity of the empty parking lot. She told me that her associates would handle any potential copulations or demonstrations in her absence. For her fifteen, Mama drove me to the track. She smoked a cigarette and ashed out the window.

"Thought you were a ghost when you walked through the double doors," she said. "Got to stand up straight." She touched my back. "You were walking hunched."

The walk had nearly taken it out of me. By the time I'd reached ProCreations, I'd gripped my side and asked for water through my swollen, cracked lips. Mama's car radio played

"Swing Low Sweet Cadillac" and I felt like I glimpsed her dreams.

"Think it over. Doesn't have to be today," she said, watching me. I leaned forward in my seat and held my seatbelt away from my stomach. "But the offer's there. I moved in this week." Mama smiled at me, trying to get some sort of reaction, but I could barely think through the throbbing. "It's nice. Not fancy, but it's nice."

I winced as she bumped over the gravel and dirt road. The walk had really messed with my bruises. Mama pulled into a handicap spot at the concession stand.

"Thanks, Mama," I said, and stepped out of the car.

"Offers there," she repeated. "Not going away."

"Want to stay for the race?" I asked.

"Wish I could." She held a hand over the low-lit digital clock in the dash. "Got to get back five minutes ago. Things'll get messy." She tapped a cigarette from a squished soft pack and pushed in the car lighter. "Go on," she said, waving me along. "Good luck." I stopped and heard the pop of the hot lighter, watched Mama light up, then she drove away.

Daddy's truck was nowhere to be seen, and I walked up toward the track. I watched the little orange dots glow and slowly approached the concession stand, still expecting to see Daddy. But nobody messed with me. Nobody cared. I was left alone without Daddy there by my side. There was no meat to pick from my bones. I grabbed a cup of Coke from the counter and offered to pay without pulling the cash from my pocket. The concession lady declined, and I drank up. A hand touched my shoulder, a small, familiar touch, and I turned around to see Sedy.

"How're you feeling?"

"I'm all right. You all right?"

"I'm all right. All good." She smiled at me. "Hoped I'd get to see you."

She glowed and I wanted nothing more than to stand there

and talk with her until my voice was all gone or the world stopped or something, but I remembered something real serious. "Hey, Sedy, got something I got to talk to you about."

"Okay," she said, a confused look on her face. She squinted and tilted her head to the side.

"Come here for a second," I said, grabbing her by the hand and pulling her around to the back of the concession stand, back near the restrooms. I pulled the wad of cash from my pocket, then put my hands around her waist. I pulled her in close and stepped on the tips of her shoes. "Sorry," I said.

She didn't respond. Her eyes were closed. I kissed her on the mouth, my swollen, sore lips bounced off hers. The taste of her lips reminded me of the red cherry wax I would eat from the ChapStick as a kid. I felt the warmth of her forehead against my own and it warmed my whole body. I inhaled all I could of her. Then I pushed the cash into the pocket of her hoodie, and stepped back, one hand still around her waist. She reached into her pocket, and I held a finger up to my lips.

"What's this?" she asked, mouthing the words and barely making a sound.

"I need you to bet on me to lose," I whispered.

"What?" She leaned back. "No," she protested and shook her head.

"You have to." I stared, still close to her, and checked the colors of her eyes—I saw the reflection of track lights.

"I can't."

"You can."

"Sedy-Jane," came the call from near the stands, "get here— *now*." The backlit silhouette pointed to the ground, and Sedy pulled away.

"That's me," she said. I watched her walk away.

I looked into the shadows and hoped for a glimpse of Daddy. I still couldn't grasp that Daddy would miss his walk up to the betting booth, much less a race. I shook off the thought that

Daddy had sensed a change. I knew that would give too much credit. As I walked to the paddock, I checked behind the tire wall and under the stands.

When I cranked the car, I held my breath and knew Daddy was nowhere around. I'd gotten a good position and pulled the car toward the front of the pack as the official lined us up. The official nodded to me as I nudged my wheels to the line. He waved me up a bit more, then closed his fist for me to stop. I dropped the car in neutral, then turned it off and took a breath. The cage smelled like exhaust. I checked the mirrors. Tom wouldn't race tonight, but George sat behind me. I caught George's eye, and he gave me the finger. The clock over the paddock ticked and the second hand bounced, seemingly unsure of its next move. The official put on his earmuffs and motioned for us all to start our engines. The roar shook the low walls of the paddock as the other engines joined mine. The official opened the gate, then waved us onto the track.

I thought about my solitude, my aloneness. All the noise drowned out the quiet of my empty house. The noise of the track was the same as the noise of my classroom and school. The noise was for others, a conversation for a pack that I could not hope to join. I was either ahead of it or behind it.

The green flag waved and the engines throbbed. Their oil pressure increased, and I lurched forward. The car spun its wheels under the low gear. The harness pressed into my bruises, but I sniffed deep, pushing out my lungs. I winced in the pain, holding it all in, the smell of the exhaust and the sharp cold of my torn muscles, but I took control, shifted, and let off the throttle. The pack approached behind me, and I eased back into them as I made a lap.

George passed me. Air wheezed from my mouth. The car throttled forward, lurched and chomped, ate it up greedily, but I quickly sucked in and held my next breath. We made laps on the track and I held on to the breath, while the car held on to the pack. As we approached the lap to make the race official, to make the results something that could stick, I still held that same breath. I tried counting, visualizing the numbers, erasing them from a board, and writing another, but as the numbers grew, my lungs burned. My eyes grew heavy and my vision blurred. The color of the signs on the stands faded and my arms tightened and cramped just before my stomach turned, but I wouldn't let go of the breath, of my one bit of control. I was resolute.

My foot stuck fast to the accelerator and I felt that the car was hungry for air and gas, but I held on. I strained to not let the breath go. I held it and my body shook. The last of my air escaped, and flat-out I refused to take another. I watched as the veins of my wrists glowed neon blue between the gap of my gloves and sleeves, then they turned gray. Everything turned gray. My vision broke into grains, tiny pixels that rearranged and swept away into the night sky. I imagined the time that we visited the fair. Me and Mama and Daddy walked into the lights and rode the Himalaya. We spun around the track, pushed into the sides of the car; the lights flashed over our eyes and I recalled the screams. "Nothing like the real deal," Daddy had shouted. *The real deal.* I no longer heard the engine noise, but I felt warm and sped up, my foot heavy on the pedal and I left the pack, angled out to my own branch of tree from the others. Even my gray vision faded as I let the car find a direct route into the wall.

Dust scattered and settled everywhere, dust slung from the bumpers and the wheels, from the hood and the frame, covering the car and the inside of my mind. It stung and it sand-blasted and blinded out the people in the bleachers as they watched the Lemon Party II flip end over end. *The real deal.* Screams hit pitch and rang out into the cold black air. *The real deal.* I rested, and the car rested, and the engine coughed itself out—even while my foot held the accelerator to the floor.

49

WILD

I drove up the dirt path bouncing, suspension squeaking all high-pitched toward the track. I was running behind, late as could be, and I tried to get there in time for the trophy and the check and the photo. But the ambulance blew by me. The flashing lights made me feel funny, had me thinking about riding, and I watched in my rearview to see the ambulance bounce along behind me. The cabin light was on, and I remembered how bright that light had felt bearing down, worse than track lights. Everything had glowed angelic like it was beamed down straight from heaven, but maybe it had been the morphine, then the pain-killers, then the— I came up on track, now with a little more fire under my tail. I pulled into the blue spots up front and left the truck running. People streamed out of stands like snakes. They passed me as I approached the betting window, but Donald met me before I could get there to knock.

"That's your boy." He waved his finger and I tried to follow it as it chased the red lights down the road. "Y'all just keep handing down broke." Donald's eyes were red, and he teared up. Looked like a big red baby.

I didn't respond. Just watched the empty faces of the crowd as they left.

"I told you and you just kept on making sure y'all let all that shit in your family tree shake down. Just can't even get close to cleaned up. Clean it up, Wild—if you even get a chance." Donald kept talking after me, but I was already back at the truck.

The drums played, pounded and beat out of tune and time, but they just kept on playing. My eyes vibrated and I kept moving.

I pulled on the door handle of the Monkey Palace, but it was locked sure enough. Nobody was around. The lot was lined with "Big Bill's" work trucks. There were at least ten of 'em and the black trucks stood big and bad. I pulled the gas tank from the back of my truck and unscrewed the cap. Took my time to dip each rag in the tank and draped them over one side of the bed rail. I was feeling too straight, needed a re-up bad. Told myself the sooner I cleaned things up, the sooner I'd get my reward. I took a screwdriver and pried open each truck's gas tank, then plugged them with a rag I pulled from the bed rail. When they were all plugged, I pulled my truck to the edge of the parking lot. I clicked my seatbelt, then looked back over my shoulder at the Monkey Palace and thought about that cage Senior had waiting. Put the truck in reverse and pushed the pedal to the floor. Truck finally came to a stop near the doors to the kitchen.

My hands were cut up and bleeding from the broken glass of my windshield. I got out of the truck and walked around to the backside of the bar. I'd just barely missed it, but that was on purpose. Pulled two beers from the cooler and wrapped a bar towel around my bleeding hand. Lava was flowing. Those monkeys were screeching and pounding the plexi. I opened both beers and drank one right then and there, then took the other and walked across the room, careful not to lose my balance and fall into the glass. I put a shoulder into the "Employees Only" door and stumbled through.

I propped the door with a barstool and drank the other beer, then pulled up each one of the wooden slats. At first the monkeys were confused as hell. They clammed up in the backs of their cages, toward the plexi, grabbing their knees and such. But when the open air found each pen, they started getting a sniff at freedom, and one by one they hopped down. They got to snorting and sniffing at each other. "Get on out of here!" I yelled at 'em. I poked at them and shooed 'em away with my gone leg. "Y'all stinking."

The monkeys ran through the bar, some got in the kitchen,

some walked out through the front doors. I took the slat with my nameplate and one more, then walked back to my truck and dropped it all in the back and grabbed two more beers and a mop from behind the bar. I knocked over a few bottles of 151, then got back in the truck, pressed the gas pedal, and turned the keys, fully expecting a fight, but it cranked on the first three spins. I pulled a lighter from my shirt pocket, put the truck in drive and pulled out of the bar. In the parking lot, I poured gas on the mop head then tossed the rest of the can into the bar. Lit the head of the mop, then hung it out the window of the truck.

"Behold the volcano god!"

A few monkeys pressed up to what was left of the windows of the bar.

"Scat!" I yelled at 'em. "Don't know your freedom from your asshole, do you?" I threw a beer out Little's window at the spectators, and watched as they scrambled away. I idled by each of the work trucks and poked their hanging rags with my flaming mop. One after another the trucks blew off their wheels. The monkeys ran into the field and then out into the dark of night. The trees glowed and jumped in our unholy ritual. I raised the flaming mop up to the night sky and watched the lava flow down my arm. The flames climbed then calmed. I tossed what was left of the flaming mop into the bar and pressed the pedal to the floor.

50

LITTLE

My breath came huge and gasping like I'd never taken one before. It was the one I'd shaken to hold-off when I was last awake. The pain in my stomach was dull and overwhelming, like I'd met a wrecking ball mid-flight and tried to hop on. I blinked and focused on all the white and chrome around me. I couldn't decide if I was dead or not. But I heard beeps of all varieties around me and wished that they would stop. My head throbbed, and when I held my hand up to my temple, I felt that my forehead was wrapped up tight. My hand had wires running from it to some unknown destination. I flapped them like reins to a horse.

"Trying to gallop out of here?" came a voice from the far corner of the room. I tried to turn and look, and gathered that I probably wasn't dead. "Lucky you didn't lose a leg. You were penned up in that cage pretty good. Said they thought they were going to find sardines once they pulled back all that metal. Took a little bit to extract you. Looks like most everything's working. We'll get that catheter out when you can stand and walk," the doctor said.

I groaned. My face felt freshly swollen, like a thousand of George's tennis shoes had booted me. "Can you talk?" the doctor asked. She walked around writing things down, checking things—from what I could tell—she did doctor things.

"Think so," I eked out.

"Good, good, good," the doctor said. "Be back," she said. "Don't go anywhere." She smiled and walked out.

A TV loomed over the room. It was off, and I willed it to come on. It didn't. Two nurses came in, one tall and hunched, the other stocky and brisk. The tall one wheeled a tray over to me. There was a cup of water and a small paper shot glass of pills.

"For your pain," she said. I drank the water but left the meds. She looked in the small cup and shrugged. "Not even one of these guys, huh?"

"He's a tough guy," the stocky one said. She adjusted things around the room, fluffed, turned, flipped things. I had trouble following her with my eyes. She moved quickly. She looked at my chart, a laundry list of broken. "Broken ribs, prior cracked ribs, broken leg, fractured foot, etc... Nothing?" The tall one shook the cup, rattled the pills.

"More water?" I asked.

"I can do that. But take it slow, okay?" The tall nurse wheeled the tray away, and the pair breezed out just as they had breezed in. The tall nurse came back a moment later, this time she didn't bring the stocky one. Mama walked in with her.

"Hey," she said, waving her hand like she would to a baby. She tried to smile, but the look made her face contort like she was also in pain.

"Hey," I mouthed. I tried again, and the word came out on the second try.

"How you feeling?" Mama asked.

I lifted one arm, then the other, one leg, then the other. "Did you see it?"

"Nope," she said, "and glad I didn't." She walked around to my other side. "Remember? I left to get back to work. Heard it was quite a thing to see though." I squeezed my hands into fists, flexing them, just to see if I could.

"That's right."

Mama slowly paced around the room, making laps, picking up and putting down a couple of standard "Get Well Soon" and "Best Wishes" cards that the hospital placed in every room.

"Didn't tell you earlier, but I got a nice new bed for you," she said, nearly blurting the words. "At the new place, I mean."

"Yeah?" I asked.

"I do," she said. "Got a couch; had to take the legs off to get in the door. A whole room for you. Place has a pool too."

"It still cold out?" I asked.

She laughed a little. "Yeah. You only been out a few hours." She picked up a gift from the counter. "This one's not from the hospital. Look here," she said. "Somebody left this for you. Kinda funny." Mama picked up the stuffed bear. It was dressed in camouflage and toted a fabric rifle. She shook it and looked at it herself, then brought it over to me and pretended to make it walk toward me, then laid it down on the bed. I turned my head and looked into the bear's black void of eyes, and nearly tumbled down into them. I searched for my own reflection, but only saw Daddy's shaggy hair and lean face.

"Guess what else," she said.

"What?"

"Got a brand new puppy."

After Mama left, another visitor came in.

"Little," Sedy said. She moved quickly toward the bed, then gave me a hug. She kissed my forehead. I hurt, but put my arm around her too.

"I'm so glad you're not—"

"Me too," I said.

"I would've missed you." She wiped her eyes with the back of her sleeve and hung on to the side of the bed. "A lot." The curls around her eyes were wet and matted together.

"How long have you been here?"

"They tried to get me to go home a while ago, but I told them *no way*." She smiled. "I brought you something." Sedy pulled a wad of bills from her pocket and quickly stuffed the money under my pillow. Her eyes flashed blue and I tried to catch them in my mind, hang onto them, till she leaned in to kiss me on the forehead again.

"Thanks, Sedy." I grabbed her hand as she pulled it out from under the pillow and held it close to my chest. "How'd you do it?"

She smiled. "George's mom took the bet. She was standing there when I tried. We were the only two in the whole place that bet against you. Felt funny doing it." She paused. "Especially when you went down the way you did." She choked up, then started crying. I tried to scoot over, and moved a smidge. Sedy buried her face next to me in my pillow. She pulled my hand to her chest, just below her neck, and I felt her heart beat a patter, soft and fast. My heart beat like a machine, warm and fluid. I could hear it, and knew that Sedy could hear it, and we both listened to the great sound, laying there quiet.

After Sedy left, I pulled the cash from under my pillow, scooped up the bear in my arm and held it close. I put the cash down the bear's camo pants and held it, then pressed the paw and listened to "We're Going on a Bear Hunt," as I stared down again into that bear's eyes. But this time I didn't see a reflection. Instead, I saw a glimmer, something brighter. In the low light of the hospital room, it seemed to me to be the small light of a star. I drifted where sleep would take me.

51

WILD

Drove till the gas ran out, the engine choked and spit and cried and whined and died.

I'd passed out at some point in the night, and woke up on the side of the road, somewhere way south, gone and gone. Driving all night wasn't easy. Things were blurry. I sat on the broken glass of the windshield. The night had been cold and chapped my face and my eyes. The morning broke and the sun cracked like an egg. I pushed open the door. My hands bled through the rag, and the blood dried the rags to my skin, like the cuts tried to eat them. Stepped down to the grass and the dirt and gravel, and it crunched under my feet in the cold. The side of the truck was cooked black. The paint bubbled in spots from the heat of the burned-up mop. It made the truck look fast, even though it rested for good.

The beating in my head thumped on the walls of my skull, veins poking out like super-highways stopped up with traffic, but it was nothing compared to any number of the beatings I'd taken in my life. Burn, burn, burn, monkey bar, burn all night like some flaming sparkler the devil was holding with his tail. Senior ever found me, he'd have me on my knees picking my switches and eating my own tail. I was sitting in the heat of some summer sun looking at my childhood in my daydreams. My hands throbbed, tired of fist-fighting my way through existing, cut up from trying to break out of my cage. All this beating and burning would make a man crawl toward extinct.

I puffed out the cold morning air and knew that the hoop snake of my childhood ate its own tail out of choice. It had taken its first bite before I ever found the stick and rolled it down the hill. I'd gobbled my own self up. Senior had broken off a piece of the family tree and rolled my ass downhill toward my own demise with the first push. But it was me. I torched that family tree like it was dry timber kindling waiting on a spark in the drought. Devil and his sparkler showed up. My soul was already ate up. Devil laughed watching all my ancestors run out into the fields and out into the night and screaming when they fell out of the tree. I wilded in the unknown, breaking limbs free in the fire.

I stepped around to the back of the truck and popped the tail-gate, slid myself up in the bed. Those thick pieces of ply, the busted-out ass-ends of the cages, were still there. They hadn't blown away in the night, in my drive. Laid them out, side by side in the truck bed. There was a handle on each one where they had been used to slap the monkey cages shut real quick. I pulled the bar towel rags from my hands and the cuts re-opened. I squeezed my hands into fists like squeezing an orange. Fresh red crept out and started to drip, then flowed free.

Worked quick, and shook in the cold. Skin of my hands went blue under all that red. Felt all the cold now that I'd stopped driving. I finger-painted streaks and letters on the boards and felt something, felt my sins released in the painting of each letter. My fingers slipped when I bent down and untied and stripped the laces from my shoes. Looped the strings through the cut handles of the boards and checked on the length to make sure that I could still fit my beating head through the gap. Laces would stretch out and get thin and hard now that they were slicked up, and I tied the knots tight. My head throbbed less, started floating while I stared there at my paintings. I looked around the truck bed. The rusted-out metal was streaked with struggle, and it looked like I'd been gone hunting in the night-time. I wrapped the rags back around my hands, pulled them tight to close up the cuts.

I stepped down just as a car drove by, too fast to read my lessons. I steadied myself on my elbows on the tailgate. My stomach was growling, talking about eating up my heart or what was left of it, and I put a finger in my mouth, something I did since I was a kid coming up short on food. But I didn't taste no salt, just tasted the rust of my cuts. I pulled the boards, one, then the other close to me, and slipped my head through the laces, turned my head between the boards. Fit me like a roll cage. I kneeled and rested my chin on one of the edges of the ply. It was warmer between the boards 'cause they blocked the wind. When I stood, the boards hung even, one on the front, and one on the back. I took my first step.

When the sign grew heavy, I stopped and knelt. The bones of my knees hurt from their knocks against the wood, but I knew this gave my walking some rhythm. I held my bound-up hands under the sign. Squeezed and wrung them. "I'm all right" with each left step and "You all right" with each right. A truck in the morning fog and dew slowed down when it rolled up on me. Right leg, gone leg, right leg, gone leg.

I stepped and slid and walked the shoulder of the highway with no laces in my shoe. *Step-slide. Step-slide*—through the trash and the dead, the cast-off and the dust. *Step-slide.*

I saw the driver read the front of the sign, mouthed out the words, "THE END." He'd know the rest when he caught it in his rearview mirror. "IS HERE."

He'd say, "Wonder what he done?"

ACKNOWLEDGMENTS

This book has its roots in my memories—a blur of the landscapes and apparitions of the South Georgia and North Florida of my youth. While the region is flawed, I hold a great gratitude for it—a reverence for its wildness, some sorrow for its brokenness, and a blind hope for what it could be in its re-birth.

Thank you to the people in my life who read this story in its different stages and believed in it: Elizabeth Hooks, Liz Van Hoose, Pam Van Dyk, Riley Manning, Josh Giles, Claire Davis, Sean Towey, George Singleton, Taylor Brown, and Caleb Johnson. A huge thank you to the Regal House team, Jaynie and Pam, for their dedication, work, and appreciation of Southern fiction. Thank you to Scott Ballew for the use of the lyrics from "High Times." Thank you to Sewanee Writers' Conference—Michael Knight, Christine Schutt, Tony Earley, and Adrianne Harun for their workshops and guidance. Thank you to Hank and Jan, Mom and Dad.

Above all, thank you, Elizabeth, Margaux, and Brer, you've waited so patiently, let's go splash Wilma T.

BOOK CLUB QUESTIONS

1. What is your hope for each character?

2. Did your opinion of the characters, Wild/Little/Nanny change as you read the book?

3. Who is the story's protagonist? Antagonist? Wild? Little? Nanny? Senior? Why?

4. What are the implications for Nanny in her attempt to breed males into obsolescence while being the mother of a son?

5. If you could buy any set of pets from ProCreations, what would it be?

6. Who was the most reliable narrator of the story? Why?

7. If you could read the story from another character's point of view, who would you choose?

8. If you could create a soundtrack for *Can't Shake the Dust*, what songs/artists would you include?

9. What would your sandwich board sign say?